MW00987424

MICHELLE QUACH

THE BOY YOU ALWAYS WANTED

KATHERINE TEGEN BOOKS
An Imprint of HarperCollinsPublishers

Katherine Tegen Books is an imprint of HarperCollins Publishers.

www.epicreads.com

Library of Congress Cataloging-in-Publication Data
Names: Quach, Michelle, author.
Title: The boy you always wanted / Michelle Quach.
Description: First edition. | New York : Katherine Tegen Books, an imprint of HarperCollins Publishers, [2023] | Audience: Ages 13 up. | Audience: Grades 10–12. | Summary: Attempting to fulfill her dying grandfather's dying wish, seventeen-year-old Francine enlists Ollie Tran to act as his honorary male heir, but the mounting lies and romantic feelings they develop complicate their plan.
Identifiers: LCCN 2022044826 | ISBN 978-0-06-303842-4 (hardcover)
Subjects: CYAC: Grandparent and child—Fiction. | Grandfathers—Fiction. | Interpersonal relations—Fiction. | Asian Americans—Fiction. | LCGFT: Novels.
Classification: LCC PZ7.1.Q23 Bo 2023 | DDC [Fic]—dc23
LC record available at https://lccn.loc.gov/2022044826

Typography by Molly Fehr
23 24 25 26 27 LBC 5 4 3 2 1

First Edition

To my bǎo bǎo

1

Ollie

THE TROUBLE ALL STARTED WHEN I MADE THE mistake of letting Francine Zhang see me cry.

It was two weeks ago, during fifth period AP US History, and we were all sitting in the dark. Mr. Romero was showing *The Deer Hunter*, which is the kind of movie you should really warn a guy about before springing it on him, especially right before lunch. If you haven't seen it, *The Deer Hunter* is about a group of American friends who go off to fight in the Vietnam War, where they're taken prisoner and forced by their captors to play Russian roulette. Some of them survive, but the violence of it—the pointlessness of it, really—horrified me, especially when I thought about how people in my family were among those caught in the shitshow off-screen, getting bombed out by the Americans.

What really got me, though, wasn't the gore or the carnage but the coming home after it. That sense of never being able to go back to whatever you were before. Something about that depressed the hell out of me, making my stomach twist up into my throat and, yes, goddamn it, forcing me to tear up.

I don't know what the hell was wrong with me that day. I mean, I'm not saying I have a problem with crying necessarily, but it's not something I really want to be doing in front of everybody. Still, the situation could've been totally fine, given how the lights were all out. I would've gotten away with it, easy—if it weren't for Francine.

There I was, about to wipe my eyes with the back of my jacket sleeve, when she somehow dropped her eraser, a rounded piece of rubber made to look like a California roll, and it came tumbling back toward my sneaker. She turned around to check where it went, and that's when she saw me.

For a second, neither of us moved. She blinked, her stare blank and penetrating at the same time. A sliver of afternoon light escaped from beneath the drawn shades behind us and cut across her nose. Her eyes were completely dry.

I leaned over in a hurry to retrieve her goddamn eraser, but really it was so I could swipe my arm over my face to hide the fact that I'd been low-key bawling. I handed the sushi roll to her without making eye contact, and she accepted it wordlessly before swiveling back around, the end credits filling the projector screen and the weird space that suddenly swelled around us.

I figured that would be it, that we'd go back to barely acknowledging each other, despite the fact that I'd sat behind her for months and recently noticed that her hair, stick straight and cut off at the shoulder, smelled kind of nice, like the tea tree oil shampoo I use on my dog, Dexter.

Francine, however, was sitting very still in her seat, as if contemplating something—and then, in an abrupt about-face, she reached into her backpack and produced a travel-size packet of tissues.

Which, to my utter mortification, she offered to me.

Desperate to avoid calling more attention to this sorry situation, I did the first thing that came to mind—I took a tissue. Anything to speed up this interaction, I reasoned. *Anything.*

But as I silently blew my nose, watching Francine refasten the flap over the tissue packet and squirrel it back into her bag, I allowed that she was just trying—in her well-meaning but unnecessary way—to be helpful. When she darted a last glance at me before facing frontward again, I think I must have given her one of those throwaway smiles, the kind that isn't supposed to mean anything to normal people.

The kind that, unfortunately, *did* mean something to Francine.

2

Francine

OLLIE TRAN HAS A DIMPLE ON HIS LEFT CHEEK when he smiles, but that isn't why I'm asking him to help me with The Plan. There are lots of reasons, real ones, though some are harder to explain than others. The discussion, however, is not off to a great start.

"*The Deer Hunter*," I blurt out, because it's the first thing that comes to mind when Ollie looks at me, clearly puzzled. "I want to ask you about *The Deer Hunter*."

Ollie scrunches his eyebrows together, like I'm speaking a foreign language, and takes a step back, small enough to remain polite but big enough to say, *Can you maybe not?* We're standing in front of his locker, which, conveniently, is just a few columns over from mine. The blessing of alphabetical propinquity has always meant that wherever Ollie is, I'm never too far behind. For years, I used to swoon over this, the fact that Tran was close enough to Zhang that, sometimes, if a class was small, there could be no one between us at all.

But it's been a while since I let myself care about that.

"What about *The Deer Hunter*?" Ollie asks, even though it seems like he'd rather not hear the answer.

"Well, I noticed it made you cry." I think back to that afternoon. "Like, kind of a lot."

Ollie's face goes pink. "I don't know if it was *a lot*."

"What's . . . your definition of 'a lot'?"

"Okay, I'm gonna just go." Ollie points two fingers off to the side and scoots away.

As I watch him zigzag between the sun-beaten lunch tables, nearly tripping over a hydrangea bush to hasten his escape, it occurs to me that maybe I could have approached this differently. But I hadn't talked to Ollie in so long—I had no idea what to say. We hadn't even interacted at all, really, until . . . *The Deer Hunter*. Still, I don't know who else to ask. I need to make The Plan happen, The Plan requires a boy, and of all the boys in my life, I've known Ollie the longest.

Our families, you see, go way back. A long time ago—a lifetime, practically—Ollie's dad grew up two doors down from my mom and her sisters. This was in Hanoi, where both our families lived for decades before the Vietnam War. If you ask any of them, they'll probably tell you they're Chinese, then turn around and speak to each other in Vietnamese. But that's how they all came to be refugees. After the Americans left, there was another war between Vietnam and China, which meant that anyone Chinese remaining in Hanoi had to hightail it out of there. We ended up here, in the United States, which is where I was born. Ollie, too. And because wàh kìuh Chinese tend to find each other no matter where they go—whether in North Vietnam or Southern California—his house is only three blocks from mine. I've known him since kindergarten, and now we're both juniors at Hargis High. A history that long has to count for something, right?

Maybe not. Ollie's halfway across the quad by this point, keys already pulled from his pocket, and if I don't say something else quick, he'll disappear into the parking lot.

"Ollie, wait," I call after him, breaking into a jog. "I . . . just want to talk to you." My voice wavers, and I hate that it does. But a few feet away, Ollie stops.

Given how precariously this exchange has proceeded so far, I figure I'd better cut to the chase.

"My grandpa has cancer," I say. "We just found out."

The news hits the way I expect it to, clumsy and heavy, and Ollie folds a little, like I've jabbed him in the soft part of his stomach. "I'm sorry," he says in a tone I haven't heard from him in at least four years. For some reason, it makes a small ball of sadness lodge in my throat.

"It's all right," I manage, even though it's not.

Ollie traces a line with his sneaker, the toe acquiring a black smudge that he doesn't seem to notice. "Is he gonna be okay?"

"No, I don't think so. It's pancreatic cancer." Ollie looks concerned, but I can tell he has no idea why that's significant. "It means he's going to die."

"They already know?"

"The doctors said he could have up to a couple of years, but probably more like a few months."

"Jeez, I'm sorry."

I struggle with how to follow up on this, and in the silence, Ollie starts to look like he feels bad about how far away he's standing. I want to tell him it's fine, that I don't expect a shoulder pat or anything. What I'm hoping for is not quite so conventional.

I take a deep breath. "I was wondering if you could help me with something."

Ollie hesitates, but then he says, "Sure."

I'm relieved, though that doesn't last very long before the doubt creeps in. We're finally having a somewhat real conversation, and in about fifteen seconds, he's going to think I've completely lost it. Like off-the-wall, bonkers lost it. Because I have to admit: The Plan is a little out there. But it's also the last important thing I can do for my a gūng.

"So," I begin, "you know how my grandpa doesn't have any sons?"

Ollie mulls this over like he has to dig real deep to retrieve this fact. "I guess so, yeah."

"He doesn't have any grandsons, either. It's really a statistical anomaly. Like, the probability of having six daughters in a row is actually quite low if you do the math out, and the probability of that *plus*—"

Ollie cocks his head, and I realize I'm rambling. *Focus, Francine!*

"The point is, there's no one to carry on the family name after he dies. And, well, I guess this is a big deal to him. Like, still."

"Even now?"

"Yeah."

"After all these years?"

I shake my head. "Yeah, I dunno."

Ollie is dumbfounded. "He's *how* old?"

To be fair, I had been surprised as well. A few weeks ago, Mom got a phone call from A Pòh, who spoke in a voice for once too quiet to eavesdrop on. Not, of course, that it stopped me from trying. Mom saw me hovering at the door and waved me in. I crawled into bed next to her, and she set the phone down on the comforter between us, a harsh rectangle of light in the darkening bedroom. We huddled over it as A Pòh spoke, her words brisk and matter-of-fact.

"Your father isn't happy," she said in Cantonese. And then, by way of explanation: "He doesn't feel well."

Suddenly, we heard A Gūng's voice in the distance. "Is that her?" he asked in faint Vietnamese. A Pòh handed him the phone, and he, too, switched over to Cantonese. "Have you eaten, Lāan?"

In my family, that question always comes first, even if it's four in the afternoon and you're not sure anymore whether you're being asked about lunch or dinner.

"Yes, Bā, how about you?" Mom replied, because that's never not the right answer, including when you're about to learn the other person is dying of cancer.

"I'm sure your mother will start cooking soon." A Gūng

shifted the receiver to his other ear. "How is my granddaughter?"

"Hóu, hóu, all good. She's right here." At this, I made an impatient gesture at the phone, and Mom cleared her throat. "But, ah, Bā, we wanted to ask . . . what did the doctor say exactly?"

There was a long pause. "Is Fōng listening?"

"Yes, I am," I chimed in. "Hello, A Gūng."

"Ah, Fōng, I was hoping not to worry you." He exhales. "I didn't want to discuss this with you, either, Lāan."

"But you *have* to tell us," I insisted. "We're family—we have to know everything. Right, Mom?"

She didn't answer the question, just reached over to smooth my hair. "We'd like to be able to help, Bā."

Sighing, A Gūng finally explained the bad news. As he spoke, Mom furrowed her brow, the lines getting deeper with each small, brittle revelation.

Into the phone, however, she simply said, "Oh, Bā."

"It's fate." A Gūng sounded like he was trying to persuade himself. "The time comes for every person. I only wish—"

He broke off then, and all we could make out was his slow breathing and the soft fuzz of static.

"What is it, Bā?" Mom asked.

His response shook me. "I only wish I had not been such a failure."

"Aiyah!" A Pòh's voice muscled through the silence. "Why must you say such ridiculous things?"

"Why else?" A Gūng sighed again. "It's true. I have no sons."

Mencius, the famous Chinese philosopher, supposedly once declared, "There are many unfilial acts, but the most unfilial is to have no sons." This makes the most sense if you understand that Chinese people talk about being filial the way Americans talk about being free. Letting your family line die out, dooming yourself and your ancestors to neglect in the afterlife—because male descendants were traditionally the ones responsible for making offerings to the dead—was the worst thing you could possibly do. You brought shame not only to yourself but also to your entire family. For eternity.

I'd obviously heard all this before, and I suspected that A Gūng, being rather ancient and very much Chinese, still believed some version of it. But I'd always written it off as an old person ailment, like progressive hearing loss or the inability to set up your own cell phone. The whole idea was clearly sexist, not to mention based on an outdated conception of gender—and anyway, who even worried about the afterlife these days?

Apparently, I guess, A Gūng.

"There won't be anyone to pay respect to our ancestors when I'm gone," he lamented. "Who will remember them? Who will take care of them?"

"We'll continue the traditions," Mom assured him. "We'll make the offerings."

"You know it's not the same, Lāan. Your duty is to the Zhangs now, and Fōng—well, she's never been a Huynh, has she?"

Mom shot a glance over at me, but I couldn't come up with anything helpful to say.

"What can we do about it at this point?" A Pòh interrupted. "In the old days, you could just find a family with too many sons and offer to take one off their hands."

"How did that work?" I asked, surprised. "Would you basically adopt them?"

"Sure, if it was a child, you might in a conventional sense," A Pòh explained. "But if the boy was older or even a young man, the adoption could be merely honorary, like if a second son agreed to take your name in exchange for an inheritance."

"Maybe we should've looked into that more," A Gūng murmured.

A Pòh clicked her tongue. "Eh, who had the money for it?"

"Don't worry, Bā," Mom put in. "None of that matters now, especially in America."

"Yes, everything is different in America," A Gūng agreed, but his voice sounded small again. "Sometimes it's strange to think how we ended up here, so far from home."

Then the line went quiet, like the void that settles over the air when the power goes out.

The conversation must have continued from there, but I couldn't get over that long stretch of emptiness. I kept thinking about it afterward, while I set the table and parceled rice into my mouth with chopsticks, and later, while I practiced four-octave scales on the piano, up and down, up and down—until, in the middle of E-flat minor, I remembered something. Years ago, A Gūng had told me he'd yearned for a piano as a kid, but only one boy in his neighborhood, the son of a doctor, had been rich enough to afford the extravagance. Many afternoons, A Gūng would walk by their house, book bag slung over his shoulder, listening for music that he would never, not in a lifetime, learn to play.

If A Pòh had been the one to share this anecdote, it probably would've been apocryphal, the type of immigrant tale concocted to make sure I appreciated the opportunities I had. But that wasn't A Gūng's way. He treated me like I would understand things, and even though I was barely eight at the time, I could tell his story was true. I knew it especially because he came to my Christmas recital every year and sat in the front row, clapping longer and harder than anyone else. And because I sometimes found him standing at our little upright, poking out the notes to "Home, Sweet Home," the only song he'd ever asked me to teach him.

I couldn't, however, recall when A Gūng had last touched the piano. I wondered if he even remembered his old dream. Instead, he seemed too busy worrying about something that I thought he'd come to terms with long ago—this pointless preoccupation with having no male heirs. Why couldn't he have a normal dying wish, like learning to make pottery or seeing the Grand Canyon? That was the kind of stuff other nonagenarians wanted, at least in the heartwarming articles you saw online. Those stories never talked about, say, how the grandpa was a little bit sexist—even though I bet a bunch of grandpas probably were. Those stories never said what you were supposed to do if you still loved them.

I slid off the wooden bench and trudged into the kitchen, where Dad, still in his mechanic's uniform, was putting away leftovers and Mom was washing the dishes.

"Do you think A Gūng really feels like he's a failure?" I asked, leaning against the doorframe.

"No, of course not," Mom replied automatically, but the way she let the water run so long over the plate meant she was lying. She did that a lot—said things just to make me feel better. Lately, though, it was getting harder to believe her.

"Why can't he see that having no sons isn't a big deal?"

Mom shut her eyes, like I was giving her a headache. "Bǎo bǎo, this is a grown-up problem. It's not something you can fix."

"I'm not trying to fix it." I was, though.

"Your grandpa is sick." Mom ignored me and wiped her hands on a dish towel. She did that for a long time, too. "We should let him be."

"But he's *wrong*, and it's making him worse." I didn't understand why she refused to acknowledge this. "Shouldn't we help him find some kind of peace?"

"That's not up to us, Francine." Dad spoke up for the first time. "It's a decision A Gūng has to make for himself."

"I know, but maybe we could distract him by getting him a

gift or taking him on vacation or . . ." Even though I knew it was futile, I found myself grasping at ideas, anything that could mean we wouldn't have to sit around, acting like hopelessness was as inevitable as death. "What about piano lessons?"

"Piano lessons?" Mom was perplexed. "Francine, A Gūng doesn't want piano lessons." She sighed and turned back to the sink. "You heard him. The situation's more complicated than that."

I slumped a bit. She was right, obviously. How were we supposed to solve a problem that only existed in A Gūng's head?

That's when it hit me. It wasn't complicated at all—the solution *also* only had to exist in his head. In other words, we didn't actually need a male heir.

We just needed to make A Gūng believe we had one.

"I know this is all super weird," I say to Ollie now. "But I have a plan."

Ollie looks down at me curiously, and once again, I'm a little nervous. At some point, we were the same height, but in the years since, he's grown nearly a foot to my measly two inches. I notice, though, that he's still got the slight under-eye bags he's always had, and the same dark eyebrows, too.

"I'm guessing the plan involves me?" Ollie asks.

"Um, yeah." My gaze slips to the frayed collar of his T-shirt, and I rush to ask the question before I lose my nerve. "Could you pretend to be my A Gūng's honorary male heir?"

Ollie shakes his head, like he couldn't have heard right. "Sorry . . . what?"

"Just for a little while," I add quickly. "Just until—" I falter as I try to say it out loud. *Just until he's gone.*

"But what do you mean by 'honorary male heir'?"

"You know, spend time with him in a grandson-esque way. Come over for tea, smile and nod at stuff he says . . ." As Ollie listens, his forehead begins to unknit. "And, um, tell him you'll change your last name to Huynh and look after our ancestors."

His brows squinch back together. *"What?"*

I explain to him what A Pòh had described, how people in the past sometimes added a boy to the family in name only. I say we'll make A Gūng believe we're going to do exactly that, so he can rest easy knowing his responsibilities to the dead will be passed on. Even though, of course, none of it will be true.

"You can't just say *you'll* do whatever he wants?" Ollie scratches the back of his ear.

"The problem is my A Gūng's convinced it's got to be a boy."

"And that doesn't bother you?"

I force myself not to hesitate. "It's not about me."

Ollie is watching my face again, but he doesn't seem to find what he's looking for. "This is a little nuts, Francine," he says, fiddling with his keys.

"So you'll think about it?"

"What? No." He goes back to sidling away. "Look, I gotta go," he says. "I'm sorry."

I barrel around in front of him, a last-ditch effort. "What if I helped you with something? Anything. Whatever you need."

"I'm good!" He throws the words over his shoulder,

high-pitched and squirrelly, then skedaddles toward the parking lot.

I let him go then, because contrary to popular belief, I *can* take a hint. Ollie clearly doesn't want to talk about this right now. But I'm sure there's a way to get him to help with The Plan—there has to be. I've just got to figure out how.

3

Ollie

THIS MORNING, FRANCINE IS PASSING OUT THE lab worksheets in AP Bio, which reminds me that it's been about a week since she told me her grandpa is dying and I've basically acted like I don't give two shits.

I feel bad. Of course I feel bad. The problem is, every time you give Francine an inch, she comes back with enough absurdity to send you to Jupiter and back. Like this thing about pretending to be some kind of honorary grandson for her a gūng. What was that all about? How did she expect me to pull off something like that?

And why me?

I had to disengage, I tell myself. For my own self-preservation. Francine's weirdness is the kind that could rub off if you're not careful. It's not so much the way she looks—if you never had a conversation with her, you might be fooled into thinking she was normal. You might even, occasionally, think she was cute. But no, Francine is always *getting involved*, jumping up to volunteer for this or that, waving her arm in your face like there's actual competition for World's Most Annoying Samaritan. Everybody at Hargis already knows the honor belongs to her.

I admit that maybe I didn't always feel that way—maybe, ages ago, I actually found her semi-tolerable. Except I haven't really thought about that in a while, and I don't feel like starting now.

Francine doesn't notice as I watch her bustling down the side of the classroom, handing out packets of worksheets to each row. She purses her lips slightly as she counts, like she's almost but not quite forming the numbers aloud. When a stack drops to the floor, pages splayed out, she stoops to pick it up with near-professional efficiency, and something about that—the way you can't tell anything's up with her at all—makes me want to wrench away the packets and pass them out for her.

"All right, loves," says Ms. Abdi, leaning over the lab station at the front of the room. She's extremely short, with long dreads and a habit of stretching out sentences into yogic-breath territory. "You all remember what today is, right?"

Half the room groans because how could we forget? Ms. Abdi gives the projector screen a tug, and it snaps up, coiling into a roll. On the whiteboard, in Francine's handwriting, are the words *PIG DISSECTION DAY* in purple marker. In the corner, she's even drawn a little pig with a curly tail, which I can't decide if I think is sort of funny or totally grotesque.

"Now, keep in mind this is a *privilege*." Ms. Abdi looks us each in the eye, and in spite of myself, I straighten a bit in my chair. "Treat this opportunity with the respect it deserves. Honor the process and your specimen." She gestures to the trays lining the counter along the far wall and then brings her hands back together, eyelids fluttering closed. I almost expect her to bow her head. "Be present."

Francine has reached the row in front of me, and I slump down again, eyes averted. While waiting for her to pass, I study the wooden panel just beneath the tabletop, where somebody in my seat, during some dreary class period, had scratched the initials "S. T. + L. D." and encircled them in a shaky heart. For months now, when there hasn't been anything better to do, I've found myself absently retracing the lines with my own pen, doing my part to preserve the mark for posterity. Sometimes I wonder about S. T. and L. D. and whether they made it past AP Bio.

Ms. Abdi is strolling down the aisle now, hands clasped behind her back. "Dissection is a way for you to gain an intimate understanding of how organisms are built," she says. "Of how *you* are built. Because don't forget, humans, too, are physical beings. We, too, are flesh and bone."

I find myself getting kind of interested in Ms. Abdi's monologue, but then my phone buzzes, and I sneak it out of my pocket. The text is from Rollo Chen, my best friend and usual lab partner, who is noticeably absent from the seat next to me.

Gonna miss lab, the message reads. **Taking care of some biz.**

I met Rollo on the first day of seventh grade, when he tried to sell me a subscription to "Rollo Pool," a rideshare service pitched as an alternative to being driven everywhere by your parents (no credit card required). I didn't take him up on the offer, but that hardly mattered: Rollo had already gotten dozens of other kids to sign up, and he would have made a killing if all his drivers—recruited from among his older cousins—hadn't quit based on claims that they were being underpaid. ("I don't see Uber paying a living wage," he said later, shrugging.)

I wasn't sure what to make of a guy like Rollo, but I ran into him again a few weeks afterward, when Mom made me go to the Welcome Dance. Everybody else was in the gym having a grand old time, but he was sitting under the bleachers by the basketball courts—exactly where *I'd* been planning to hide out until it was time to be picked up. "I know you're gonna find this hard to believe," Rollo said, remarkably smooth for a kid who was crawling out from under a metal bench. "But I can't dance for shit!" Then he grinned, a big chipmunk-like smile crisscrossed at the time with braces, and somehow, in that force field of his shamelessness, I felt a little bit less alone.

Right now, though, Rollo is nowhere to be found.

Me: **Dude, it's the pig dissection. It's like 50% of our grade.**

Rollo: **Relax, you got this.**

"Ollie," says Ms. Abdi. "You need a partner, don't you? This isn't one you can do by yourself." She skips her eyes over Rollo's empty seat to land on Jiya Jain, who pushes back a lock of magenta hair and removes an earbud in the same sleight of hand.

"Um," I stall. "Rollo might be . . . late."

Jiya slouches a bit as she leans forward, though on her, the habit is almost intimidating. Other than a nose ring, she dresses like a child from the nineties, but don't let that fool you. Her vibe is definitely too cool for school. Right now, she pulls her notebook closer, flipping to a fresh page as if preparing to jot down whatever Ms. Abdi is about to say, but the giveaway is the intricate pattern of thick lines bleeding through from her drawing. She's basically always drawing, often very intensely, which is why I avoid saying much to her. Also, she scares me.

"Tell Rollo he needs to see me about all the classes he's missed." Ms. Abdi rubs her chin, like she's tallying how much Rollo has let her down. "And then can you please put your phone away, Ollie?"

I scramble to stuff it back in my pocket.

"You'll work with Jiya today," Ms. Abdi decides, and before I can convince myself it won't be that bad, Francine, now empty-handed, skips up and slides into her seat at the end of the row.

Right next to Jiya.

"Oh, yes," adds Ms. Abdi, nodding like I'm in for a real treat. "And Francine, of course. You girls don't mind?"

This is another reason I don't really talk to Jiya: she and Francine are best friends. It's as true as it is inexplicable.

They both glance over at me now, and Francine raises her chin slightly. "Sure," she says, her voice a shade more apathetic than I expected. "Ollie can be in our group."

"Wonderful," says Ms. Abdi. "Let's get started, then."

Francine, of course, is the one who jumps up to get first crack at the pig fetuses. I stay in my seat, as does Jiya, who flips back to her artwork-in-progress. The drawing, done elaborately in black and gold Sharpie, features an Indian American girl with dark-rimmed eyes, like Jiya herself, whose face is being grabbed by a hand wrestling its way out of a phone screen. The effect is a little alarming.

"So, you and Francine always work together?" This is not the most unnecessary thing I could have said, but it's up there.

"Yup." Jiya's head is still bent over the page, like she can't even be bothered to notice how inane my comment was. "She's usually the one who does the heavy-lifting, though. She loves labs."

As if on cue, Francine reappears and sets a tray on the tabletop with a clink. Our pig, encased in its shrink-wrapped sarcophagus, teeters a bit, and I try not to look at it.

"Here," says Francine, handing me an apron. She's already got hers on, along with goggles and gloves, and before Jiya and I have time to follow suit, she cuts a straight line across the bag and frees the pig from the plastic. Unceremoniously, she lays it onto the paper towels nestled in our tray, and the three of us stare down at the rubbery form.

"Are you okay, Ollie?" Francine nudges her goggles up her nose. "Is it the smell?"

"No." I grip the edge of the table, wishing I'd thought to lie about having a religious reason to get out of this. "I mean, yes,

I'm fine." The smell is vaguely chemical but less pungent than I'd imagined. The issue is more that it's a *fully formed* piglet, complete with skinny legs that end in little hooves, eyes resting in the appearance of sleep, and—the thing that really gets me—fuzz along the top of its head.

"Are you sure?" says Francine. "Do you want to just be the instructions reader?"

I would like nothing better than to be the fucking instructions reader, but I can feel Francine's concern settling around my shoulders, trapping me like a heavy cloak I don't need.

"No," I say again. "I said I was *fine*."

"I'll be the instructions reader," Jiya pipes up, grabbing one of the lab packets. When I shoot her a look, she raises an eyebrow. "Well, someone's got to."

"Jiya's a very good instructions reader," Francine assures me.

"Great," I say. "Terrific."

"I think we should name him." Jiya inspects our pig fondly. "Any ideas?"

Francine shrugs, and they both turn to me. Unfortunately, I'm too nauseous to come up with anything good. "How about . . . Piggy?"

"*Piggy?*" Jiya appears to notice me properly for the first time, and it's not a positive assessment.

Francine decides to riff on my suggestion. "What if we made it . . . Pig*by*."

"Pigby," repeats Jiya, thoughtfully this time. "That's better." And I guess it is.

Francine, however, is already moving on. "Can you lift up

the tray, Ollie?" She knots together two rubber bands and tugs them taut over Pigby's head. "I need your help tying him down."

Somehow I recover enough to do as she asks, which enables her to slip the linked elastics under the tray. But when she stretches one loop toward me, I balk. "Can you at least hold it?" she sighs.

I take it reluctantly. "You're awfully chill about all this," I observe, hoping she doesn't think I'm impressed. Even if I am.

Francine wraps her side of the rubber band chain around Pigby's front right leg. "I'd like to go to med school someday, so I'll have to get used to a lot worse."

Ugh, I should've known. Every time I hear about an Asian kid who's planning to become a doctor, I could throw up. "Do you really want to, though, or is it just what your parents want?"

"Both, I guess." She points at Pigby's other front leg, and even though I'm still feeling squeamish, I follow her example and secure his limb to the tray.

"What kind of doctor?" I ask, curious in spite of myself.

"Primary care," Francine answers without hesitating, and I picture our family doctor, the ancient Dr. Nguyen, whose office in a boxy Little Saigon medical building is adorned with faded posters about handwashing and heart attacks (courtesy of pharmaceutical companies). He's the only doctor I know personally, and I wouldn't want to be him at all.

I flick another rubber band across the table. "Doesn't that seem kinda boring?"

"There's a shortage of family physicians nationwide," Francine explains, and I don't know whether that's better or worse than if she'd just said her parents made her. "Can you lift the tray again?"

Seeing no other choice, I help her tie down the pig's remaining legs. Together, we make sure poor Pigby, strung up as if in a medieval torture device, won't be going anywhere.

"Now cut a V shape," Jiya reads from the instructions. "Under the pig's neck."

Scalpel in hand, Francine squints over her shoulder at the diagram on her lab sheet. "Okay," she says, feeling her fingers along the skin where she's about to make the incision. "Here goes—"

"Wait," I say. "We're gonna . . . just like that?"

Francine's scalpel is still hovering over Pigby. "Yes?"

"But his entire existence has been about nothing. We didn't even let him make it out of the womb alive. His sole purpose was being a specimen for dissection."

Both Francine and Jiya seem surprised by my outpouring. I'm a little surprised, too.

"That's not nothing," says Francine. "His sole purpose *would* have been being a byproduct to the pork industry."

"They raise the sows for meat," Jiya clarifies. "And then they remove the fetuses to discard or use as fertilizer." She turns to Francine. "I guess Ollie's kind of right? If it weren't for the meat industrial complex, Pigby could have grown up to be a happy adult pig."

"If it weren't for the meat industrial complex," Francine replies, "Pigby wouldn't exist."

"How do you know, though?" I mean for the question to be combative, but instead it limps forward, practically begging everyone to feel sorry for it.

"Are we talking about . . . pig souls?" Francine sets down the scalpel, and there's a whiff of incredulity in her question.

"I'm just saying, we don't know. We don't know where life comes from, or where it goes, or how it gets allocated. But you're just standing there, with death in front of you, and you're not even thinking about it."

Francine studies me for a moment, and then the full weight of my douchebaggery hits me as I remember: her grandpa. Her grandpa's fucking dying and I'm asking why she isn't thinking about questions of life and death.

I try to fumble together an apology as Francine picks up the scalpel again. But instead of going back in for the cut, she pauses and drops her hands, clasping one wrist over the other. "Would you like to say a few words for Pigby?"

"What?" Coming from anyone else, this would surely be sarcastic, but from Francine, it's hard to tell.

"Like a prayer or something," Francine prompts. "Whatever you want."

I look over at Jiya for help, but she only shrugs. "I don't believe in God."

I'm not sure I believe in God either. My parents are technically Buddhist, but I have no idea what Buddhists would say for a pig who's about to get sliced open.

"I don't know," I stammer.

With the air of somebody who realizes she has to do everything herself, Francine bows her head. "Thank you, Pigby, for being our specimen and giving us a chance to learn about mammalian anatomy. We don't know where your soul is headed, or if you even have one, but what matters is that you were alive once. Your life, though short, was given over completely to the service of others, which is the most anyone can aspire to. You had, and always will have had, a purpose."

She straightens up again. "How's that?" she says generally, but her eyes are asking me.

I'm astounded. Francine's speech, unfussy yet strangely thoughtful, was somehow appropriate, its poignance buried beneath the breezy pragmatism. It's clearly more than I was able to muster and much more than I was expecting from Francine.

But I don't know how to say any of that, or even if I want to. So I cross my arms and turn toward the window because it's easier than looking at her.

"It's whatever," I mumble. "Can we just get this over with?"

4

Francine

ON SUNDAY, WE DRIVE UP TO LA FROM ORANGE County to my a gūng and a pòh's house. We all act as if everything is normal—Dad with his hands perfectly placed at ten and two o'clock on the wheel, Mom listening to some staticky Cantonese radio station with her eyes closed, and me in the back seat, watching the gray landscape whiz by.

Usually, when traffic is really bad (which is often), I like to pass the time by peering into other cars. People do all kinds of things when they don't realize anyone's looking—argue with wild hand gestures, bite into sloppy sandwiches, dance to music I can't hear.

But today, I don't notice anything because I spend the whole drive thinking about Ollie.

Was I totally deluded for believing he would help me with The Plan? Has he somehow, over the years, become an actual jerk?

I lean my forehead against the window, letting the road

jostle my face against the glass until it hurts. My mind drifts over everything I know about Ollie, the details I've kept packed away like my old stuffed animals, safe but out of sight. When I was younger, I went to his house a lot more because my cousins and I often got dragged there by our parents. I remember the kitchen most, narrow and rectangular with sunny tile countertops that in later years got replaced, like a betrayal, by two slabs of green marble. My aunts, along with Mom, would help Ollie's mother amid the steam and smoke of wok oil, wrapping Chinese-style egg rolls with Vietnamese-style filling. The men would be in the adjoining dining room, noisy and rambunctious, speaking three different languages—Vietnamese, Cantonese, and occasionally Mandarin—and somehow, saying nothing at all.

As for me, I mostly got ignored: by Ollie, who escaped to his room before I even toed the threshold of the front door; by Ollie's brother, Isaac, who was already in high school and interested only in video games and basketball; and by my cousins, especially Lauren, the oldest, who for some reason was not at all intrigued to learn that when she turned bright pink around Isaac, it was the veins in her face overreacting to adrenaline.

Once, when I was ten, I found the three of them—Lauren; her sister, Ava; and my other cousin Sandy—huddled together on Ollie's front steps, where they'd gone while I'd been laying out The Game of Life. "Sure," Lauren had said, when I'd offered to set it up. "You do that, and then we'll come back and play." But twenty minutes after I'd counted all the money, arranged the bills along the sides of the board, and plugged the plastic people into four car-shaped pieces, I was still sitting there on the carpet, alone.

Outside, only Ava turned around when I pushed open the screen door.

"Oh, hey, Francine," she said, her voice slightly more high-pitched than usual. "You want to join us?"

Except there wasn't any room left on the steps, so I hovered behind them, watching Isaac as he dribbled a basketball around another Asian kid in the driveway.

"What are you all up to?" I asked after a minute.

"Nothing," said Lauren.

Isaac made a shot just then, which sent him jogging in a circle, arms pumped in the air, while the other kid laughed and shook his head.

I eyed Lauren, who was paying very close attention to the proceedings. At the time, she was fourteen, like Isaac, and had lined her eyelids with dark strokes, the outer edges swooped out and up. She looked pretty, but even I could see that Isaac wasn't going to notice that while she was sitting all the way over here. Especially when he was so immersed in basketball.

"If you want to get Isaac's attention," I offered, "wouldn't it be better if you asked to join the game?"

"We're not trying to get anyone's attention," Lauren snapped.

This seemed false, but arguments with Lauren were consistently unpleasant when she was wrong.

"Okay, well," I said, shrugging, "do you still want to play Life?"

"Lauren says Life is boring," Sandy piped up.

I stood there for another minute, observing Isaac as he tried to steal the basketball from the other kid, and wondered, genuinely, how this was any less boring.

"Maybe you should move closer to the hoop—"

"No one's asking you, Francine," said Lauren.

"No one ever does," added Sandy, and the three of them exchanged a look.

Now it was the veins in my face that were reacting to adrenaline, though I couldn't tell you exactly why.

Back inside, I sat down at the coffee table, surveying the Life board spread out before me. I decided to play the game on my own—it wasn't like I hadn't done that plenty of times before. As an only child, you got used to that kind of thing. It was only sad when other people saw you doing it.

"Uh, Francine?"

I looked up, my hand over the spinner. Ollie, on his way back from the kitchen, had paused reluctantly, chrysanthemum tea drink box in hand. His dog, Dexter, a great big husky mix the color of cream puff pastry, crashed to a halt against his heels.

"Are you playing Life . . . against yourself?"

I resumed my spin of the wheel, which whirled so fast the rainbow of colors blurred together. "Seems like."

Ollie shifted from one foot to the other, glancing around the empty living room. "How's it going?"

"Good," I replied, pushing one of the car pieces forward seven spaces. "I'm winning."

That made Ollie laugh—a quick, barely there exhale of surprise—but then he immediately sobered, stealing a glance out the window as if to check for any witnesses. All we saw was Isaac lunging for the basketball.

"Do you need, um . . ." Ollie was having trouble getting the question out. Already, too, he was inching away, like he hoped more than anything my answer would be no.

I decided to save him. "Sure, if Dexter wants to join, he can. I know Life can be a complicated game for a dog, though."

We both looked down at Dexter, who wagged his tail guilelessly, glancing from me to Ollie. Then Ollie stared at the floor so long that I decided to go ahead and spin the wheel again. But instead of leaving me alone, he sat down next to Dexter.

"Okay," said Ollie. "He'll play." Patting Dexter's back, he kind of smiled at me, and that's when I noticed his dimple for the first time.

I nearly fell over.

Everyone always says that between the two of them, Isaac is the handsomer brother. But I've never thought so. Ollie's deeply hooded eyes, set off by delicate lashes, are large and serious—Mom often insists they were wasted on a boy. A Pòh's assessment, though, is not as generous: "That one looks like he suffers," she says. "His older brother took all the good fortune." When I try to argue that you can't tell that just from someone's *face*, A Pòh dismisses me. "The point is, you're always better off with an oldest son."

But that gloomy air my a pòh found so inauspicious was exactly what I liked about Ollie back then. I was sure it meant he pondered things that other people didn't, things that I hoped to understand. Even when he smiled, a twinge of melancholy would remain, like a bit of salt in chocolate milk—and boy, that wasn't something you got over fast.

Now, though, I wonder, if I'd been imagining something that had never been there at all.

"We're here, Francine," says Mom, and I blink.

A Gūng and A Pòh live on a sloped street just north of Chinatown, off a thoroughfare lined with shuttered tire shops. Despite the constant sunshine, there's no escaping the industrial pallor that lingers right around the corner. Their neighbors are mostly Mexican families, squeezed into beautiful old houses that have been cut up into apartments. White people have started to move back into the surrounding neighborhoods, but this one's a holdout—for now at least.

My grandparents' house was originally built for somebody rich, though it's kind of hard to see that now. You can still make out little details, like the crown molding in the living room or the archway that leads into the dining room, but most of the grandeur is now buried. Literally, because A Pòh is a bit of a hoarder. The porch is dense with potted plants and piles of boxes, plus stacks upon stacks of weekly ad circulars.

"Every time we come, it gets worse," Mom says to no one in

particular, kicking aside a tray that once held Asian pears. She says it in English, in case A Pòh overhears.

Lauren, who can be wise about such things, once told us younger cousins that the hoarding is a result of a lifetime of surviving war. "Think about it," she said. "First the Japanese came to Vietnam. Then the Americans. Imagine what that does to your *psyche*."

When A Pòh opens the door, however, she seems scarred neither by war nor, for that matter, the more recent trauma of A Gūng's diagnosis. "Hallooo!" she cries, as loud as ever. It's how she always says hello.

"A Pòh hóu," I reply dutifully.

"You need to eat more," she tells me, rapping my shoulder blade with her knuckles. "What is this? You're all bones!"

Gratuitous (and inaccurate) assessments of my weight aside, I like A Pòh. When I was a little kid, she was the only person who never got tired of talking to me. I'd ask any question—say, "Why are crows black?"—and she would always have an answer, no matter what. She liked to explain things, and I found it magical.

These days, she still enjoys talking to me, but the stories are more often things she learned from reading the Chinese newspaper—like the time some elderly woman got her purse stolen at a Monterey Park intersection. So, you know, it's not always as nice.

Normally, A Gūng would be finishing his qigong exercises around now, standing in the center of the living room with his arms outstretched. The giant TV, a gift from Lauren and

Ava's parents and probably the most expensive thing in the house, would be tuned into one of his usual news programs (at this hour, usually a Mandarin one beamed in via satellite). The smell of Folger's instant coffee would waft out from the kitchen, where A Pòh would be puttering around as she assembled A Gūng's midmorning meal—a bowl of porridge, a bit of boiled choy sum, and a soft banana.

But today, everything is eerily still. For the first time, I notice the worn patch of hardwood floor where A Gūng's feet shuffled every day. The TV, control of which has been ceded to A Pòh, is playing a black-and-white Jimmy Stewart film with the sound off. A Pòh has a gift for comprehending movies without needing to understand a word—though right now she isn't really watching this one.

"Where's Bā?" Mom asks. In response, A Pòh puts a finger to her lips and points toward the bedroom. Two roller suitcases sit right outside the door.

The thing about today is we're not here just to visit A Gūng and A Pòh. We're here to bring them to stay at our house, where it will be easier for Mom or Dad to take A Gūng to his various appointments. And although nobody says it out loud, it also means he'll get to spend more time with us. Until, I guess, there isn't any left.

"Lunch will be ready soon," A Pòh says in her normal voice, and disappears into the kitchen.

Dad settles into the La-Z-Boy by the fireplace while Mom hovers in the dining room, picking through the oranges and apples heaped on the table. A Pòh is always buying fruit to make offerings to the Guanyin Buddha and our ancestors, but she never eats it fast enough afterward, so most end up going to mold.

"Mà! Why don't you throw these away?" says Mom, chagrined.

A Pòh comes back out and picks up an orange, holding it close to her nose. She takes off her glasses to inspect it, but after only a second, shakes her head. "Aiyah, it's not a big deal!"

Mom and I exchange a glance, and my limbs feel inexplicably heavy. Maybe it's the worry that A Pòh wouldn't have realized on her own that the fruit had gone bad—or worse, that she refuses to acknowledge she clearly hadn't noticed this time.

"Fōng," she commands now. "Go wash your hands and get ready to eat."

My mind is still on the fruit, but I obey her and trudge toward the bathroom. I'm suddenly not sure I have the energy anymore for anything, much less The Plan. In the hallway, I pause in front of the photos on the wall. They're ones I've seen before, of course, mostly color portraits of Lauren, Ava, Sandy, me, and other people in our family. A few are of A Gūng and A Pòh from when they first came to America, looking serious and already old, though maybe not so gray.

Then there's a sepia-toned photograph that's smaller than the rest, taken when A Gūng and A Pòh still lived in Vietnam. Squeezed within the serrated borders are much younger versions of themselves—A Gūng's forehead broad and unlined,

A Pòh's hair still raven black—along with six girls of various ages, including a small baby who is Mom. No one is smiling, exactly, and A Pòh's expression is particularly unreadable. A Gūng's, though, is more open. In the slick of his pomade and the heft of his glasses, there's a determined optimism that gives him the appearance of a Cold War intellectual. You can see he still believes, despite the poverty that's tailed him his whole life, that all circumstances, surely, can be triumphed over.

I try to square this A Gūng with the one I'm familiar with, but it's hard. The face that I know, clouded over with wrinkles, hardly seems like it ever had the space for such ambitious faith.

A few steps down the hall, A Gūng's door is slightly open, so I tiptoe over and peek in. The shades are drawn, darkening the room against the sunlight that might have filtered through the window. A Gūng is facing away from me, the top of his head obscured by a flannel sleeping cap, so all I can see is an inert form lost in the covers, slumped into a curve of defeat.

I back away quietly, my chest stinging. I refuse, however, to cry. A Pòh always tells me there's no point to crying, and I'm inclined to agree. What *does* have a point is taking action. I already know the one thing that will make me feel less sad is to help A Gūng feel less sad. He may have given up, but I'm not going to.

Which means I'm not giving up on Ollie yet either.

Ollie

ON MONDAY, I ALMOST FORGET THAT I'M SUPposed to meet with Ms. Mirza during fourth period, so I have to sprint across campus to make it to the counseling office in time. I was assigned Ms. Mirza randomly, which was a lucky break because as college counselors go, she is super chill. In fact, she probably wouldn't even mind if I were late, but you know—I don't want to be that guy.

I'm a little winded when I skid to a stop in front of the office door, so I'm not really prepared when I swing it open and find, behind a desk piled high with stacks of envelopes, Francine. Her student aide badge hangs on a lanyard around her neck.

"Ollie?" She sets down a small plastic bottle topped with a sponge, which I guess she'd been using to moisten the envelope flaps. "What are you doing here?"

The way she's asking, though, makes it seem like she's glad to see me. Like me showing up here is just the pleasant surprise she was waiting for.

I blush. I'm one of those people who blushes easily, often for no reason. Sometimes all it takes is somebody talking to me—they could be saying "Are you finished with that?" or "Where is the bathroom?" and it wouldn't make a difference. In most cases, it doesn't have anything to do with who the person is. Like right now, which *definitely* doesn't have anything to do with Francine. We haven't spoken outside of class since the pig dissection day, which is as it should be, though I have sometimes found myself thinking about her Pigby speech and the whole sad thing with her grandpa, and I kind of wish I'd reacted differently that afternoon.

"I'm here to see Ms. Mirza," I say, hoping she doesn't notice how pink I've gotten.

"Oh," says Francine, frowning. "She's out sick today."

"Wait, really?" I scroll through my phone to see if I missed an email. "Was I supposed to reschedule?"

Francine opens a calendar on the computer and clicks a few times. "No, you're fine. You've been reassigned to Ms. Lane instead."

I want to tell Francine that this is far from fine. Ms. Lane is the other counselor at Hargis, and she's worshipped on campus for getting kids into top schools. She's got a resting face as severe as the part of her hair, which is streaked with gray even though she's not actually that old. People say she once intercepted a Stanford interviewer at a SoulCycle class in Huntington Beach just to make someone's case. Basically, she's dedicated AF and that's not exactly the best fit for me.

Before I can react, however, Ms. Lane appears in her doorway. "Good morning, Ollie," she says. "You're late."

I glance at Francine, who looks sorry for me, and then the clock on the wall. In the time that we've been talking, it's become two minutes past eleven—which means I *am*, technically, now late.

"Sorry," I say, shuffling over to take a seat in Ms. Lane's office. As she shuts the door, I remove my backpack and hug it to my chest, then change my mind and drop it on my shoes, then change my mind again and kick it under my chair. Ms. Lane watches all of this without a word, and only when I finally sit still does she speak up.

"All right, Ollie," she begins. "This meeting is for you. What questions do you have for me?"

I'd been under the impression that this would be a quick check-in—a simple requirement for all juniors at this point in the semester—so I obviously have no questions. "Um," I venture. "I guess I'm wondering how I'm doing, college-wise?"

Ms. Lane opens a manila folder on her desk and pulls out my transcript. Of course she has her shit together, despite being saddled with me pretty last minute. "Your grades look competent," she observes with a sniff of surprise. "Quite competent."

This is not an accident. I discovered long ago that getting decent grades was a surefire way to keep my parents off my back, so I always make sure to do just well enough to fly under their radar. It's one of the few useful things I've learned from

Isaac, who has perfected the practice into an art. In high school, he was the poor man's golden boy: earned straight A minuses, played varsity basketball but didn't make captain, got nominated for homecoming court but wasn't crowned king. He was, and still is, slightly below above average in all aspects of his life and generally affable about the whole situation. Somehow, though, he's now a junior at Berkeley, so I guess it worked out for him.

"Your extracurriculars, in contrast, are extremely weak," Ms. Lane continues. "We'll have to fix that if you're hoping to get into a certain tier of school."

I shift uneasily. My activities are nothing stellar, though they always seemed fine enough for getting by. Especially considering I'm not even trying to pull off an Isaac. But Ms. Lane is looking at me expectantly, so I say, "You mean, like, join more clubs?"

Ms. Lane shakes free another sheet of paper, this one a form I'd filled out with a summary of my extracurricular experiences. "Not necessarily. Colleges want to see depth, not breadth. They're particularly interested in evidence of initiative and commitment." She places the page in front of me. "To be frank, I'm not seeing a lot of that here."

I look down at my list, which includes some basic stuff like Key Club and National Honor Society—organizations that are impressive sounding, but so big that nobody notices if you don't show up to a meeting. The reason Ms. Lane isn't seeing a lot of initiative and commitment here is that there isn't any.

"I can work on it," I say, because I feel like the quickest way out of this conversation is to agree with everything.

Ms. Lane doesn't buy it. "What exactly are your goals, Ollie?" she asks, leaning forward suddenly. The question is suspiciously similar to one of my dad's favorite topics, which is what I plan to do with my life if I don't want to join the family business. My parents run a company importing and exporting Chinese medicinal herbs, and we all expect Isaac to be in charge someday. The problem is, the only thing that interests me less than medicinal herbs is working for Isaac.

"I'm not sure," I say blandly.

Ms. Lane's gaze stays fixed on me, and I remember another rumor I'd heard about how her eyeliner is tattooed on. How or why this came to be known is anybody's guess, but Ms. Lane shockingly settled the matter by corroborating the story. "It's much more efficient this way," she supposedly said—which, in retrospect, seems on brand.

"I can tell you have a lot of potential, Ollie," she says, which is one of those things adults want you to think is a compliment but actually means they're about to make you do a lot more work. "It seems to me, though, that you are in grave danger of wasting it." She folds her arms across her desk. "But don't worry—you're one of my students now. Which means it's my job to ensure you make the biggest impact you can."

I gulp, because that's exactly what I was afraid of.

"I think the key for you is to invest in something other than yourself." Ms. Lane waves a hand over my transcript. "Grades are important, Ollie, but I want to know: Are you willing to step up for others? Are you passionate about your community? Do you *care*?" I shrink a bit in my seat because I don't know how to answer those questions. I mean, if she puts it like that, then sure, I care. Don't I?

Ms. Lane, however, is already closing my folder. "Decide on an activity you'd like to get more involved in and bring me a plan of action when I see you next week." When I look bewildered, she adds, "It's already March, Ollie. You don't have much time. Let's get more substantial experience under your belt before the year is over."

I manage to mumble a positive response, then almost as quickly as I was diagnosed, I'm dismissed. I can't quite wrap my head around how Ms. Lane's interest in my college prospects seems both way too aggressive and, at the same time, totally perfunctory. Either way, it blows. I have no idea what I'm going to report back to her. It's not like Key Club is suddenly going to let me be their treasurer or whatever—kids spend years working up to those positions. I, on the other hand, have never been comfortable putting myself out there like that. I'm not one of those people who always feels the need to make some big contribution. After all, I'm not—

"Francine, geez!"

She jumps backward, flailing but recovering quickly, as I almost trip over her. I wasn't expecting her to be right outside Ms. Lane's door.

"How was it?" she asks, like she wasn't just listening in on the whole thing.

"I don't know." I'm partly disoriented and partly annoyed. "Why don't you tell me?"

"Well, if I'm being honest," Francine replies, "it didn't sound too good."

Reflexively, I get defensive, but then I realize that I literally asked for it. Sighing, I rub the back of my neck. "The gist is that Ms. Lane thought my extracurriculars were shit."

Francine nods solemnly—you would've thought I'd said I was getting expelled or something. "And are they?"

"No," I snap. Then I pause. "I mean, maybe they are, but it's whatever. What's it to her? She barely asked me about my interests and basically stopped listening when I didn't have an immediate response. Now she's expecting me to conjure up more 'substantial experience' out of thin air. How the hell am I supposed to do that, especially this late in the year?"

"That's fair." Francine nods again, weirdly agreeable. "Did you tell Ms. Lane how you feel?"

"Did I tell Ms. Lane?" I repeat, faltering, and it occurs to me then I've kind of been going off, which I hadn't meant to do three feet from Ms. Lane's office and certainly not to Francine. I don't know what about her right now is making me blab on like this. Blushing again, I take a step toward the main office door. "No, I guess I didn't."

"Oh," says Francine, but you can tell she really wants to ask *why not?* It's another question I don't have an answer to, and

I'm thankful when she instead goes with "Maybe it won't be as bad as you think. I'm sure there are lots of clubs that would love to have your gung-ho spirit!"

Her exaggerated you-can-do-it fist pump is so ridiculous that it makes me laugh, and I forget for a second why I was embarrassed. "Well, tell them to get in line," I joke just as the bell rings.

"Sure thing." Francine grins at me. "I'll draw up a list."

As I reach for the door, I decide against my better judgment to wave, and at first it takes Francine by surprise. Then she waves back energetically, and I smile to myself as I step outside, shaking my head. She always was a funny girl.

6

Francine

"I'VE GOT IT!"

I scamper up the steps of the amphitheater stage, where Jiya is sitting on the concrete with her legs stretched out, an empty bento box container by her knees. Her sketchbook rests on her lap, and she's drawing something as I approach.

"Got what?" she asks, sliding off her gargantuan headphones. The music's so loud, I can tell she's listening to Violet Girl, her latest obsession.

"A solution to the Ollie problem." I plop down next to her. "I have it all figured out."

Jiya lowers the volume and gives me exactly the look I was expecting. "The Ollie problem, huh?"

Most people are surprised when they find out Jiya and I are best friends, which is reasonable. Sometimes I'm surprised myself. My first impression of Jiya was that she was the kind of person who didn't need friends. It was freshman fall, and I'd been passing out flyers for the Teacher Appreciation Pancake

Breakfast when I discovered her here, on the outskirts of campus, having lunch alone on the amphitheater stage. Despite the empty seats, it felt like a bold move, putting her solitude on display like that. Still, I figured she'd enjoy pancakes as much as the next person, so I looked past her piercings and then-orange hair and asked if she wanted to buy a ticket. "The proceeds go to a good cause," I explained when she gave me the once-over, raising her headphones barely half an inch. After a long silence, during which I began to question whether Jiya had ever eaten gluten in her life, she broke into a grin. "Sure," she told me. "I'd love to."

Since then, we've met for lunch in the amphitheater almost every day. No one else ever comes here, so it's a peaceful spot—sometimes you can even hear the sparrows tittering in the shrubbery. It's a good place to talk about important stuff.

Like, for instance, the Ollie problem.

"I've got an idea for how to win him over," I say, ignoring the question Jiya is really asking. She knows, of course, that I used to have a crush on Ollie even though it was from before she and I were friends. But she *also* knows that I don't anymore, so there's no need for us to get into it now.

Jiya twirls her pen between two fingers, clearly contemplating whether to follow up on this thread. To my relief, she just says, "Okay, tell me."

I describe this morning's encounter with Ollie in the counseling office, as well as the concerns Ms. Lane identified with his extracurriculars. I leave out the part about overhearing most of the conversation through the door.

Jiya shakes her head. "Francine, were you eavesdropping again?"

"It's fine! Ollie didn't seem to mind. He basically *asked* for my help figuring out which clubs to approach."

"Did he though?"

"Okay, maybe not directly, but I really think this could work, Jiya. I could totally figure out a plan of action for him. I am *all* about plans and action."

Jiya watches me unscrew my thermos and scoop up some pasta salad. "You've already started, haven't you?"

I have. While walking over here, I sent out a mass email to literally every club president asking what they could use help with this month, and what do you know, I've already gotten replies. Mostly from smaller, more obscure groups, but there's nothing wrong with that. This isn't nearly as hard as Ollie thought it would be. I've been passing along his name to all interested parties, so I'm sure he'll have loads of opportunities soon.

"You know," Jiya says gently when I outline all this for her, "even if Ollie finds this useful, it doesn't mean he's going to help with The Plan."

I look down at my pasta salad and jab the spoon around. "Yeah, that's probably true."

"And you know that would be okay, right? Like your grandpa will be fine even if you don't pull off this whole honorary-male-heir scheme."

"Well, he won't be fine, even if I do. That's the point."

Jiya sinks back into a slouch, and I realize I sounded a lot more down than I wanted to.

"But maybe Ollie will agree," I add, taking a bite of the pasta even though it's no longer as cold as it should be. "Guess we'll see."

Jiya still seems skeptical, but an unexpected figure has appeared at the edge of the amphitheater and is beginning to make their way over.

"Is that . . . Rollo Chen?" I say, squinting.

It is, in fact, Rollo. I immediately wonder if Ollie is with him, but no, it's just Rollo. As usual, his hair has been blow-dried to a poufy height, and his white Allbirds sneakers are spotless. Today he's also wearing something bulky on his back that, upon closer inspection, turns out to be an expensive-looking cooler. He hauls it up the steps with agility, then eases it onto the ground like it's precious cargo. The whole contraption, admittedly, is more stylish and streamlined than my actual backpack.

"Jiya Jain," Rollo announces as he whips out an iPad. He beams at her, flashing his very straight teeth. "Just the woman I was looking for."

I have three classes with Rollo, but it feels like this is the first I've seen him in a while. "What's all this, Rollo?" I ask, examining his cooler.

"This, Francine," he says, waving his hand, "is a week's worth of inventory for Rollos and More, Hargis High's first ever candy delivery subscription service." He points at the *Rollos and More* screen-printed on the waterproof fabric.

I glance at Jiya, who doesn't look nearly as confused as me. "He came by orchestra class one morning to take orders," she explains. To Rollo, she adds, "Didn't you say it was called Rollo & Co.?"

"That didn't test as well with my target audience," Rollo replies. "Too Millennial sounding."

Jiya shrugs one shoulder and nods, like maybe she agrees.

Rollo unzips his cooler and rummages around in the main compartment. "All right, let's get you the goods! Gummy bears, was it?"

"Gobstoppers," Jiya corrects.

"Oh, yeah, gobstoppers." He pulls out a box of them and does a fancy toss behind his back. Jiya is surprised but reacts quick enough to catch it anyway.

"I thought we weren't allowed to sell candy on campus?" I say as Rollo taps away at his tablet. A few years ago, Hargis instituted a campus ban on junk food, and as far as I know, student fundraisers aren't exempt.

"We're not," Rollo confirms. "It's been *great* for business."

Jiya stuffs a gobstopper in her mouth before offering me one, but I decline politely. "Aren't you worried you'll get caught?" I ask Rollo.

He's already got his stash packed up again. "You sound like Ollie," he says, chuckling, and slings the cooler over his shoulders.

At the mention of Ollie, Jiya pops in another gobstopper and darts a look at me. But I know she won't reveal that we were just talking about him. Instead, she turns back to her sketchbook, a sign that she's finished with the conversation.

"Hey," says Rollo suddenly, peering down over her shoulder. "Did you draw that?"

Jiya's working on a painting of two girls in a surreal embrace, which she said is meant to be "like a Violet Girl song meets Gustav Klimt, but with an ancient Indian art aesthetic." She doesn't bother to share any of that with Rollo, though. "Yup."

"Isn't she good?" I show him the front of my binder, which features a cool metallic illustration of sunflowers. The artwork is in her usual style, but because she painted it especially for me, the vibe is a bit more cheerful than her other stuff. "She did this, too."

"Dang, Jiya." Rollo looks from one drawing to the other. "Tell me you've considered monetizing your skills."

Jiya pauses over her sketch. "How do you mean?"

Rollo reaches into his back pocket and pulls out a sleek nylon wallet. "We should talk," he says, handing her a business card. "I have tons of ideas."

Jiya holds up the thick cardstock, which would look fairly professional if it didn't include the printer's logo conspicuously in the bottom-right corner. The front of it reads *Rollo Chen, Art Agent.*

"Who are your other clients?" I inquire, taking the card from Jiya.

"It's a side hustle," Rollo assures me, which both does and does not answer the question.

"I'll consider it," says Jiya.

Then Rollo's Apple Watch buzzes. "Looks like I gotta run," he says. "But yeah, let me know!"

As he traipses down the steps, skipping over the last couple with a big jump, Jiya regards him with mild curiosity. "What do you think?" she says, pushing the gobstoppers around in her mouth. "How legit is Rollo, really?"

"Hmm," I say. "Hard to know."

"Well, I can always ask Ollie." Jiya grins when I look up, startled. "Aren't you two gonna be hanging out a lot soon?"

"Oh, right," I reply, hoping that saying it aloud will make it true. "We sure are."

7

Ollie

ON WEDNESDAY MORNING, WHEN I SPOT FRANcine hovering by my locker, I'm weirded out by two things. The first is that I don't immediately turn around and walk away, which would've been my usual instinct—and, I always thought, the correct one.

The second thing is that Francine doesn't actually seem to be waiting for me. Instead, she's standing there chatting with Jared Morales-Smith, her hair swishing as she nods, like it's not even my locker she's blocking. Before I can approach them, she's already bounding off, giving Jared a friendly wave that skims his shoulder, not once realizing I was behind her the whole time.

Like I said, weird.

Before I can process what just happened, Jared notices me and breaks into a grin. "There you are, Ollie!"

Jared is a band geek, but as I recently learned, the kind you should also pick for your team in PE class: stocky and well-built underneath the floppy hair and glasses, he definitely works out more than me. I don't remember what instrument he plays, but I bet it's something large and heavy, like a tuba. I wonder if that's Francine's type now.

"Um, hey," I say to Jared. We've never discussed anything beyond "Pass it, I'm open!" so his enthusiasm is unnerving.

"The team is so stoked to have you, man." Jared thumps me on the back. "You're exactly the type of guy we need."

I assume he must somehow be referring to PE, but we're currently on the golf unit and that's not a team sport. "What—"

"It's so rare to find someone new who has real appreciation for the game. Most people don't take it seriously because it's so easy to pick up. They think it's a cakewalk just because our main competitors are seniors."

Now he's totally lost me. "You only play against seniors?"

"Yeah, senior citizens. But you'd be surprised—those old people are really good! We all compete in the same league because there aren't enough high school teams."

"Right." I nod like I understand. "What game are we talking about again?"

"Lawn bowling." He holds up a cylindrical leather bag. "What else?"

I have no clue where Jared got the idea that I wanted to get into lawn bowling because this is the first I've heard that Hargis has a team. I don't even know what a lawn bowl looks like.

"Actually, I don't really do competitive sports," I say, hoping that will end the conversation. “Besides, I’d probably just drag you all down.”

“No way!” Jared follows me as I start walking. “You’re being way too down on yourself, dude. All you need is a little more confidence.”

“How about I get back to you?” I step around him and hurry off to class.

I don’t think much more about any of this until lunch, when I’m waiting in line outside the cafeteria. Rollo brings food from home, so he doesn’t even need to be there, but he likes to take advantage of the time to play his favorite game.

“How much would you pay,” says Rollo, “to have someone stand in line to get lunch for you every day?”

“Zero dollars,” I reply, swiping my ID. “It takes like thirty seconds.”

“What about when it rains, though?” Rollo looks up at the sky, blue and cloudless over the palm trees.

“You know it barely rains here. And when it does, they usually just move the line into the multipurpose room.”

“Okay, what about this. How much would you pay”—Rollo watches me consider the two options of the day, teriyaki chicken bowl or PB&J sandwich—“to have someone decide what you get for lunch every day?”

“What? Negative dollars.” I go with the PB&J. “Why would I want that?”

“Um, hello? Decision fatigue, only the dominant affliction of modern life.”

As Rollo gets ready to hit me with another conundrum, I feel a light tap on my shoulder. When I turn around, I'm accosted by—I kid you not—a group of mimes.

"What the—" I clutch my lunch tray to my chest as the ensemble begins their performance, which is led by a girl I recognize as another junior, Rita Lopez.

"Wait, is this a promposal?" asks Rollo, mesmerized.

That seems unlikely to me, considering Rita is not someone I've had a full conversation with since that time she got assigned to be my Spanish partner in freshman year. Not to mention, prom isn't for two months. So I have absolutely no explanation for why she is pointing and gesturing at me.

Everybody else in line is watching now, and I'm increasingly unsettled. I finally give in and take a step toward Rita and the mimes, and as soon as I do, they all jump for joy. A couple of them even do splits in the air, which would impress me if I were not so mortified. Finally, Rita comes up to me and digs out a small square of paper from her pocket. She makes a big show of unfolding it again and again until it's only got one crease left, and that's when she hands it to me. I open it, because that's clearly what she wants, and it reads *JOIN US* in thick black lettering, with a date and time printed in smaller font below.

I look up at Rita, confused, but all she does is give me a wave, which is instantly copied by the rest of the mimes, and then they scatter dramatically.

"Did you say yes?" someone calls out.

"It wasn't a promprosal!" I bellow, stuffing the paper into my backpack. Geez, what is up with people today? I can't seem to go anywhere without getting interrupted—

"Hey, you're Ollie Tran, right?"

I've barely taken two steps when another kid I've only seen a few times around campus appears in front of me. He's wearing a red T-shirt that says *I like big bugs and I cannot lie* and carrying some kind of terrarium covered with a blanket.

"I'm Marcel Cooper, president of the Hargis Entomological Society. I was told that you'd like to get involved with our arachnology committee."

"Arachnology?" I repeat, swallowing.

"Doesn't that have to do with spiders?" Rollo comes around to get a better look at the terrarium. "If so, then you've definitely got that wrong. Ollie *hates* spiders."

"Really?" Marcel seems surprised. "That's not what it sounded like."

"Hold on." I try not to think about what's hidden under the blanket. "Where did you even hear about me at all?"

"I got an email blast from Francine Zhang," explains Marcel, furrowing his brow. "She said you were looking for a new club to join. Like, you needed better extracurricular activities?"

"*What?* Why would she do that?"

"I don't know, but when I wrote back saying we needed someone to take charge of cleaning Gwen's terrarium, she said you'd be highly interested." Marcel, who is looking more uncertain, turns away slightly to put some distance between me and Gwen, like I'm the dangerous one in this conversation. "Are you?"

"Gwen is a cute name for a spider," Rollo coos, lifting the edge of the blanket. "Can I—"

"Wait," says Marcel, pivoting to keep her out of reach. "She's temperamental!"

Unfortunately, this is the exact moment that I've also thrust out my arm to swipe Rollo's hand away—because I want to leave Gwen alone as much as she wants to be left alone—and what happens instead is I collide into Marcel and send the terrarium soaring into the air, forcing me to lunge forward in an attempt to break its fall.

Which is how I find myself lying on the asphalt, my face inches from a very large, very hairy, very stressed-out spider.

"Shit!" I yelp, scrambling backward. It comes out like a high-pitched shriek, and only when I hear snorts of laughter do I look around and realize that all of this, to my utter humiliation, has played out in front of a crowd that now feels like it's grown to half the school. This means I've just publicly laid bare one of my worst fears while experiencing basically my *worst* fear of all.

I jump to my feet and run.

"Maybe you need to have a talk with Francine!" Marcel shouts after me, as he tries to corral Gwen back into her terrarium.

I don't stop to tell him that's *got* to be the understatement of the year.

***

Somehow, I miss Francine in all her usual places that afternoon, which only fuels my frustration—especially because I end up having to fend off several more invitations from random clubs. Eventually I run into Jiya, who insists she can neither confirm nor deny that Francine is avoiding me *per se*, but after a lot of prodding, admits that yes, they heard what happened and yes, Francine probably could say a thing or two about it. When I learn that she volunteers at the library after school, I storm across the street to find her, clearing the wide, flat steps four at a time.

"Children's Room," the librarian tells me when I ask about Francine at the check-out desk. Before even hearing the response, I see her through the double doors, just beyond the magazine display. She's sitting in a kiddie chair with a stack of picture books balanced on her knees, looking almost Disney-level cute and totally innocuous. Man, is that a joke!

I stomp across the gray carpet. "Francine!" I yell in a decidedly non-library voice.

Francine looks up, but that's when I realize she's not alone. Slowly, I turn my head to see that ten other little pairs of eyes are also fixed on me.

From the children's information desk, another librarian peers at me sternly, and it's likely that I'll be forcibly removed from three o'clock story time in about forty-five seconds.

"Everyone," says Francine brightly. "This is Ollie."

"Hi, Ollie," responds the kid Greek chorus.

One boy, wearing a T-shirt screen-printed with Mister

Rogers's face, shouts, "How are you feeling, Ollie?"

Befuddled, I glance at Francine. "We've been learning about emotions," she explains, holding up a book with an illustration of a pissed-off moose on the cover. It's called, appropriately, *Moose Is Mad*.

A girl with curly hair raises her hand. "Ollie looks mad!"

"Yeah! Yeah!" everybody agrees.

"Should we try to help him?" Francine seems to forget momentarily that *she's* the reason I'm mad. "What is something that Ollie could do?" She taps her chin as if deep in thought, and I can't believe she's turning me into a fucking teaching moment.

"Time-Out Tent!" another kid calls out, and the rest of them find this to be a positively phenomenal suggestion. They cheer and then stare at me eagerly.

"Um," I say. "Francine, why don't you show me the Time-Out Tent?"

Francine raises a *one moment* finger to the librarian, then leads me to a large play tent set up in the center of the room. A few minutes later, I'm sitting on the floor with my knees pressed together and my head up against the sloped canvas, crowded in way too close to Francine.

"This is where we send kids to take a break if they have a tantrum," Francine whispers. "That's why it's called the Time-Out Tent."

"I don't care why it's called the Time-Out Tent!" I hiss, and Francine looks at me like I definitely belong in the Time-Out

Tent. I throw my hands up in the air. "Can you just explain why the hell you spammed the entire school about me?"

We're so cramped in this tent that I'm kind of in her face, and it's warm enough that the last two inches between our foreheads suddenly seems like a lot less. I can tell she feels it, too, from the pink flush in her cheeks and the way she appears, for once, to be at a loss for words.

That doesn't last long, though.

"I was trying to be efficient." Her voice is squeaky but resolute. "From our last conversation, it sounded like you needed some help. Fast."

"Okay, except this wasn't helpful. This was the opposite of helpful." I feel my irritation boiling up again. "What made you think I'd be interested in any of those clubs? Like, *entomology*? Seriously?"

"To be fair, I had no idea you were *that* scared of bugs."

"I'm not—"

"And have you even tried lawn bowling? It's actually quite calming. You'd probably get a lot out of it."

"I'm not gonna lawn bowl!"

"Then what *are* you going to do?"

As usual, I don't have an answer to that, so I slump back and groan. "Damnit, Francine, why can't you just mind your own business?"

She leans forward. "Listen, I'm sorry that this didn't turn out as . . . low-key as I was hoping. But you should really give one of these activities a try."

"Um, no, thanks. I'm not interested in hanging out with a bunch of weirdos."

"How are they weirdos?" Francine frowns. "Like, okay, maybe their interests are a little out there, but that doesn't make them weird. They're just passionate about what they like, and they're not afraid to show it. That's admirable."

"Well, great, but that's not me."

"I don't think that's true."

She's giving me that look again, the hopeful one from yesterday in the counseling office. The one that suggests *she* thinks I have a lot of potential, too. The one that makes me want to get up right this second and do whatever she says at the same time that I want to shut down completely.

"What's it to you, anyway?" I ask peevishly. "Why do you care so much?"

"Because we're . . . friends." She hesitates for a moment, and while I'm contemplating the accuracy of this statement, she adds in one big rush, "Also, I thought maybe if I helped you with this, you might help me with my grandpa."

What the hell? *That's* what all this is about? I'm still trying to decide how the fuck to respond to that when she says, "So . . . you really didn't like any of those clubs?"

Without another word, I get up on my knees and dive through the tent flap—only to come face-to-face with the Mister Rogers kid.

"You still seem mad," he observes.

"I—"

He points a finger at my nose. "Francine says you should always do something productive about your feelings," he tells me. "*Even* if you're a boy."

I glance back at her and see that she's got her hand outstretched, as if to quiet the kid, but then she slowly drops it, because there's no point.

"I guess I still have a lot to learn from Francine," I say, and stalk out of the room.

8

Francine

JIYA DOESN'T SAY "I TOLD YOU SO," BUT SHE PROBably should.

I guess I might have to rethink The Plan, I text her as I walk home from the library. **It's seeming kind of unlikely at this point.**

Jiya's reply is diplomatic: **You tried.**

I know Jiya thought The Plan was unnecessary, and I get it. Maybe I would, too, if I didn't see firsthand how awful things are for A Gūng. He and A Pòh have been at our house for a few days now, staying in my bedroom. Meanwhile, I've moved to the spare room, where I sleep on an old, narrow mattress that has seen multiple aunts and second cousins through their first night in America. I don't mind, though, because there's no question that A Gūng is too sick to be anywhere but here. His cancer, I learn, is unresectable, which means chemotherapy is his only treatment option, and though he's had just one injection so far, he's already experienced many of the typical side effects: fatigue, headaches, nausea, poor appetite. The one I didn't expect? Anger.

"Why did you give me so much?" he complained yesterday when A Pòh served him porridge in bed. "How am I supposed to eat all that?" Before she could reply, he slammed the spoon into the bowl and sloshed glutinous liquid all over the sheets. I ran in and offered to clean it up, but A Pòh shooed me out of the room. "At least he still has enough qi to talk so loudly," she told me, unfazed.

Given that outburst, I'm surprised to find A Gūng standing calmly at the dining table when I arrive home this afternoon. As I get closer, I realize he's in the process of placing offerings of fruit onto our household altar.

"Hi, A Gūng," I say, dropping my bag on the floor. "Do you need help?"

"Thank you, Fōng, but I am fine." He sets a plate of apples in front of our Guanyin Buddha figurine, and she smiles down at us, kind and serene, from behind incense sticks.

"Are you sure?" I watch as he struggles to reach the bottom shelf, home to Deih Jyú Gūng, the Lord of the Landlord.

"Of course." He waves me off and makes a point to stand up on his own. "I'm just doing a little bit to lend A Pòh a hand. She plated all this fruit but hasn't had a chance to offer it."

"Did she ask you to?" I'm highly skeptical that A Pòh would have given A Gūng any kind of task, but I'm also relieved that his mood seems to be somewhat improved.

"Aiyah, you know her," says A Gūng. "She is always trying to do everything herself."

He picks up another plate of apples, but before he sets it on the middle shelf—the level for ancestors—he pauses to consider the black-and-white photos of Dad's parents, my a yèh and a mā, which flank a memorial tablet in the center. I can't read most of the Chinese characters printed on there, but I do recognize the one for my last name, Zhang. For the first time, I'm struck by the fact that this is a space reserved for *Zhangs*.

"You must remember to pray to your ancestors," A Gūng reminds me as he edges the plate onto the crowded display. "Make sure to ask for their protection. I want you to have a good life."

His conviction unsettles me, and I glance back at the photos of my other grandparents. "We should make room for the Huynh family here," I say suddenly, pushing aside one of the flower vases. "There's plenty of space—"

"No, no." A Gūng stops me before I can touch the picture frames, and his grip on my wrist is gentle but firm. "Don't worry about that, Fōng. I shouldn't have troubled you with it."

At that moment, however, he closes his eyes like a rush has come over him, and though he tries to grab the table for support, he misses and stumbles. I catch his arm in time but also crash into the altar, knocking an apple to the floor with a bruising thump.

"Are you okay, A Gūng?" I ask, alarmed.

"I was only a little lightheaded," he says after a couple of breaths. "It's nothing." But he lets me help him to a chair and doesn't quite meet my gaze. Instead, he points to the brown welt on the apple. "Don't tell A Pòh," he adds, attempting a smile.

"I thought you were going to rest!" As if conjured by his words, A Pòh emerges from the kitchen with my after-school snack, a steaming bowl of instant ramen noodles topped with choy sum and slightly too salty stir-fried pork.

"I'm going, I'm going." A Gūng leans toward me, his voice conspiratorial. "You see how she orders me around?"

I do my best to look amused for his sake, but it's hard to ignore the slow, stiff way he rises to his feet and plods toward his room. After he's gone, I sit at the dining table and slurp my noodles quietly, trying to wash down my dread.

"You should drink the soup today," says A Pòh, noticing my silence. "Your mother had a whole chicken in the fridge, so I decided to make some broth. It's very good for you—I simmered it for several hours."

"I will, A Pòh."

"You know, back in Vietnam, a chicken like that wouldn't be so easy to come by. You'd have to get a live bird and break its neck yourself, then pluck all of its feathers, too."

I know A Pòh is chattering to fill the space that A Gūng left behind, so I go along with it, nodding as she launches into a detailed explanation for how to butcher a chicken. She loves to share instructions and advice for activities that may or may not be particularly relevant to your life, and I admit that I do sometimes tune her out. Today, though, I find her minutiae comforting.

"You've probably never done anything like that here," A Pòh declares eventually, after she's outlined the butchering process from start to finish. "There's so much American kids don't have to know."

I reflect on this for a minute. "I guess the other day I did dissect a pig in science class."

A Pòh's eyes widen in surprise. "A whole pig?" she says. "By yourself?"

"Well, it was a small pig," I explain. "And I was working with some other students. You know one of them—Ollie Tran. He was in my group."

As soon as I mention Ollie, I wish I hadn't, but of course that's what A Pòh picks up on.

"I didn't know Ollie Tran was still in your class," she muses. "How is that young man?"

"Oh," I say. "He's all right."

"He used to be so skinny." A Pòh squints at the memory. "Is he still?"

Without meaning to, I think of Ollie in the Time-Out Tent, crammed close enough for me to learn he must still like peppermint gum, and I feel an old desire to defend him. "He's not too skinny," I say before I can stop myself.

"That's good," A Pòh concludes. "A boy ought to be made of sturdier stuff."

While I'm wondering if there are any circumstances in which Ollie could be plausibly referred to as "sturdy," a jangling at the front door is followed by the crash of keys hitting the ground and, finally, a faint sigh. Moments later, Mom appears in her blue 88 Value Market vest, lunch bag slung over her arm. She's just gotten home from her job as a cashier manager, a promotion she earned a few years ago partly because she speaks so many languages—useful at a place like 88 Value Market, which is Taiwanese owned but caters to all kinds of Asians.

"We haven't seen Thằng An in a while," A Pòh says to Mom. She means Ollie's dad, but she refers to him familiarly, using his Vietnamese name *An* instead of Andrew, which is what he goes by now.

"He and Mai have gotten so busy," Mom replies. "And since the kids have gotten older, they haven't had time to play together anyway." She kind of looks at me when she says this, because she's always suspected I liked Ollie and worries I never got over him. When I catch her, she pretends to study the strap on her lunch bag.

"A Gūng seemed better today," I pipe up, trying to redirect the conversation.

"Did he?" Mom doesn't do a good job of hiding her doubt.

"Yeah, I thought so." I make my voice extra upbeat. "I bet he'll keep improving, too."

A Pòh sits down next to me. "Fōng, I've been meaning to show you something. I found it when we were packing to come here." She motions to Mom, who jumps up as if glad to have something to do. From her bedroom, she retrieves a small box made of textured red cardboard, similar to what you'd get from a jewelry counter in the Asian Garden Mall. The gold chain inside, however, isn't secured as if it were brand-new.

Instead, it's bunched up in a corner of the cotton fill, and A Pòh has to straighten it gently as she lifts it out.

"Do you know how your A Gūng and I met?" A Pòh asks, and I shake my head. Strange that I've heard all about stuff like A Pòh's experience with poultry, but not this. "We were both in the same Vietnamese class, and he sat in the seat behind me. At the time, I was only a little bit older than you."

My mind immediately goes to Ollie sitting behind me in history class, and then I blush, because that's obviously not the same thing at all.

"During the French occupation of Vietnam, they made us study their language, but it was all very disorganized." A Pòh seems thoroughly dismissive of French imperialism. "Only after they left did we learn Vietnamese. You had to if you wanted to find any work."

"You mean you and A Gūng didn't know Vietnamese before you were my age?" I'm amazed, because you definitely couldn't tell that now.

"No, we lived in the Chinese part of Hanoi, so there was never any need," A Pòh explains. "Funny how our paths never crossed, though, until we took the class together." She chuckles. "That's what you call yùhn fahn."

In Chinese, yùhn fahn is a concept similar to fate, but it applies specifically to relationships between people. If you and someone else have yùhn fahn, it means the two of you were destined to meet. They say the inevitability of such a friendship transcends lifetimes.

"When we got married, your a gūng gave me a necklace," A Pòh continues. "Twenty-four karat gold." She lays the chain across her lap. "That was very valuable in those days. He was quite poor, but it was important to him that I have it."

"This is the one?" I examine the willowy thread of gold, which winks in the last bit of sunset coming through the window. It's beautiful, but a little short to be a necklace.

"After the war, as we were preparing to flee Hanoi, A Gūng and I couldn't take your mom and aunts together, so they were sent with other relatives to all different places," says A Pòh. "That's why A Gūng decided to have the goldsmith melt down the necklace to create six bracelets. One for each girl." She holds the chain up now. "So they all had to be as thin as this."

I nod, but something catches in my throat. Maybe it's the idea of A Pòh's wedding necklace disappearing forever in the chaos of war, dissolving into pieces that were scattered across the globe with my mom and her sisters, possibly never to be seen again.

Mom has been quiet this whole time, but she speaks up now. "I remember you sewed mine into my jacket," she says. "Right here." She pats her chest, close to where her heart is.

"Yes, that was to make sure no one could take it," says A Pòh. "Because gold is gold, you see? If needed, it could always be sold."

I see then that the necklace was never just a sentimental token. For A Gūng and A Pòh, it was a hedge against an uncertain future—protection in the event that safety could be bought.

"I'm glad you didn't have to sell yours," I tell Mom, marveling at everything the bracelet went through to make it here to America.

"Me too," she says. "Because A Pòh and I think you should have it."

Surprised, I glance between the two of them. "Really?"

"Of course," says Mom. "You're my one and only bǎo bǎo." She wraps me in close for a hug, and I'm comforted by the familiar smells of fried fish and produce that linger on her vest. "Don't ever forget that."

I'm probably too old to still find solace in such a babyish endearment, but Mom has called me bǎo bǎo since before I can remember, and I don't want to let go of it just yet. "Thanks, Mom."

A Pòh takes my hand and wraps the delicate gold around my wrist. "I know you are sad because you're afraid of what will happen to A Gūng," she says, securing the clasp. "But no matter what, you'll have this to remember him by."

I tilt my hand back and forth, admiring the way the bracelet shimmers as it dangles. It's so slight, yet also so permanent—and I'm grateful it will always be something solid to hold on to, even when everything else feels like it's falling apart.

Ollie

"DAMN, SO IT WAS ALL FRANCINE?"

Rollo and I are at the Costco food court, our usual after-school hangout. It's situated outside the store, which means you can eat there even if you don't have a membership—crucial because neither Rollo nor I do. Today, though, Rollo needs to replenish inventory for Rollos and More, so he's borrowed his cousin's card. He does this every month, which is why he's confident he won't get caught: "I'm way better-looking than Nick, but they probably think all Chinese people look the same anyway."

The Costco food court is great because it's (1) only a two-minute drive from Hargis and (2) home to the best hot dog you can get in Jacaranda for $1.50 or less. It's the kind of food that's such a great value, the price actually starts to affect the taste—in a good way, of course. Rollo is a fan of the cheese pizza and also the berry smoothies. He does love himself a berry smoothie.

He's sipping one now, eyebrows raised, as he listens to me recount the Francine situation. We've settled into our favorite patio table in the corner, one of the few with a functioning umbrella, and I scoot over to take advantage of the shade.

"Yeah, it was Francine," I gripe, unwrapping my hot dog. "I don't understand why she can't just act like a normal person."

Rollo slides his smoothie back and forth on the table. "I mean, her recruitment strategy was painful to watch, but you gotta hand it to her—it got the job done."

"Yeah, by *humiliating* me in front of everybody at school." I tear open a packet of relish, squeezing out the contents forcefully. "And I still have nothing to report to Ms. Lane next week."

"That's *your* problem, though, isn't it? She identified a million options for you. In, like, less than twenty-four hours." Rollo sounds almost impressed.

"Do you not remember the options?"

"Dude, just pick something. There's got to be some activity that won't require too much work. Here, let me see the list she gave you."

I've been steering clear of Francine since our confrontation in the Time-Out Tent, but this morning, I found that she'd slipped an envelope through the vent of my locker. On the front, she'd drawn a sad-looking spider with a speech bubble that said *Sorry*, which felt kind of like a troll move even though it probably wasn't. Inside, there was a page printed with all the clubs who had responded to her email blast, along with the people I was supposed to contact if I was interested. *Hope this helps*, she'd written at the top. *XO, Francine*.

"XO, huh?" Rollo grins when I hand him the printout.

"Come on. You know it's just like another form of 'sincerely.'"

"Uh-huh," says Rollo suggestively. *"Sincerely."* I lunge over to swipe the list back from him, but he holds it above his head. "Okay, relax, I'm kidding. Although—" Rollo squints one eye at me. "She *did* used to like you, didn't she?"

I take a bite of my hot dog and chew glumly. "Don't remind me."

For obvious reasons, I've never discussed this even with Rollo, but I still remember the exact moment Francine and I met on the first day of kindergarten. I couldn't bring myself to let go of my mom's hand, but Francine was already running around the playground like she owned the place. When she spotted me, she bounded right over, her pigtails flying. "Hi, I'm Francine!" she said. "Do you want me to hold your hand so you won't be scared anymore?"

In response, I did the only reasonable thing I could think of: burst into tears.

Luckily, nobody else has any recollection of this, and even if they did, I'm sure they wouldn't hold it against me, considering I was five. Personally, I've gotten a lot more sensible in twelve years. The same cannot be said for Francine. She never seemed to learn basic stuff about being a kid—like how you really don't want to be teacher's pet, or how people sometimes don't need your advice even if it's good. For a while, it wasn't such a big deal because she was equal-opportunity over-the-top to everybody, but at some point in fifth grade, I started to get the *special* Francine treatment.

I'm pretty sure it was this one time when she and her cousins came over to our house, and instead of ignoring her like usual, I played some board game with her. And sure, it was kind of fun. She had a weird sense of humor, but I laughed a lot, and it was actually nicer than being cooped up in my room the whole time. On the following Monday, I even said hi to her at school. I thought it was a more or less chill thing to do.

The problem was that Francine had no chill. In what I would come to recognize as true Francine fashion, she was suddenly extra nice to me, all the time. No amount of avoiding her, or mumbling one-word answers, or eventually, even straight up snapping, would deter her. As the years passed, I was only just managing to stave off insinuations that she liked me or, God forbid, that I liked *her*.

Then, in eighth grade, there was the Mr. Marchand incident.

Mr. Marchand was a substitute teacher who we had pretty regularly—every couple of months, you'd see him pop up in one class or another. Pale and soft-spoken, he was young for a teacher, though for some reason completely bald, and he wore dress shirts that were slightly too big. I always thought he was an okay guy. Once, when he was the sub for Mr. Valdez's algebra class, he caught me reading a sci-fi novel under my desk instead of doing the work we'd been assigned, but all he said was, "Oh, Isaac Asimov? He's great, isn't he?"

The thing about a teacher like Mr. Marchand, however, is that he's often just one bored kid away from being totally punked. That's exactly what happened this one time he subbed for Ms. Yee when she was out a whole week for jury duty. He made the extremely ballsy (or reckless, depending on who you ask) decision to show up to a middle school wearing a bike helmet tricked out to look like R2D2's head. Before the morning announcements were over, a plan to steal it was hatched.

Our period led the charge, and everybody was in on it—well, everybody except Francine, because it was automatically assumed she would ruin this and every prank. But that left me alone to wrangle with the question of what to do when the guileless Mr. Marchand, upon discovering the theft, asked us, "Have any of you guys seen my helmet?" I didn't say anything, not then, and not when, much to the class's surprise and irritation, it reappeared magically on his desk the next day, as if it had never been missing at all.

"What a relief," Mr. Marchand said, and in fact, his brow no longer shone with the consternation of the day before. "I guess I owe a thank-you to whoever found it!"

I was feeling pretty good, too, until Francine raised her hand. "It was Ollie," she announced.

All heads turned to face me, and I could sense the social calculus shifting in real-time. I had been one of *them*, somebody who could be counted on. But now, I was skidding toward the realm of Mr. Marchand or, worse, Francine. I had to do something fast.

"No," I lied. "It wasn't me."

"Yeah, it was," Francine insisted. "I heard Corey and them bragging about how they stole it, but Ollie brought it back. I saw him."

"Oh," said Mr. Marchand, his smile genuine and wide. "Well, thanks, Ollie!"

"Yeah," said Corey. "Thanks a *lot*, Ollie."

At the end of class, as we were all leaving, I pulled Francine aside in the hallway. "Why'd you have to go and say all that for?" I demanded.

But before she could respond, Corey strutted by. "Yeah, Francine," he said. "Are you in love with Ollie or something?"

Francine stood up straight. "I was just trying to do the right thing." Then, glancing from Corey to me, she added in a voice that was only slightly smaller, "And so what if I like Ollie?"

Corey was delighted. I was mortified. "Did you hear that?" Corey whooped. "Ollie, is Francine your *girlfriend*?"

That's when I cracked.

"No!" I yelled. "Francine is *not* my girlfriend. We are not even *friends*."

At this, Francine's gaze stopped me in my tracks. It wasn't that I could tell she was angry or upset, because she was neither—it was, unusually, that I couldn't tell anything at all. It was like she'd shut a book I hadn't quite finished reading.

"Okay," she said simply, and that was it. Afterward, she continued to be her strange, unabashed self, but she no longer tried to talk to me, and that meant I could stop thinking about her. Mostly.

"You don't find her kind of cute?" Rollo says now, sucking up the last of his smoothie. "Don't get me wrong—she's *definitely* weird. But also cute."

"That's irrelevant."

"Aha!" Rollo points his straw at me and waggles his eyebrows. "You didn't disagree."

Ugh, Rollo. So what if I think Francine is cute? Sure, maybe there's a tiny part of me that was glad—or relieved, anyway—she was acknowledging me again. Maybe that tiny part did want to help with her ridiculous plan. But I can't. Because even though Corey Nguyen isn't in my math class anymore, he's still around. Guys like him are always gonna be around. And Francine's always gonna be Francine.

"I thought you were gonna tell me what to do," I say to Rollo, jabbing at the list. My face is obviously full-on red.

"All right, let's take a look." Rollo sets his smoothie aside and leans over the sheet of paper in front of him, humming as he runs a finger down the first column. He stops when he gets to an item near the bottom. "Bingo."

I tilt my head to read what he's pointing at. "Multicultural Club?"

"They're the ones who put on that Multicultural Dinner every year. That's all they do. I'm sure it'll be super chill if you join. Like just sign up to bring a bunch of bánh mì or something."

"I guess that seems fine."

"It'll be more than fine." Rollo returns the list to me, and I fold it back up before slipping it in my pocket. Then he tosses his smoothie in the trash, turning all business. "Now, let's go buy some candy."

When we get to the store entrance, however, we're stopped by a burly white man in a Costco vest. His name tag says Vincent. "Can I see your ID, please," he says, and it's not a question.

Rollo is clearly surprised, but he takes it all in stride. "Slow day?" he asks, handing over his cousin's membership card.

"Your ID, sir," repeats Vincent, inspecting the photo on the back of the card.

"What gives?" Rollo hedges. "I've been here a ton of times, and I've never needed my ID before."

Vincent nods back at the food court. "Those two individuals have informed me that there is a high likelihood you would be using this membership card fraudulently." When we whip our heads around, a freckled girl and boy wave impishly from the patio tables before they scramble away.

"Agh!" Rollo mutters. "The Doherty twins!"

"Sir, if you cannot produce your ID, I'm afraid I will have to ask you to leave." Vincent is still holding the membership card. "And I will be confiscating this, since it is being used in violation of the membership terms and conditions."

Rollo is appalled. "No way, man," he says, snatching the card back. "This is bullshit."

"Sir . . ." cautions Vincent, who makes a grab for it.

"Ollie, run!" Rollo yowls, and we tear off into the parking lot, leaving Vincent shouting after us.

"What the hell?" I ask, panting, once we've reached Rollo's car. "Who were those kids?"

Rollo bends over, pressing into his side as he tries to catch his breath. "They're freshmen," he explains. "The little snots! First they ripped off my idea. Then they tried to undercut my business." He shakes his head in disgust. "Now they're playing *dirty*?"

I start laughing. I can't help it. "Calm down," I say. "They look twelve."

"Don't underestimate the enemy!" Rollo unlocks his car with a furious beep. "This can't go on like this—I need to come up with a retaliation plan before they bleed me dry." He pats his windshield affectionately. "Do you think a beauty like this pays for itself?"

"No, I think your parents do."

"I gotta strategize," he frets, ignoring me. "They've got a real advantage with the two of them, since they can cover more ground."

"Well, maybe you should just find somebody to help you," I suggest, sliding into the passenger seat. "Somebody more helpful than me," I add, when he looks like he's about to ask.

"You're right, I need a partner with better follow through,"

Rollo agrees. Then his face brightens. "Hey, what about Francine?"

"Seriously?"

"Kidding, bruh." Rollo chuckles and starts the car. "Kidding!"

10

Francine

ON FRIDAY, MS. LANE HAS A LOT OF PINK SLIPS FOR me to deliver, so I spend most of the period crisscrossing campus instead of sitting in the counseling office. I'm glad, because this type of task—the kind that forces me to get up and move around—always makes me feel extra productive. Which, considering how unproductive I've felt since taking a break from The Plan, I'm thankful for.

"You know what you should do?" Jiya asks, thumbs hooked in the pockets of her khaki overalls. "Listen to the new Violet Girl album. It'll cheer you up, I promise."

Jiya's fourth period is Trigonometry, which is maybe the only class she cares about less than AP Bio, so when she spotted me on her way to the bathroom, she decided to join me for a stroll.

"Sure, I'll listen." I'm not nearly as well-versed as Jiya in all things Violet Girl, but I do like her music, too.

"I read this interview where she mentioned one of her new songs is about coming out as trans. She didn't say which one, but I think it's 'Bumblebee.'"

"That's really cool." I make a mental note to check out that track specifically, but Jiya is already sending me the link.

"I'm just glad she's finally getting big." Jiya repockets her phone. "It's so awesome people are appreciating her stuff."

"Hey," I say, sensing an opportunity. "Have you been considering what Rollo said the other day? Would you want to start selling your art?"

"Stop right there, Francine." Jiya points a finger at me. "I see what you're doing. Don't turn this into one of your helpful projects."

"It's just a friendly question!"

"Well, the answer is, I haven't decided." Jiya loops one of her dangly earrings around her finger. "I guess it could be fun? I've never had anyone pay me to draw before. Like, who would?"

Jiya sounds flippant, but I know she actually feels uncertain. Both of her parents immigrated here from Mumbai to be software engineers, and their idea of supporting her artistic side has been to suggest—enthusiastically—that she become a front-end developer.

"I'd pay," I assure her. "Whatever you end up doing, I'll be your first customer."

Jiya brushes me off. "No way," she says. "We're friends."

"All the more reason I should value your work."

"I don't know." Jiya studies her boots as we walk. "The whole business angle also makes me think about art differently.

I've always drawn stuff for myself, and I didn't care if anyone else liked it. But now, having other people like it would be the point. And I kind of hate that."

It's true—Jiya refuses to even post her art on social media for this reason.

"I'd basically be putting myself out there to be judged in this really concrete way." She thrusts her arms out, letting her chunky bangles slide down to her wrists. "Like I'm *asking* to be told my work isn't worth it."

"Do *you* think it's worth it?"

Jiya seems surprised by my response, and she doesn't answer right away. "Me?" She looks up at the palm trees overhead. "I mean, sure." But she doesn't sound sure.

"Maybe it'll get less weird asking others to believe that," I say, "if you get used to believing it yourself."

We're approaching the math building now, and Jiya's trig class is up ahead. "You're being very astute," she says as we slow down in front of the door. "Maybe even . . . *helpful*."

"Yeah, so you should tell Rollo you're interested."

Jiya laughs. "Okay, I take it back."

Just then, Ollie rounds the corner, walking fast. He's bent over his phone and doesn't notice we're standing there until he almost trips over us.

"Oh, sorry." He's so distracted that he forgets he's been trying to avoid me, and of course my antennae go up. Something must be going on.

Jiya points at the door and mouths, *See you later*, and right before she disappears into the classroom, she glances toward Ollie and then winks at me. As the door closes, I hear Mr. Bello say, "Ms. Jain! We thought we'd lost you."

Meanwhile, Ollie has rushed on, and I hesitate, considering the two remaining pink slips that still need to be delivered. Impulsively, I stuff them in my pocket and follow him.

"Hey, Ollie," I say, catching up to him. "Is everything okay?"

Ollie wrinkles his forehead. "Do you happen to know where I can find"—he scrolls back up on his phone—"the 'big broom closet'?" When I look confused, he shows me his screen:

Rollo: **SOS SOS SOS**

Ollie: **What's up?**

Rollo: **Get your ass down to the big broom closet NOW.**

Ollie: **Where is that??**

Rollo, however, hasn't responded for several minutes, which is both unhelpful and slightly worrying. "What do you think happened?" I ask.

Ollie is about to answer when the ". . ." flashes, and we lean our heads in together to watch the screen. I catch a whiff of Ollie's peppermint gum again, and I get a lot antsier than I expected waiting for Rollo's reply.

Finally, it appears.

Where they keep the brooms!!!

Ollie face-palms, but then I realize something. "Wait, maybe he means the custodian's office, near Sciences. Should we check?"

We run across the quad, and sure enough, we can hear

Rollo's voice just on the other side of the science building. As we approach, I motion to Ollie and we hide by the open door.

"Mr. Reyes, I'm telling you," Rollo is saying. "This isn't what it looks like."

I peek inside and see that Mr. Reyes, our vice principal, is standing with his back to us, the walkie-talkie on his belt beeping every so often. Mr. Reyes wears his hair in a man bun and thinks Hawaiian shirts are business casual ("They're button-downs," he's joked more than once), but the way he's crossing his arms at Rollo right now suggests he is not in a relaxed mood.

"What it looks like is you're using school property to store candy you've been selling on campus," says Mr. Reyes. "None of which is allowed, dude."

"I know, but you have to understand. This"—Rollo gestures at the stacks of boxes on the floor—"has nothing to do with me."

"But these all say *Rollos and More*," Mr. Reyes points out. "That's *Rollos* as in . . . you, isn't it?"

"Yeah, but I didn't put them here! I'm being framed by the Doherty twins—I would never have picked a location with such suboptimal temperature control."

"So where *have* you been storing all this?"

Rollo is silent.

Mr. Reyes sighs. "Rollo, I'm sorry, but I'm gonna have to confiscate this candy. And you need to put the kibosh on the whole enterprise."

"Aw, but, Mr. Reyes, that's exactly what the Dohertys want! They're trying to corner the market by getting rid of me. They've been out to get me this entire time."

When I glance up at Ollie, my hair accidentally brushes across his nose, and he jumps back, blushing like *he's* the one who's been caught in the middle of something. But there's no time to find out what. "How do we help Rollo?" I whisper. "He's really digging himself into a hole."

Ollie takes out his phone and struggles for a moment before typing: **Just say you're sorry and you'll quit selling candy!** I peer over his shoulder as he hits send. "I don't know what else to tell him," Ollie whispers back. "We can't even be sure he *wasn't* the one who put the boxes here."

There's a faint buzz, and we see Rollo check the message. To our amazement, he begins typing a response right in front of Mr. Reyes.

"Rollo, are you texting right now?" Mr. Reyes can hardly believe it either. "We're in the middle of a discussion."

That's when Ollie's phone pings, and before we get a chance to read Rollo's reply, Mr. Reyes turns to look at the door.

"Hold on, I promise this is relevant." Rollo runs over to poke his head out, and the sight of us fills him with relief. "This guy will vouch for me," he declares, dragging Ollie inside. "Go on, Ollie, tell Mr. Reyes how unreasonable the Doherty twins are."

Mr. Reyes looks at Ollie and then at me, clearly baffled by our presence. Ollie, however, is unable to produce any explanation, and the silence goes on for so long that Mr. Reyes gets ready to shut it down.

So I decide to speak up.

"Mr. Reyes, I think it's worth looking into the Doherty twins' situation."

Both Rollo and Ollie gape at me. They're probably surprised because I don't even know who the Doherty twins are. But somehow, I get the feeling that Rollo, despite his track record for sketchiness, is telling the truth. A guy who is willing to spend money on a fancy wearable cooler probably *wouldn't* store his inventory in an un-air-conditioned closet.

Rollo recovers first, giving me a nod that is the equivalent of an air high-five, but I'm not done.

"Rollo, though, has stopped selling candy," I continue. "He's decided to explore other business ideas instead."

"Yeah, that's right." Rollo latches on immediately. "I was getting to that."

Mr. Reyes taps a few of Rollo's boxes with the side of his Converse. He doesn't really believe us, but he wants to. "Well, that's good to hear," he says at last. "Sugar kills, man."

"Totally." Rollo bobs his head vigorously.

"Get this stuff out of here before the end of the day," Mr. Reyes orders. "I don't want to see it anywhere on campus, okay?"

Rollo salutes. "Yessir."

Then Mr. Reyes remembers Ollie and me. "Did you two need something?"

"Oh," I say, pulling out the pink counseling slips. "I was delivering these and happened to be passing by."

"And I, um . . ." Ollie manages to start a sentence this time but still isn't sure how to finish it.

"Ollie just likes to hang out with Francine." Rollo's voice lowers as he leans towards Mr. Reyes. "You know how it is."

Ollie flushes all the way to his ears, and my heart does a little skip even though I know Rollo's lying.

"All right, get to class, all of you." Mr. Reyes herds us out of the room, but he smiles fondly at Ollie and me, like he does know how it is.

At lunch later that day, Jiya has an Art Club meeting, so I decide to switch it up and eat in the bio classroom. Ms. Abdi is usually game to discuss whatever article she last read in the *New York Times* science section, and that's always a good time.

Today, however, the room is empty when I get there, so I settle down in my usual seat and decide I may as well get some homework done.

"Francine!" Barely a minute later, Rollo materializes in front of me, drumming his fingers on my laptop. "Just the woman I wanted to see."

"Hey, Rollo." I smile back at him. "What's up?"

Rollo grabs a chair and swings it around so he can sit opposite me. "I never got the chance to say thanks," he begins. "For earlier, with Mr. Reyes."

I shrug him off. "It was no big deal."

"Sure it was," Rollo argues. "I would've been toast otherwise."

That's when I notice that he's unpacked his lunch and spread it out fully on the table. He's eating gỏi cuốn filled with shrimp, rolled up neatly in rice paper, complete with a peanut dipping sauce. All of it looks pretty good, considering he's not even Vietnamese. "My mom got the recipe from Ollie's mom," he explains when he sees me looking. "I love spring rolls."

Before I can react, Ollie himself pops his head through the door. He takes in Rollo's setup before glancing at me, and it's clear he's as confused as I am. After Rollo's rescue, the two of them had left together while I'd hurried off to finish delivering those last counseling slips. Ollie hasn't said a word to me since, even though we had fifth period together, so I assumed we were supposed to go back to how things were.

"Ollie, my man." Rollo waves him over. "Have a seat. There's plenty of room."

"Um, sure." Ollie moves toward us tentatively, balancing his lunch tray on one hand while throwing Rollo a look that very obviously says *What the hell is going on*?

I, too, would like to know what is going on, because what it *seems* like is something I never would've expected in this or any lifetime: I'm about to have lunch with Rollo and Ollie.

"I was just telling Francine she's a real lifesaver," Rollo says to Ollie. To me, he adds, "Not like this guy, amirite?"

Ollie scowls. "I sent you a text with some very reasonable advice!"

"Yeah, exactly," Rollo says. "You sent me a *text*."

"Well, all I did was tell Mr. Reyes the truth," I say. "You *are* considering other avenues of business."

Rollo blinks, processing this for a second before he breaks into a grin. "I like the way you think, Francine."

He seems to have misunderstood me, so I attempt to set him straight. "But you are actually going to quit selling candy, right?" I reach for my sandwich, then put it back down without taking a bite. "If not, you definitely should."

Rollo suspends his spring roll in mid-dip. "I mean—"

"You already have a lot on your plate, Rollo." I fold my laptop screen down so I can focus on him. I know it's no skin off my nose, but I can't just stand by and watch him continue to make bad choices. "I think it would be better if you stuck to stuff that isn't against the rules. Like the art agenting."

Ollie raises an eyebrow at Rollo. "Art agenting, huh?"

Rollo gives Ollie the hand. "I'm working on it."

"Yeah, so stop wasting your time with the Doherty twins, whoever they are," I tell him. "If you ask me, they seem like trouble."

At this, Rollo glances at Ollie, who seems oddly smug. "Also reasonable advice," Ollie observes before biting into an apple.

Rollo, however, is not particularly fazed. "You know what, Francine? You're right." He chomps thoughtfully. "As an entrepreneur, sometimes you gotta know when you've been outcompeted and be willing to make a pivot." He snaps his fingers. "That's what I'll do. Pivot."

I'm not entirely sure what Rollo is talking about, but I'm pleased he's taking my advice. "That sounds great," I say. Meanwhile, Ollie crunches a little more loudly on his apple.

Now a beep emits from Rollo's watch. "Ah," he says, checking the screen. "It's been real, friends." He shoves another spring roll into his mouth and gathers up his lunch as efficiently as he'd laid it out. "Especially you, Francine. Seriously, have you ever thought about becoming a life coach?"

Again, he leaves no time for a response, only points a finger gun at me and winks as he hops out of his seat.

"Hey, where are you going?" Ollie leans all the way over his chair, lobbing the question at Rollo's back. There's a note of concern in his voice.

"I've got a meeting." Rollo turns around to face us, but he keeps walking away, just backward.

"With an artist client?" I call after him.

"No," Rollo replies right before making his exit. "A prospect for a new side hustle."

As the door swings shut with a thud, the classroom goes completely quiet except for the hum of the wall clock, and suddenly, I'm sitting alone with Ollie.

"Rollo seems nice," I say because nothing else comes to mind.

Ollie has hollowed out his apple, but he nibbles at the part near the stem, like he's reluctant to put it down. "In his own way," he agrees.

I notice the faintest impression of his dimple—which is

all that shows when his smile is a little crooked, the way it is now—and I feel a familiar kindling inside my chest. I snuff it out real quick, though, because this is Ollie we're dealing with. Ollie, who is so hard to be friends with. Ollie, who up until earlier today, refused to even speak to me.

Except I guess we're talking now.

"Do you think he'll actually quit the candy business?" I ask.

"I don't know," Ollie admits. "I can't predict what he's gonna do half the time." Then he kind of chuckles. "Rollo has always been . . . an acquired taste."

"Yeah, well," I joke, "a lot of people would say that about me, too."

This catches Ollie off guard, and he twists his apple stem for a while until it breaks off. "Listen, Francine," he says finally. "I've been kind of a dick, and I'm sorry." He flicks the stem into his lunch tray. "I overreacted to the whole thing with the clubs—I know you were just trying to help. And I know you've been having a rough time with your grandpa." Ollie's eyes look more melancholy than usual. "I'm sorry about that, too."

This is a long speech for Ollie, and I'm not sure how to respond. "It's okay," I say. I remember that I haven't started on my sandwich, so I pick it up again, chewing quietly. After a bit, I swallow. "And I should've checked in before sending the mimes after you."

Ollie laughs. Unexpectedly, he points at me with both hands, nods, and gives a jerky thumbs-up.

"What's that supposed to be?" I'm amused but also perplexed.

"I was miming 'You can say that again!'"

"Really?" I snort into my sandwich. "Because that definitely seemed more like 'Great work, Francine!' to me."

Ollie's laughing again, too, and when the weight at the bottom of my stomach explodes in a giddy burst—like a dandelion scattering itself in the wind—I realize, with a start, that I haven't felt this light in a while.

"How is your grandpa?" Ollie asks, his voice more subdued.

"Oh," I reply. "Not that great. I'd still like to figure out something I could do for him." I study my sandwich. "I know no one else thinks it's a big deal, but I do."

"I get it," says Ollie. "I do think it's a big deal." But then maybe I look a little too hopeful that he might change his mind about The Plan because he adds, "*No*, Francine."

"I know, I know." I rest my chin in my hands. "Don't worry, I've been trying to brainstorm some other options. My grandparents' anniversary is coming up, so I thought maybe I could throw them a surprise party. Or maybe I could organize a concert with performances of A Gūng's favorite music. Or maybe—"

"Francine," interrupts Ollie. He pushes his lunch tray away, and his apple core, finally abandoned, rolls around inside it. "I'm just . . ." He falters, then tries again. "Are you okay?"

I sit back in my chair. "What do you mean?" I say. "Sure, I'm okay."

"I don't know. Maybe you should give yourself a break."

I run my finger along the edge of my laptop, rubbing hard at a smudge I find on the lid. "Why would *I* need a break?"

Ollie looks uncomfortable. "Well, your grandpa's sick."

"I *know* he's sick." Without understanding why, I want to throw something at Ollie. "*That's* why I can't take a break. What if I run out of time?" My voice escalates to an unprecedented pitch. "What if I'm *already* running out of time?"

I don't mean for the question to come careening out that way, but Ollie lets it hang in the air, like he wants me to take it back down and examine it more carefully. Only I can't even look at him. It's so strange. I feel as though I'm finally getting close to him, close enough for him to see me, and all I want to do is run away.

"I guess I'm trying to ask if you want to talk about anything," Ollie says at last. "Not necessarily with me. Unless you want to. Then, um, sure." He is floundering a bit, but he manages to pull himself back together. "I just wonder if that could be more helpful than worrying about the things you mentioned." Though he doesn't say it, I know he thinks my new ideas are as ill-advised as The Plan. "Maybe you should forget about all that stuff."

"You haven't even seen my grandpa lately," I shoot back. "How would you know what would help him?"

Ollie crumples a napkin and tosses it into his tray. "I was talking about what would help *you*, Francine."

Suddenly, I'm really tired. "I already told you how you could help me, Ollie," I say flatly. "Except you didn't want to. And that's fine."

He frowns. "It's not that I didn't want to—"

"But just because you're willing to sit around doing nothing even when someone needs you, that doesn't mean I am."

Ollie goes still for a moment, but then he stands up so fast, the chair skids backward against the tile floor. "Fine," he says, before grabbing his tray and stomping out of the room.

I lift my laptop screen so violently that the hinge creaks, but I hardly notice. Instead, I open up a blank document and start writing down the alternative plans I'd listed to Ollie earlier, pounding on the return key each time.

Only after I've typed the last bullet point, watching the cursor flashing at the end of the line, do I wonder how a conversation so alive with possibility turned into an argument.

11

Ollie

WHAT THE FUCK IS FRANCINE'S PROBLEM?

I tell myself I should just forget about her and all her ridiculous ideas. What's it to me, anyway, if she can't deal with her grandpa dying? Why should I care if her attempts to cope are misguided? The girl is obviously beyond help. I mean, look what happened at lunch—the one time I actually try to be nice to her, she flat-out dismisses me. Which is just rich, considering I was only there because Rollo told me to meet him for lunch without explaining that said lunch would involve Francine. If it had been up to me, I would've been perfectly happy to not have shown up at all. So it's whatever.

I try to put the whole thing out of my mind as I head to my first meeting with the Multicultural Club. They gather after school, which is kind of unusual—most of the other groups on campus meet at lunch. Twenty-five minutes and it's over. But Amanda Moreno, the Multicultural Club president, told me they switched to after school—on Fridays, no less—because they found they "always had so much to cover!" This should have tipped me off that Rollo might have been mistaken about how "chill" the Multicultural Club is. Well, that and the fact that Amanda introduced herself by naming all the languages she speaks, along with her proficiency in each ("Spanish, native; Mandarin, fluent; Arabic, basic; Gaelic, aspiring"). I'm starting to understand why Ms. Lane was so thrilled when I told her I was joining the Multicultural Club—Amanda definitely seems like her kind of girl.

"Under the old leadership, the only thing we ever did was plan an annual dinner," Amanda is saying now. "But this year, with all the new members I recruited, we've really turned the organization around. We've started all kinds of new initiatives, including advocating for dual-language immersion programs at Hargis, organizing international pen-pal exchanges, and raising money to buy foreign language books for the library."

Amanda talks fast. Like, really fast. Like her-entire-life-is-a-debate-tournament fast. She's got mad-scientist hair topped with a floral bucket hat that she is, against all odds, pulling off, and her gestures are so big I learn pretty quickly to stay out of her way.

"Of course," she continues, "we're by no means abandoning the Global Gala—which is what we're calling it now, by the way—because it's our biggest fundraiser of the year. That's what we'll need your help with."

I look around the room and people are nodding at me, so I take a seat and nod back.

"This year's theme is 'Family Stories,' so we're adding a component to the gala that we believe will help bring important context to the food being served. Damien?"

I've known Damien Figueroa since freshman year because he sits next to me in homeroom, and we've always been friendly—he drinks his morning tea from a Japanese stoneware mug and sometimes shares his fancy scones—but I didn't realize he was in Multicultural Club, or any other club. I guess I never asked.

"So excited to have you join us, Ollie!" Damien exclaims. "I'd be more than happy to get you up to speed." Turning businesslike, he adjusts his wire glasses and pulls up a PowerPoint slide with a map of the gym. On one end, there's a box marked as the stage, while the center is filled with circles—probably to indicate dining tables—and the perimeter is lined with rectangles.

"These will be booths showcasing students' family histories." Damien indicates the rectangles with a laser pointer. "They'll also include relevant food dishes, all organized by country and region."

"It's great that you're participating because we really need more representation in the Southeast Asian corner," Amanda says to me. "Your family's Vietnamese, right?"

"Yeah," I answer. "Well, Chinese Vietnamese. Does that count? It's kind of complicated, but I guess it does. Yeah, it does."

I really need to figure out when to stop talking.

"Don't worry, you can tell us all about it in your booth," Amanda promises.

"Wait," I say. "I'm getting my own booth?"

"Yeah, of course." Amanda examines me like she's just realizing maybe I'm a bit slow. "Is that a problem?"

Somehow, I don't think explaining that I wasn't expecting to get such a big assignment so soon will score me any points with Amanda. I consider what would happen if I told her I've changed my mind—that Multicultural Club isn't for me after all—and hightailed it out the door. But Damien is already typing my name into one of the little rectangles, and in what is clearly meant to be a welcoming gesture, he adds two smileys at the end.

Meanwhile, Amanda is striding over to me, pushing up her billowy sleeves in a way that suggests she is fully prepared to dig deeper into my issues. In a desperate act of self-preservation, I squawk, "Nope, all good!"

Much to my relief, she takes me at my word, and we are free to refocus on the agenda. I relax into my chair, grateful for the return of my status as a nobody—until I realize, belatedly, that if there *was* a window to back out, I just closed it. There's no way I can get up and leave now, not unless I want to make an even bigger fool of myself.

I don't know how I managed it, but I'm stuck.

When I get back home later that afternoon, no one's there except for Dexter, who bounds up at the crack of the front door, jumping to greet me with a jubilant bark. He's seven now, but he still gets pretty good air. Even though I know you're not supposed to let dogs climb all over you like that, I don't stop him because it's nice to feel like your arrival is worth that much excitement every day, especially when you're returning to an empty house.

As I open the fridge and rummage for something to eat, I think about how Isaac used to be around more before he left for college. I do kind of miss him occasionally, but he can also be a real asshole. Like if I told him everything that was going on right now, especially the stuff about Francine, he'd a hundred precent just make fun of me. His favorite story is the time when, completely out of the blue, Francine left me a strawberry Yan Yan on the front steps with a note saying she'd heard it was my favorite flavor. I was too embarrassed to touch it, so Isaac ended up scarfing down the whole thing (everybody, even Isaac, knows strawberry is the best flavor). From then on, whenever we heard she was coming over with her family, he'd turn to me and ask, "So when's the wedding?"

"Forget Isaac," I say aloud to Dexter, who wags his tail because he thinks I'm about to give him a treat. I break off a piece of week-old kale from the crisper drawer and toss it to him. "He didn't deserve that Yan Yan." Dexter only munches in agreement.

I wish it were easier to forget Francine, but my mind keeps going back to our conversation at lunch, the way she kept running around in circles, trying to escape how upset she really was. I can't shake off the way her voice lurched upward when she threw that question at me: *What if I'm already running out of time?*

I didn't tell her this, but sometimes I've thought about that kind of stuff, too. Every so often, when I'm walking Dexter around the neighborhood, treading the same old sidewalks around the same old blocks, it'll hit me. Dexter will be sniffing that same old fire hydrant on the corner, always like he's never seen it before, and I'll remember that one day, I'll probably still be here, but he won't.

I kneel on the floor and pet Dexter now, trying to memorize the warmth of his back as he leans against me, or the way his left ear twitches when I scratch his neck. He looks so happy still, like he doesn't notice his joints are already a little stiffer and his fur isn't quite as shiny as it used to be. That's the thing that gets me, I guess. He's oblivious.

It's goofy, I know, to get worked up about something like this, especially over a dog. Isaac definitely wouldn't understand, despite the fact that he's the reason my parents got Dexter in the first place. But it's not only about Dexter. Not really.

I give up on my snack because the pickings are just too pathetic, and maybe I'm not that hungry anyway. Dexter follows me into the family room, where I flop down on the leather couch, which is a little cold, like it usually is. I turn on the TV, letting the sound echo against the empty walls, but I don't watch it.

Instead, I think about A Mā, my grandma on my dad's side. She lives in San Francisco, and we see her just once a year. Every December, she consults some Chinese almanac to pick an auspicious travel date and then take the Vietnamese bus down to Orange County to spend the holidays with us. While she's here, I usually don't have much to say to her—my Cantonese is bad, and my Vietnamese is worse. I feel sort of awkward holing up in my room to read or game or do whatever I would be doing normally, but I feel even more awkward hovering around her, unsure of how to act as she busies herself with the cooking and cleaning that none of us do enough on the regular. Before I know it, the two weeks are up, and we drive her back to the bus stop so she can go home.

But at the end of this last visit, Mom and Dad were too swamped at work to take her, and Isaac had already flown back to Berkeley, so I had to do it. I'd just gotten my license earlier in the year, and it was the first time I'd driven A Mā anywhere. She seemed really pleased to have me as her chauffeur, and as we stood there in the Vietnamese market parking lot, right before she was about to board the bus, she reached up and cupped my face in her wrinkled hands. "Good boy," she told me in Cantonese. "You've grown up." I was too startled to summon any words besides "m̀h"—that workhorse syllable of agreement that masks all Cantonese deficiencies—before she shuffled into line behind other people's grandmas and grandpas, her layers of outerwear hiding her thinness but not the slight hunch of her shoulders. She was old enough, I realized, that each time she left now could be the last time I saw her. As the bus rolled away, I was struck by the sense that there hadn't been enough time to figure out what I really wanted to say.

I wish I could tell you that I've called my a mā every week since, and that I've been practicing my Cantonese more so I can have a real conversation with her, but I haven't. I don't know why. I'm not Francine, I guess, who would probably *move* to San Francisco if she thought it was what her a mā wanted. She's so extra, she'd probably do it *tomorrow*.

But then, maybe she wouldn't have to feel so shitty about all of it.

My phone pings with an email, one I don't really care to see right now—from Damien, with details about my Global Gala booth. Apparently I get a table, but all other supplies or materials, I'll have to buy or make myself. An attached PDF shows where I'll be located in the gym. Turns out Amanda was being very literal when she said "Southeast Asian corner."

I toss my phone onto the cushion next to me and cover my eyes. How is somebody like me supposed to fill a whole booth with my family history? I barely even talk to my parents. Most nights, I don't see them before seven, and sometimes they're on the phone with people in China late into the night. This has been the case for at least five years now, ever since Dad's idea to get into the skincare market really ramped up business. Lately, even weekends have been pretty much shot because there's some new product launch coming up that I should probably know about but don't. On the plus side, they've done well enough to turn our previously modest ranch house into a first-generation immigrant new-money wet dream—Dad has never met a room he felt couldn't be improved with a lot of marble—so I guess there's that.

My point, though, is that the chance of them sitting down with me to have an in-depth discussion about where we came from is basically nil. I know the general gist of events—after leaving Vietnam, Mom's family resettled in Toronto, while Dad's ended up all over the place, including LA—but neither of them ever made it a priority to explain the details, and Isaac and I never thought to probe further.

When Mom gets home later that evening, bearing a stack of Styrofoam takeout containers, I wonder if I should broach the topic now.

"Where's Dad?" I ask, helping her set the food down.

"Still in the car." Mom drops a pile of disposable utensils and napkins onto the dining table. "He was in the middle of a call."

Typical. I sit down and open a container to find *cơm tấm sườn nướng*, a Vietnamese dish of grilled pork chops and broken rice. It smells like lemongrass and garlicky fish sauce, and my stomach rumbles.

"How was school?" Mom sounds a little distracted as she frowns at an email.

"Fine," I say, which would normally be the extent of my response. But today, after a couple bites of pork chop, I point at the cơm tấm and ask, "Is this something you used to eat in Vietnam?"

Mom stops typing and sets her phone down, her manicured nails clinking against the table. "You know, I don't remember." She takes a closer look at her rice. "It's been so many years."

I do know that Mom left Hanoi earlier than Dad—she was probably twelve or thirteen when she first moved to Canada—but I'm kind of surprised by her answer. We eat cơm tấm all the time now, so I just assumed it was something she would've had when she was younger.

"It's a southern Vietnamese dish, so I don't know if it was very common in Hanoi when I was a kid," Mom says, getting thoughtful. "At least, I don't think I ever had it. I do remember bún chả, though. And phở, of course. And bún chả giò, though in the north, it was called bún nem."

"How come you and Dad don't call it bún nem?"

"Oh, we've lived near Little Saigon so long now, we've picked up all of their phrases." Mom chuckles. "I can't even keep track anymore whether I'm using the northern or southern terms for things."

I, of course, had no idea there were language differences between the regions, so I try to remember all this in case I have to explain it to other people. I was thinking of bringing egg rolls to the Global Gala, so I'd better know what to call them. Plus—and this is the real truth—I'm so desperate, I'll take any content.

"Do you have any old family pictures? Like from Vietnam or China?" This had been Rollo's suggestion when I chewed him out for his faulty intel on the Multicultural Club. **Just turn your booth into a giant photo collage**, he'd texted back. **People will eat that up.** A few minutes later, he added, **No pun intended LOL.**

Mom glances around the dining room. "I might have a couple somewhere, but I'm pretty sure most are with your grandma in Toronto."

That's not great. My a pòh refuses to learn how to use a smartphone, and it would probably cost her a fortune to mail me the photos via Canada Post, so that's a no-go. Besides, I've talked to her even less than my a mā.

"What about Dad—does he have any?"

Mom shakes her head. "Not here either, I don't think." She pauses, and it's clear she's wondering why I'm suddenly full of questions. "Is this for a school project?"

"Sort of," I say, and give her a quick rundown on the Global Gala. I decide to encourage the impression that I'd "volunteered" to get involved.

"I didn't realize you'd joined the Multicultural Club," Mom says. "When did you become interested in that?"

"Oh, I'm not, really." But then I realize that answer might invite more questions, so I keep talking. "Or I mean, I guess you could say I'm trying it out. I heard about it from Francine originally. You remember her, right?"

Unfortunately, this seems to spark Mom's interest even

more. The *wrong* kind of interest. "Yes, of course," she says eagerly.

I feel my face warming up, so I rush to blurt out the next thing that comes to mind: "Actually, she told me her grandpa has cancer."

"Oh no." Mom's face falls, and I feel bad because I know she was thinking the conversation would go in a different direction. But it's too late to take it back.

"Yeah." I poke at a cucumber slice with my fork. "I don't think he has much time left."

Mom reaches for one of the utensil packets and delicately pulls it apart at the seam. "We should tell your dad," she says. "He'd want to know."

"Really?" This is unexpected. Why would Dad, who barely has time to take an interest in his own family, care about Francine's?

"After your a yèh died, Francine's grandparents helped their family a lot," Mom explains. "As a kid, your dad ate many meals at their house because there often wasn't enough food at home."

I glance over at the third Styrofoam container that sits at the end of the table, unopened. "I didn't know that."

"Yeah," says Mom. "In those days, if a father passed away, it was really tough for a family. With no way to make any money, they often lost everything, even their place in the community." She slices her pork chop into small, thin pieces. "You see, although Francine's family was also poor, they at least still had her grandpa to provide for them. They were still respectable."

This makes me remember my a mā again, and suddenly I don't feel like swallowing the spoonful of rice I've just stuffed in my mouth. All those times she's been here, and I never thought about how hard things must have been for her or my dad, who was one of five kids. It occurs to me that maybe there's a lot I don't know. "How did A Yèh die?" I ask.

"He drove a delivery truck for a living, and there was some kind of accident," Mom replies. "Your dad doesn't like to talk about it."

As if summoned, Dad appears in the doorway. "I'm starving," he says in English, like it's just a throwaway phrase. "How's the *sườn nướng*?"

Dad's a lot like Isaac, who has the same fill-the-room bluster and Cary Grant smile—although I've always felt that Isaac's version, which is more mellow, takes up less space. In case it wasn't obvious, other than slightly too-large ears, I didn't inherit too much from Dad.

"The meat is a little dry today," Mom tells Dad in Vietnamese as she dips a piece into the fish sauce. She wrinkles her nose a little. "I probably could've done a better job."

I consider asking Dad about A Yèh, but when he sits down and opens his laptop even before his *cơm* container, I can't bring myself to form the question.

Instead, Mom decides to mention Francine's grandpa. "M̀h," is all Dad says when she tells him about the cancer. His expression is hard to read.

"At least he lived a long life," Mom concludes, sighing.

"It's true," agrees Dad. "Not everyone does."

Then he turns back to his computer, Mom gets another email that she has to respond to, and the three of us eat in silence until I get up and leave the table because I can't sit there anymore.

I wake up early the next morning even though it's a Saturday, because Dexter waits for no man when he feels entitled to a walk. Normally, I'm fighting off grogginess as I scrounge around for his leash, and only occasionally do I remember to throw on a hoodie over my PJs before I leave the house.

Today, however, I feel wired before I open the door. As Dexter runs around me, I pause in front of the gilt-edge mirror that Dad had installed in the foyer. It's one of the few pieces of wall décor in our house, which has been in a state of half-furnished potential for years—just a scattering of expensive stuff waiting around in emptiness. I try not to notice this particular dud most days, but now, as I peer at my reflection, I wonder if it could reveal what might be up with me.

Nope. I look the same as usual, if maybe like I didn't sleep that well last night. I ruffle my hair a little bit, which doesn't do a whole lot, and lead Dexter outside.

The sun's already out, which means we're in for a hot afternoon, but right now the air still feels cool and fresh. It's the kind of nice weather I'm never sure what to do with. Between that and this weird energy I want to burn off, I decide it might be a good day to take Dexter on a new route.

Our neighborhood was built on old orange groves, mostly in the fifties, so the houses are pretty uniform: one story, rectangular, unassuming. The exceptions are those that have been remodeled and bloated beyond recognition, like ours, or the few that were here long before the subdivision existed. Dexter and I find ourselves approaching one of the latter, a white Victorian with peeling paint and a wraparound porch that sags in the middle. The lot is huge, but there's no getting around the fact that the place is a real eyesore. I've passed it many times before, usually in the car, and I've always thought it might have been a cool house once. But now it's so rundown, I can't imagine it would possibly be worth saving.

Dexter is frolicking through the yard's overgrown grass when I notice the sound of somebody watering the lawn across the street. It takes me a second to realize that somebody is Francine.

Somehow, without intending to, I've ended up on her block.

My usual impulse kicks in, and I want to hurry away while I can, but Dexter has found some fascinating smell deep in the weeds and won't budge, even when I tug hard on his leash. "Come on, Dexter," I whisper. "Time to go!"

When he refuses, I give up and stand there for a moment, thinking. Then, before I can change my mind, I start walking toward Francine's house. "Come on," I repeat to Dexter, and this time, he hops right to it.

Francine has her back to us, so she doesn't know we're there until I say, "Hey, Francine."

She turns around so fast, I almost expect us to get blasted with water. But she takes her thumb off the hose in time, so the spray becomes a mellow stream pouring into the grass next to her.

"Oh!" she says. "Hi, Ollie." She doesn't seem mad at me anymore, maybe because I've caught *her* off guard for once—and I admit there's a little bit of satisfaction in that. But then I realize she's waiting for me to say something. Like maybe why I'm there or why we're having this conversation. Except . . . I have no idea either.

"Watering the plants?" I say, then congratulate myself on hitting it out of the ballpark with the inane comments *every single time*.

"Oh," says Francine again, checking the hose. The water is forming a muddy pool by her shoes, so she aims it back out over the lawn. "Yeah, I do it in the mornings because the afternoon sun is too hot and dries up all the water before the plants can get it, but in the evenings, the water doesn't dry up fast *enough*, which can cause fungus to grow in the roots—" She sucks in a deep breath. "Guess that was more than you asked." Her laugh is slightly uncomfortable, and for the first time I feel like I actually understand what might be going through her head.

"It's all good," I say. "Dexter wanted to know."

The look she gives me is funny, like she's just learned something new about me, but it's not bad. She glances down at Dexter, and a grin slowly blossoms across her face. "Good ol' Dexter, huh?" She backs away to turn off the faucet, then bends down to pat her knee. "Come here, boy!"

Dexter immediately trots toward her, but as Francine watches him, she frowns. "What's wrong?" she asks, inspecting his left side. "Does something hurt?" To me, she says, "Has he been limping for a while?"

I must really be out of it because I hadn't noticed anything. "He seemed okay this morning."

Francine lifts Dexter's paw and peers into it, separating the pads of his foot with her fingers. He jerks away at her touch, which *is* weird—he never minds that usually.

"Ah," she says. "There's a burr stuck in here." She jumps up and heads toward her front door. "One sec." When she reappears, she's got a pair of tweezers, which she holds out to me. "Do you want to do it?"

"Go ahead," I tell her, and she kneels on the ground in front of Dexter. Calmly, she picks up his paw again, speaking to him in a low voice. I try to help by stroking his back, but that seems to make him more nervous, so I quit it and let Francine do her thing. Dexter squirms some more, whimpering, but Francine stays composed. Just a few minutes later, the operation's over and she's got the burr out.

"All done." She rubs Dexter's chin. "That wasn't so bad, was it?"

"You'd make a good doctor," I say as Dexter pants happily, restored to his old self. I mean for it to sound light, like I'm joking, but it comes out mostly sincere. I'm embarrassed until

I see Francine smile again, and I decide it's not that bad. Her smile, I guess. And being the reason for it.

"I walk our neighbor Mrs. Henry's dog sometimes when she's not feeling well." Francine gestures at the knee-high grass in front of the old Victorian. "Nero loves shrubbery, so he's always getting burrs."

"That place has been abandoned for a while now, hasn't it?" I almost add that somebody should just tear it down already, but Francine is sighing as she gazes at it, and not in a yeah-what-a-dump kind of way.

"Someday," she muses, "I'd like to live in there."

I look back over to see if I'm missing something, but I only notice patches where the roof shingles need replacing. "It's pretty old."

"Yeah, but I like that," says Francine. "I like that old houses make it easier to imagine the people who came before you. It's nice to feel as though you're part of a bigger story."

I picture our house, where my parents—especially my dad—have worked so hard to scrub away all traces of anything old. They obviously wouldn't agree with Francine. They couldn't even be bothered to keep old family photos around. But as I examine the Victorian again, this time trying to conjure up images of who might have lived there, I do kind of get what she's saying.

"Anyway, it wouldn't look bad if it were all fixed up," Francine continues. "My mom would love to spend evenings on that porch, chatting away with my a pòh. My dad could turn that big yard into a Japanese garden, which he's always dreamed of having the space for. And—"

All of this makes me realize something. "Is that what you'd really want?" I ask. "To live across the street from your family?"

"Sure, why not?" She surveys her block, like its charms are obvious. "Wouldn't you?"

"No way." I recoil so hard that Dexter gets up from where he's been lying on the sidewalk and shakes himself out.

"Oh yeah?" Francine leans down to scratch him behind the ears. "How come?"

It's such a Francine question—the type of thing anybody else would find self-explanatory but she asks anyway, forcing you to think more about it than you planned.

"I don't know if I like spending that much time with them," I say eventually, kicking a pebble into the street. "And maybe they don't like spending that much time with me."

That second part just slips out, and it makes Francine go quiet. She studies me carefully. "Of course they like you," she declares even though I wasn't saying they didn't.

My silence seems to remind her of something else, and she takes a deep breath. "I'm sorry about yesterday," she says. "I didn't mean to go off on you like that." Dexter, sensing her discomfort, noses her knee, and she pets him absently.

"It's okay." I shrug. "Maybe you weren't totally wrong about me."

"Don't say that," Francine insists. Then she looks like she's about to launch into a reassuring speech that I'm sure will make me feel self-conscious, so I hurry to change the subject.

"I've been meaning to tell you I joined the Multicultural Club," I say. "Thanks for, uh, suggesting it."

"That's great!" Francine takes the bait, her face brightening. "How do you like it?"

I almost just say fine, but something about her earnestness makes me tell the truth instead. "Harder than I expected," I admit, explaining how unhelpful my parents have been with the whole family history thing. "I probably can't even fill up a single poster board with our photos."

Francine's brow furrows as she listens, and then she gets an idea. "We have lots of old pictures," she says. "You could use them if you want."

In that moment, as I watch her tuck some hair behind her ear, it occurs to me that Francine, unlike most people, isn't full of shit. What I mean is that Francine doesn't have an agenda other than the one she broadcasts loud and clear. She doesn't do the things she does to gain nice person points. And when she does expect anything in return—like with The Plan—it's usually for somebody else.

"Did you know my dad used to spend a lot of time with your family?" I say suddenly. "When they were living in Hanoi?"

Francine searches my face, like she's trying to figure out why I'm bringing this up. "Yeah, of course."

"Did you know they basically took care of him after my a yèh died?"

"Well, sort of—" But I can tell from her expression that she knew.

"He probably would've starved without them." Out of nowhere, I'm getting worked up.

"I'm sure that's not true," Francine says, because she thinks it will make me feel better, but that's not exactly what I'm looking for.

"How come you didn't mention it?" I ask her.

She looks confused. "Why would I have?"

In a way, she has a point—maybe that history isn't really relevant anymore. And it does feel weird to be talking about it as we loiter here in the sunshine, me on this sidewalk, Francine on her lawn. The whole thing seems so far away, like something that couldn't possibly have happened. Yet it's actually one of the reasons we're standing here at all. She could've said, *Remember what my grandpa did for your dad? Can't you do one thing now for him?* But of course she didn't.

"I had no idea," I say, even though that doesn't explain anything.

Francine, however, nods like she gets it, and her hair looks shiny in the morning light. "I'm sorry," she says simply.

I glance up at the sky, which is blue and clear, and all at once, I feel overtaken by an impulse I hope I won't regret.

"I'll help you with The Plan."

"What?" Francine is stunned.

"You want me to hang out with your grandpa, right?" The idea is coming together as I speak. "Maybe he can tell me stuff about Vietnam and my family. And I'll also take you up on the offer for the photos."

"Wait, really?" If I thought she looked happy earlier, her face now is a goddamn illumination.

For once, though, her lack of chill doesn't bother me. Instead, I let myself catch some of her joy, the fervor of it growing into a warm flush in my chest, and I don't remember why I resisted it so much before. Because it feels good, being looked at the way she's looking at me. Maybe I wouldn't mind it more often.

"Yeah," I tell her. "Of course."

12

Francine

IT'S A LITTLE EARLY TO BE PRACTICING THE PIANO, but I decide to go for it anyway, running through all my scales. The complicated ones, I've found, are the most comforting: E flat major. C minor. C minor harmonic. And so on. The morning has been so odd that I'm glad to lose myself in something that requires mostly muscle memory. There is, after all, a lot to think about.

First question: What in the world has gotten into Ollie?

Not that I'm complaining, of course. Because, amazingly, he's agreed to help me with The Plan! It's particularly surprising because I wasn't even trying. All I did was snap at him at lunch, and the next thing I knew, he was showing up at our house to talk to me. If I'd known that's all it would take, I would've tried being a jerk to him ages ago.

Boys certainly are strange.

But it's fine—he's on board, and that means we can get going with logistics. Tomorrow's Sunday, so it might be a good day for him to come over and kick things off. I wonder how

A Gūng will react. Based on what I've seen, he likes to have people visit, but he doesn't necessarily want to *do* anything with them. There's a lot of sitting around, demonstrating filiality. Which is easy enough, but not very exciting. I hope Ollie doesn't mind.

I remember then that I'll probably be seeing a lot more of Ollie now, and the thought makes me stumble a bit over the keys. To be totally honest, I'm still feeling a little jumpy from our encounter. I hadn't been wrong about him, it seems. He is, in his own way, as nice as I recalled. But that's *not* necessarily a reason to start liking him again, I remind myself. Not really.

I pick the scale back up from where I left off, this time getting enough into the zone that I stop thinking about Ollie and A Gūng altogether. It's almost meditative, practicing like this, and I go on for so long that I don't even notice until afterward that Mom, A Pòh, and A Gūng have returned from their morning walk. As I head to the kitchen to get a glass of water, I overhear them talking in the bedroom.

"She has to practice so much, doesn't she?" says A Gūng. "So many hours."

That's odd—A Gūng is annoyed by my practicing? I thought he liked listening. Maybe I'd gone a little overboard with the scales, but I couldn't have sounded *that* bad. Plus, I didn't realize he was already home, or else I would've checked to see if he wanted to sleep or something.

"It's okay, Bā." I hear Mom's voice now, though it's softer. "She likes to practice."

This is true, although it must be said that the piano lessons were not originally my idea—Mom got the inspiration from some of her regular customers at 88 Value Market, the ones who spoke Mandarin and immigrated from Taiwan. They knew about things like classical music and Harvard admissions and being well-rounded, and they encouraged Mom to make those my pursuits. Mom isn't so sure about Harvard ("It's so far! And cold!"), but she agreed to the piano because she likes to imagine me one day coming home from my job as a doctor and unwinding—perhaps at a shiny baby grand—to the calm notes of "Für Elise." Even now, after I've learned to play everything from Bach to Mozart to Rachmaninoff, Mom still only really appreciates "Für Elise."

I, however, enjoy it all well enough. My teacher, Ms. Kuo, says I have excellent technique, though I could work more on my "expression." I practice every single day without fail, so I hope I'll eventually get as good as she wants.

In the meantime, maybe I'm not good enough for A Gūng either.

"I'm just concerned that she's always so busy," A Gūng says to Mom. "Don't you think it's too much, with school, piano, volunteering, and everything else? She should be allowed to take it easy."

"That's how kids are these days," Mom replies. "If they want to get into a good college, they have to do a lot."

I hurry over to the closed door, intending to go in and assure A Gūng that Mom is right—that I don't like taking things easy anyway—when his response makes me stop.

"But she's a girl. Why does she need to worry so much about that?"

I'm not surprised, exactly, that A Gūng would say such a thing. I guess I'm more surprised at the way it hurts.

"What nonsense!" A Pòh has been quiet so far, but she cuts in now. "You know girls can go to good colleges now, too."

I try to slink away from the doorway, but as soon as I take a step, the floor creaks. Suddenly, everyone inside the room registers that the piano has been silent for a while.

"That might be Francine," Mom whispers. "She's always listening in."

The door opens before I can escape, and Mom appears in front of me. "Your a gūng is tired," she announces. "We'll let him rest."

"Don't listen to anything he says," A Pòh calls over Mom's shoulder. "Old people are always dō jéui. They should not talk so much."

A Gūng is sitting in the ancient gray armchair Dad moved in here for me last year, after we finally got a new living room set. He does look tired, but what alarms me most is the way he seems to disappear into the upholstery, his legs frail inside loose trousers, his hands gripping the armrests as if that alone could stop his limbs from dissolving into wisps.

I decide then to put aside what A Gūng said for now, because to change his mind would take much more time than he's got left. And anyway, at the end of the day, he's still family, isn't he?

"I have something to tell A Gūng," I say.

Mom doesn't seem to think this is the best idea. "Maybe you can wait until later—" she begins, but A Gūng interrupts her.

"If my syūn wants to talk to me, then of course I will listen." His voice is weak, but it is nevertheless a proclamation.

I slide past Mom and kneel on the carpet next to A Gūng. A Pòh gives me a gentle smile, and I greet them in my usual way: "Morning, A Gūng. Morning, A Pòh." I speak to them almost exclusively in Cantonese, but certain English words—like *morning*—have made it into the mix.

"How are you doing, Fōng?" A Gūng pats me on the head. "You're always working too hard, aren't you?"

He's showing that he cares, I tell myself. He just wants what's best for me—he always has. Is that enough? I'm not sure, but I hope so.

"I have some good news." I avoid Mom's eyes as I address A Gūng. "I found a boy to be your honorary male heir."

For a moment, there's a shocked silence all around me. Then Mom says, "Francine, what are you talking about?" while A Pòh says, "Aiyah, Fōng . . ."

But A Gūng once again commands the discussion. "A boy?" he asks. "Who?"

"Pìhng," I say, using Ollie's Cantonese name. "The one from the Tran family."

A Gūng turns this information over in his head. "The second son of Thắng An?" he says, more to Mom than me. She glances in my direction, clearly uncertain about how to answer.

Trust me, I telegraph to Mom, willing her to play along. *Look at how hopeful he seems already!* And it's true, there is a glimmer of interest now that cuts through A Gūng's weariness. It's obvious to all of us, including Mom.

She finally gives in. "M̀h," she answers, though not very persuasively. "That's the one."

A Gūng is quiet for a long time before he speaks. "You talked to Thằng An?" he asks, and for a second, I *am* concerned that The Plan won't hold up to his probing.

"I don't see why the Trans would need to agree to this, since they have so much money now," A Pòh remarks, and it makes me wish she were not always *quite* so matter-of-fact.

"Well, maybe it's not about the money for them," I rush to say. I think of the conversation I'd had with Ollie and add, "Maybe it's just to honor the history between our families." I pray that's enough to convince A Gūng.

But I needn't have worried because he responds by leaning forward, propelled from the armchair with the energy of someone ready to believe a miracle at any cost. "I'd like to see him."

"Okay, sure, I'll ask Ollie—I mean Pìhng—to come over." I scramble to get up so I can text him immediately.

"An, too," says A Gūng, catching me mid-motion. "I would like to speak to An as well."

I hesitate, still balanced on one knee. I wasn't necessarily counting on Ollie's dad to be involved, and I'm not sure if he'd be down. But the look I send over to Mom, who still doesn't know what's going on herself, is returned with a helpless shrug.

It's fine, though. I'll talk to Ollie and we'll figure out the details together. "Of course," I tell A Gūng cheerfully. "I will arrange that, too."

"All right, let's give A Gūng some peace and quiet," Mom says. "I mean it, Francine." She tilts her head toward the door and waits for me to leave the room first, so I go ahead and do as she says.

In the kitchen, however, when we're out of earshot, Mom crosses her arms. "What on earth is going on, Francine?"

A Pòh, unusually reticent, goes to the sink and puts on gloves like she might as well get the dishes done, but I know she's waiting to hear what I have to say, too.

So I explain it all—about The Plan and Ollie and how he's agreed to help. Mom doesn't interrupt me, but her forehead gets more and more wrinkled as I continue.

"Why didn't you talk to me about this before mentioning it to A Gūng?" she asks when I'm finished. Her eyes are closed so tight, it looks like she's wincing.

"Well," I say, folding my hands behind my back. "I wanted to get the details sorted before bothering you." That's mostly accurate—I thought there was a higher chance she'd go along with The Plan if it seemed actually possible.

Mom, though, isn't really listening. "I think we should tell A Gūng that there's been a mistake and Ollie won't be going through with this after all," she says. "It's too much."

"We can't do that!" I cry. "A Gūng will be so disappointed.

Didn't you see him? He seemed better just hearing about it."

"Francine," says Mom, rubbing her temples. "It's times like these that make me realize you're really still a child."

She doesn't sound angry, just frustrated, but I step back from her anyway, unsure of how to respond.

A Pòh studies me before speaking up. "Lāan," she says to Mom. "Fōng has her heart in the right place. Why not let the children try their idea?"

I was never one of those kids who minded when adults told me I was too young to do this or that—for the most part, I found their assessments reasonable. I *was* a child, after all. This time, however, the way Mom and A Pòh are talking about me makes me bristle even though I can't quite pinpoint why.

"Mà—" Mom tries to argue, but A Pòh stops her.

"At this point, there are worse lies," she proclaims, and turns on the faucet.

Curiously, Mom doesn't say anything further—probably because in this exchange, *she's* the child.

And just like that, The Plan is on.

It's almost two fifteen on Sunday afternoon, and I'm pacing around the spare room, sitting down on the bed and then getting back up again. The mattress creaks every time, a wheezy metronome for my impatience. I've shut myself in here so I don't bother anyone else, but one minute more of this and I might burst.

I peer out the window just in time to see Ollie walking up

the driveway, head down and phone in hand. A second later, I get his text: **Hey, I'm here.** I don't bother responding before sprinting for the front door, leaving the vertical blinds swinging in my place.

"Hi," I say. Through the metal screen door, I can see Ollie is wearing a button-down shirt that's been ironed, though inexpertly, and he's also combed his hair. The look doesn't quite come together, but my heart swells involuntarily at his effort. I decide not to mention that he's late.

"Hi," he replies, and when I let him in, he takes off his sneakers and lines them up next to our shoes. As he straightens up, I notice that he smells different—not peppermint, but something else. I could be wrong, but it kind of reminds me of his brother, Isaac. In a nice way.

"Thanks for coming," I chirp, trying to cover up the fact that my heart is beating a little fast. I blame adrenaline, but it's probably just from the uncertainty of whether we'll be able to pull off the ruse.

"You're still sure about this?" Ollie runs a hand through his hair, which musses it up and, at the same time, returns it closer to its normal state. He looks better, and also more familiar, and I relax.

"Of course." I pause at the edge of the foyer. "You haven't changed your mind?"

"No," says Ollie, looking not at all confident about his answer.

"Come on," I say, leading him down the hallway. "My a

gūng is in his room." As I raise my hand to knock on the door, Ollie glances up.

"Isn't this your room?" he says.

For some reason, that makes me I blush. I wasn't expecting him to remember something like that.

"Yes, but it's where my grandparents are staying for now," I explain, and rap my knuckles loudly against the wood.

"Come in," A Gūng calls out.

Ollie hangs behind me as we enter the room, and I literally have to step aside in order for A Gūng to see him.

"Pìhng is here," I announce.

"A Gūng hóu," Ollie says, using the honorific for *grandpa* like we'd discussed, but his voice is barely above a mumble. I nudge him with my elbow, willing him to move closer. Doesn't he know that A Gūng is hard of hearing?

Ollie, however, seems to interpret this to mean that he's said the wrong thing, so he tries again, switching from *hello* to *how are you*: "A Gūng, néih hóu ma?"

But A Gūng doesn't seem to mind whatever Ollie says. "Hóu, hóu," he replies, all smiles. He waves his hand around. "Sit, sit."

I settle cross-legged on the bed, but Ollie hesitates, looking to me for direction. I'm not sure what to tell him, because the room is small and there really isn't anywhere else to sit. He ends up sinking down gingerly next to me, his arm accidentally grazing my knee. That's when it hits me—I never imagined, after all this time, that I'd find Ollie and me sitting together *anywhere*, let alone on the edge of my mattress.

Especially not with my grandpa a few feet away.

I make an effort to scoot over without anyone noticing, while A Gūng asks Ollie a series of basic questions: how his parents are doing, how business is going, how his brother is liking college. At first, Ollie is able to answer everything with the Cantonese word for *good*: hóu, hóu, hóu. Then they get to a topic that requires slightly more vocabulary.

"What do you hope to do in the future?" A Gūng says.

Ollie throws me a pained glance. "Why does everyone always want to know that?" he whispers in English.

"M̀h sīk tēng a?" A Gūng asks if Ollie doesn't understand, and for the first time during this visit, he sounds a little disappointed.

"Just say what you're considering, maybe," I suggest.

"Like what, though?" Ollie seems to be more at a loss than usual.

I try to figure out which thing A Gūng would disapprove of less—Ollie's inability to speak his ancestral language or the fact that he has no direction in life.

I decide to go with the former. "Ollie's Cantonese is very bad," I explain.

Ollie shoots me a look of betrayal, but it couldn't be helped. I had to say *something*.

A Gūng responds with a sound that's a cross between comprehension and regret. "Ohhh." Then, in an aside, he switches to Vietnamese. "This boy only knows English." He shakes his head. "It's too hard."

My mind races, searching for a way to save this conversation, and I'm just about to volunteer to be their full-time translator when Ollie jumps in.

"I do understand." His Cantonese emerges slowly, halting but not incorrect. "I understand both Chinese and Vietnamese. But the speaking—I need to practice."

At this, A Gūng's smile gets bigger than I've ever seen it before. "Very good!" He chuckles. "What do you have to worry about? You're excellent."

I wrinkle my forehead slightly because I don't know if I would go *that* far. Not to mention I've also been speaking Cantonese to A Gūng this whole time—and all the time—but he's never told me I was excellent. But I guess the important thing is that A Gūng is happy, right? That's why we're here. That's why we're doing this.

"Yes, Ollie will get better in no time," I agree pleasantly.

Ollie is caught off guard by the praise but also pleased, and it seems to encourage him to try out more Cantonese. "And about my future . . ." he ventures. "I'm still thinking about it."

I wish Ollie had realized he should've dropped the subject if his answer wasn't going to be doctor, lawyer, or engineer—but once again, he doesn't get the reaction I expect.

"You have plenty of time," A Gūng declares, reaching over to thump him on the shoulder. "You're a smart boy. You'll figure it out."

His words make me feel a pinch somewhere deep down, but then I notice Ollie, whose cheeks have turned fully pink, slipping me a shy smile—and suddenly, I'm not sure what exactly is causing the strange sensation in my stomach.

Later, after we've chatted with A Gūng for a while, A Pòh insists that Ollie can't leave before eating something, so the two of us move to the living room. She brings out a plate of oranges, peeled and separated into neat wedges, and sets it in front of us. "They're from the tree in the backyard." She points through the window. "Very sweet."

"Thank you," says Ollie in English, apparently feeling bashful about his Cantonese again.

But A Pòh obviously knows that phrase, and she smiles at him. "Eat, eat," she urges, handing us two mini forks. "M̀h sái haak hei." *Don't be polite.* Then she leaves us alone on the couch.

To buy myself some time to think, I pop basically half an orange into my mouth, while Ollie uses his fork to spear a single wedge. "That went pretty well, right?" he says, swallowing.

Somehow, it did—A Gūng seemed to like Ollie a lot. Strange emotions aside, I do feel a sense of relief. "Yeah," I reply. "Good job."

"So what's next?" He leans back on the couch, the synthetic leather squeaking under his pants. Though he glances down at it, he doesn't make any comment.

"Nothing very complicated. Maybe you could come over once a week?" Then I remember A Gūng's other request, which

I need to bring up at some point even though it probably won't go over well. "Also . . ." I add, bracing myself for the worst. "Do you think your dad might be able to come for a visit?"

At first, Ollie seems more confused than annoyed. "My dad?"

"My grandpa is hoping to talk to him about The Plan." I eye the plate of oranges, which is nearly empty now. "The details and such."

"But there *are* no details." Ollie swivels to face me, like he wants to—yet simply cannot—believe the depths of my outrageousness. "The Plan isn't real."

"I know, but I was wondering if your dad could, you know, be in on it."

"We're talking about *my* dad, right?"

"Yeah."

Ollie looks like he's definitely going to say no, but as he stares at me, something convinces him to change his mind. "All right," he decides. "I'll ask."

"Okay, great!" How strange it is, interacting with this new, agreeable Ollie. Awkwardly, I rub my hands on my knees, then a second later, slide them under my legs. Without realizing it, I start bouncing on my heels and have to will myself to stop.

While I fidget, Ollie rests his elbow on the armrest, drumming his fingers. He seems nervous, too. When he notices a framed photo on the side table, he picks it up. "Is this your a gūng?"

"Yeah, with my mom." I love that picture of them—they're in

a park somewhere, standing on a bridge, and A Gūng is smiling serenely into the camera while Mom, no older than I am now, leans over the railing, laughing so hard her eyes are squeezed shut. I've always wondered what she found so funny in that moment, but when I asked her, she couldn't remember anymore.

"They look a lot alike," Ollie observes.

"Everyone says that," I tell him, grinning. "People also say I don't really look like my mom. I think the auntie consensus is that she was prettier at my age."

I expect Ollie to laugh at this, but he's still looking at the photo. "I don't know if that's true," he says, and I feel my face go warm.

I push myself up to the edge of the couch. "You said you needed old pictures, right? We have loads more—one sec and I'll grab them."

Grateful for the task, I run to the spare room closet to find the giant album where I last left it—in a cardboard box on the floor, tucked next to a stack of outdated Thomas Guides—and haul it back to the living room.

"It's kind of falling part," I say apologetically, setting the book on the coffee table. Some of the sheets are coming loose from the metal rings, and I have to slide them back into place. "I've been meaning to get a new one, but I haven't had the time to look. Did you know it's hard to find one made from materials that are actually acid-free? That's what prevents the pages from becoming discolored, because the chemicals break down over time and—"

I stop myself because I realize I'm going into way too much detail for anyone who isn't, say, A Pòh, but Ollie sits down on the floor next to me and nods, like I've told him important info. "They'd damage the photos," he says. "Makes sense."

"Yeah," I say, surprised that he was actually listening. "Exactly."

I open up the album between us so that we can look at it together. Years ago, I'd taken it upon myself to arrange all the photos in chronological order, so the oldest ones are at the front. "Wow," says Ollie, studying the sepia images, "these are really cool." Then he gets to a picture that makes him stop. It's one of A Gūng and another young man posing in front of a motorcycle, both wearing dark sunglasses and shirts with short sleeves. A Gūng is standing with his hands on his hips, a typical pose for him, but Ollie is focused on the other figure—the one leaning against the bike with his arms crossed.

"Who's that guy?" Ollie asks me.

I glance down at the photo. "I'm not sure, actually."

Just then, A Gūng emerges from the hallway and makes his way over. "What are you two up to now?" he asks. His face is wan as usual, but the optimism from our earlier conversation lingers in his voice.

I gesture at the album. "I'm just showing Pìhng these photos."

"Ah!" A Gūng touches the worn gray cover, then chuckles and shakes his head. "Why would you bother him with all that old stuff?"

I figure it's too complicated to describe Ollie's situation with the Multicultural Club, so I just say, "Pìhng asked me to."

Like magic, A Gūng suddenly seems much more amenable to the whole prospect. "Pìhng is interested?"

I pretend not to notice that and slip the photo from its plastic sleeve. "Yes, he was asking who this is."

"Let's see." The yellowing paper curves slightly as A Gūng holds it up to his eyes. "Bring me my magnifying glass," he says, and I jump up quickly to retrieve it. As he peers through the thick lens, his recognition gives way to more chuckles. "Ohhh, no wonder you are interested in this photo."

Ollie and I watch as he sets everything back down on the table. Of course, now I'm curious, too.

"Pìhng," A Gūng says, handing the photo to Ollie. "You don't recognize your own a yèh?"

Ollie looks surprised, but as he examines the picture again, understanding dawns on him. I look over his shoulder to reconsider the young man, and it's true—he does kind of look like Ollie's dad.

"Was that your motorcycle, A Gūng?" I ask. "Or did it belong to Pìhng's grandpa?"

"Oh, no." A Gūng's eyes crinkle up, and for a moment, it's almost possible to forget he's sick. "That wasn't either of ours. We just knew it was always parked there at the same time, so one day we decided to take a picture with it. I was terrified that the owner would show up and chase us away."

Giggling, I try to imagine the scene: both of our grandpas

in their cheap sunglasses, all wiry instinct and undernourished limbs, preparing to bolt at any second even as they smirk into the camera. I spy a grin growing at the corner of Ollie's mouth, and I don't know if he realizes it, but at that moment his a yèh kind of looks like *him*.

"Bā," A Pòh sticks her head out the kitchen doorway. "Come here and eat your banana."

"Aiyah, can a man never have a minute to himself?" A Gūng complains, but he nods at her in his jokey way, and I know he's not really mad. In fact, right before leaving the room, he turns back to beam at us tenderly, like he can't quite contain his joy, and waves of it wash over me as well.

Ollie, who also seems relatively cheerful, continues to flip through the photo album. "Do you think I should scan a bunch of these, and maybe blow them up so they're larger?" he asks. "That would probably work for the booth, right?"

"Yeah, I can probably find a scanner app," I answer, pulling out my phone. But then I notice Ollie is getting near to the end of the album, where the pictures are recent enough to feature me. "We can skip those," I say quickly, reaching over to shut the cover.

Ollie bats my hand away, laughing. "Let's not."

And that's how we end up going through a bunch of *my* old pictures, in all their bad-childhood-haircut-and-awkward-pose glory. There's me with my face screwed up in a wail, a large jade pendant around my neck. There's me riding a tricycle wearing a misspelled "Mikey Mouse" T-shirt and yellow sweatpants. There's me in our old apartment, sitting on shaggy green carpet while I listen with a plastic stethoscope to the heartbeat of a doll.

"Even back then," says Ollie, sounding amused.

He's still chuckling as he leafs through the rest of the album, taking (unnecessary, I might say) care not to skip over any pages. "You know, these aren't *that* bad," he tells me. "They're not, like, naked-baby level embarrassing or anything."

"Well, unfortunately—or fortunately, depending on your point of view—the photos from that era of my life are gone," I say. "They got lost when we moved."

"Oh yeah?" says Ollie. "That's too bad."

"Yeah, I used to be more bummed about it. My mom said she searched all over, but in the end, she couldn't find them. We didn't have a digital camera or smartphone then, so what can you do?" I pat the album affectionately. "But don't worry, there's plenty of cuteness left here."

"Good to know." Ollie grins and returns to the album, and apropos of nothing, my heart skips all kinds of beats.

A couple of pages later, he suddenly leans forward. "Hey, I'm in this one," he says. "When is this from?"

I check where he's pointing. "Oh, that's the first day of kindergarten."

"Ah." Ollie steals a glance at me, then studies the photo for a long time.

"You're actually in some other ones, too." I flip directly to another picture, a few pages later. "That's when we went to Irvine Park for a field trip, and you got assigned to be my buddy. Remember we had to link pinkies because your hands were too sweaty?"

"No." Ollie's laughing again. "I do not remember that."

"Here's another one." I turn the page again. "That's from your sixth birthday party."

In this photo, I'm off to the side, posing with a cheesy grin next to some other kids, clearly hamming it up for the camera. As for Ollie, he's front and center, holding a stuffed panda and also smiling wide. He seems elated to be standing next to his dad, who's holding up bunny ear fingers behind his head.

"My dad looks a lot younger than he does now," says Ollie, mostly to himself.

"Yeah, he used to wear those polo shirts a lot," I say. "The pastel ones."

Ollie is quiet for a little while longer, then slides down so his head can rest on the couch seat cushion. His mood seems to have shifted a bit. "You have a good memory for all this stuff."

"Only because I've gone over these photos so many times," I admit. "It's how memory works, you know? The process of going back to things is what makes you remember. Your brain prunes away the stuff you don't think about." I straighten the photo of Ollie's birthday party inside its sleeve. "That's why I like to revisit old photos—it makes me happy to remember good times, and I don't want to forget them."

Ollie glances at the picture again. "Doesn't it also make you sad, though? Because the past is over?"

I fold my hands into my lap and ponder this. "Photos, though, *are* something that last. At least for a while."

"But they could get damaged." Ollie is weirdly insistent. "Or lost. Like your baby pictures."

I finger a piece of the protective plastic that is coming off the page. "That's true. Sometimes I do worry that could happen with these ones, too. Especially those that traveled such a great distance to get here." I turn back to the Hanoi pictures and wonder if the negatives still exist somewhere an ocean away.

Ollie must notice that I look troubled because he reexamines the spread in front of us. "What if we scanned all the photos?" he says after a moment. Before I can answer, he adds, "Or I mean, I can do it, since I'm the one who needs them for my booth. That way you'll be able to preserve them. Maybe not forever, but for a long time."

His sentences come out in a disjointed rush, like he might change his mind about what he's suggesting any second, but I feel like I could hug him anyway.

I flip over to the snapshot of him and his dad. "Here," I say, removing it from the album. "You should have this."

That seems to make him uncomfortable. "What would I do with it?"

"Whatever you want."

"It's fine, I'm sure I already have a ton of pictures from that birthday." He crosses his arms.

The photo flutters as I hold it out to him. "Well, it's yours if you want it."

A few seconds of silence elapse before Ollie finally says, "Okay, sure." He takes the picture and tucks it carelessly into his inside jacket pocket, like it's a receipt he didn't ask for. "Thanks."

But when I get up to take our empty orange plate to the kitchen, I pause in the doorway and spot him sneaking the picture out for another look.

13

Ollie

WITH A FAMILY LIKE MINE, IT'S PROBABLY NOT surprising that I've never really been a photo person. For me, the idea that you should live in the moment instead of squandering your time trying to capture it for posterity—that always made more sense. Plus, with smartphones, it's easy to take too many pictures and then never look at them again. So what's the point?

Physical photos could be a little different, I guess. But the only ones I really remember seeing are from when I was a baby, and I have no idea where they are now. It's been ages since I went back to them. Since anyone did.

In the last week, though, I've been thinking about what Francine said. About how memories are formed and how she's always looking back. I want to write it off as just another kooky Francine habit, but then I pull open my desk drawer, where I've stored the print that she gave me.

It's been a while, but I do still remember that birthday. I wanted to see the giant pandas in San Diego, so Dad convinced everyone to drive down to the zoo. I'm not sure how he managed because it's two hours each way and tickets weren't cheap even back then, but he did it—organized the carpools and everything. Maybe it's easy to get Chinese people excited about pandas. Dad, at least, was surprisingly into them. "That one is an American like you," he joked, pointing at the bear that had been born in the zoo.

Afterward, without even needing to be asked, he bought me a stuffed panda toy from the gift shop. He seemed really pleased to give it to me, and in that moment, I was sure birthdays didn't get better than this. Before we left, Francine's mom asked a zoo employee to take a picture of everyone, and I guess that's how she ended up with this photo.

What isn't shown, however, is something else I remember: at the end of the day, when all of us kids were super sleepy from so much sun, I saw Francine getting a piggyback ride from her dad. That seemed like a great idea to me, so I asked Mom to pick me up, too. But Dad stopped her.

"You're a big boy now," he told me. "You're far too old to have your mother carry you." When I started to whine, pointing out that Francine was still getting the treatment, Dad took both of my shoulders and said, in a way that I instinctively knew not to argue with, "Ollie, you can't act like a girl."

A few years later, as we were decluttering to get ready for the house renovation, Dad rounded up a bunch of Isaac's and my old toys into garbage bags and threw them all away. The stuffed panda was among them, and he didn't even notice.

"Hey, are you there?" Dad's outside my room now, and

I push the drawer closed in a hurry and dive for my backpack. I'm about to announce that I'm heading out to school, but when I step into the hallway, Dad points at his Bluetooth earbud. "Hello?" After a second, he takes out his phone and frowns at it. "Can't hear a thing," he says to me, like I'm a stranger sitting next to him in the airport.

My first reaction is to roll my eyes and slip by him like usual, but then I remember I'm supposed to tell him about The Plan. Ugh, why the hell did I agree to that? Francine herself knew how unlikely it was—it was so clear from the way she asked me, all sad-eyed except for that tiny trace of hope I couldn't bring myself to crush.

"Uh, hey, Dad?" I linger outside my room, waiting for him to glance up from his phone.

"What's up, Ollie?" He does that thing where he looks at me but doesn't stop typing.

"Do you think you might have time to go visit Francine's grandpa soon?" I begin, because that sounds reasonable enough. "She told me to ask you."

"Oh, yeah, of course." Dad's fingers finally pause, though it's probably only because he's just finished his message and another one hasn't come through yet. "How's he doing? Does he need anything?"

This is lucky—Dad's perfunctory concern is the perfect segue for me to bring up The Plan. "Actually," I say. "I'm helping Francine with something for her grandpa. It's kind of weird, but also kind of makes sense because her grandpa is super old? But anyway, we're pretending like you've agreed to let me be his honorary male heir, since he's depressed about not having any sons and all. So when you see him, can you just go along with it?"

Dad's eyes are back on his phone, so I repeat, "Dad?"

"Sure thing, Ollie. Was this your idea?" He's typing again. "I'm on board with whatever you suggest."

It's not entirely clear to me whether he heard everything I said. "Wait, so you're agreeing to do it?"

Dad's phone rings then, and he puts up a finger. "Hold on, I have to take this."

Glancing at my watch, I see that it's almost eight, which means I'm going to be late for school unless I leave now. I don't usually feel the need to have defined end points in my conversations with Dad, but today—maybe because I find myself thinking about Francine and what I want to tell her—I push to pin down a response.

"Dad," I say again, even though I can hear the other person talking on the other end of the line. "This is important. Are you saying you're cool to help us?"

"Yeah, of course, just let me know when," Dad replies, muting and then unmuting right away.

I jump in quick before he can move on. "What about, like, in two weeks?"

"Not a problem, John," Dad says into the phone, while giving me a thumbs-up.

I'll be annoyed if Dad makes me brief him on the situation

again, but at least he *did* seem like he was open to helping. Just that alone surprised me, if I'm being honest. I've grown so used to him not being involved that I forget what it's like when he is.

As I back out of our driveway, I wonder if Dad's visit with Francine's grandpa is going to be awkward. At least Francine will be there to diffuse it with her own awkwardness—I never knew I'd ever feel grateful for *that*.

Up ahead, I catch sight of a girl walking fast along the sidewalk. I look back at her without thinking, and I don't register it's Francine until a second later—a disorienting second that makes me blush even though I'm alone in the car. She hasn't seen me, so I could drive past her and act like I didn't know it was her, but weirdly, I don't want to.

I slow the car and roll down my window. Francine is clasping her backpack straps with both hands, her elbows flapping out with every step, and now that I'm closer, I can see the Francine-ness again. She turns her head when she senses my car, and I don't notice I'm grinning at her until she notices it, her own smile blooming in response.

"Hey, Ollie," she says, popping out her headphones. She comes over and rests her arms on the window. "How's it going?"

"Not too bad." I glance around the empty street, which is quiet except for my idling car. "Do you walk to school every day?"

"Yeah, it's a good time to listen to podcasts." Francine indicates her phone, which is paused in the middle of an episode of

Wait Wait . . . Don't Tell Me! "And it's better for the environment, obviously."

We both consider my car, which is an SUV. A small one, but still.

"Guess you probably don't want a ride in this thing then," I joke.

Francine looks down at the empty passenger seat, then back at me. She grins. "Well, if you're going to guzzle all that gas anyway . . ."

As she swings her legs into the car, I see that she's wearing shorts. It's hard to explain why I noticed because they weren't even *that* short, and besides, she's worn shorts a thousand times, hasn't she? Maybe I'm distracted by the fact that she's also wearing a long-sleeved tee, which is one of those things girls do that makes no sense to me—if it's hot enough for shorts, then why bother with long sleeves? I especially didn't know that it was the kind of thing Francine did.

She pushes up her sleeves now, like she's self-conscious about them, and I spot a thin gold chain on her left wrist.

"Is that new?" The bracelet *is* something I haven't seen her wear before, and I latch on to it, hoping she hasn't realized what else I've been checking out.

"This?" Francine holds out her arm, shaking it so the chain lays smooth against her skin. "Not exactly." She tells me the story of how the bracelet came to be, and I'm impressed. "I just decided to start wearing it more," she says. "I know it doesn't look like much, but I like it."

"I think it's pretty." The comment slips out before I've had a chance to consider whether I should be telling her things like that. When she smiles at me, the answer doesn't get any clearer.

"So, um, about my dad," I say in a rush, because no other topic kills a moment quite like that one. "I talked to him about visiting your grandpa, and he said okay."

Francine doesn't seem to mind the abrupt change in subject. In fact, she seems thrilled. "That's amazing!" she exclaims. "Maybe we can all have a nice dinner party. I'll send you guys a calendar invite."

Now I really hope Dad was being serious this morning. I don't tell Francine that it's been years since I asked Dad to do anything, so I can't guarantee his word is any good. But she looks so optimistic, I can't help but feel hopeful, too.

"Hey," I say, holding out my USB cord. "Do you want to finish your podcast?"

Anytime I think Francine's face can't get any brighter, I'm wrong. There it goes, up one more little notch. "Sure!" she replies, and plugs in her phone.

Normally, I think of *Wait Wait* as something you listen to in snippets—it's perfectly fine if it happens to be on the radio, but I never imagined anybody downloading episodes intentionally. Francine, though, is one of those people. She knows all the answers, most of the time even before the contestants. She *loves* the show. It's hilarious.

When we get to school, I'm kind of sorry the ride was so short. "That's another downside to driving," says Francine as she gathers her books into her lap. "You barely get any listening time in."

She's kidding, but it's true—the trip, all in, took barely five minutes. Short enough that I probably wouldn't mind another segment of *Wait Wait*.

"Well, I can listen on the way back, too," I say. Then I realize it sounded like I was offering to drive her home, which I wasn't. Was I?

Francine looks like she's wondering, too. We're standing outside my car now, and even though there's a bit of a breeze, it's another warm morning. I notice she's got her hair tied halfway up today, a few of the strands falling over her face, and her cheeks are already brushed pink from the sun.

Once again, I see my chance to back off—to make it clear, maybe, that I meant I'd download the episode myself later, or to claim that I didn't actually enjoy the show. But I don't do either of those things. Instead, I lean on to the hood of my car and say, "That is, if you're willing to get in this gas guzzler again."

Francine pretends to mull this over. "All right," she says. "But only because you're clearly such a big fan."

Grinning, I lock the car and follow her out of the parking lot. "I think I'm coming around."

"What did I tell you?" Rollo appeared at my locker a few minutes before AP Bio, so we're walking to class together. "Piece of cake, right?"

He'd asked me how things were going with the Global Gala,

so I mentioned I was using his idea of a photo collage—which naturally meant he claimed credit for solving the entire problem.

"Um, only because Francine is letting me use her photos," I say. "My parents were useless on the family history front."

"Oh, yeah, how'd the visit with her grandpa go?"

Rollo has so far been very supportive of my decision to help Francine with The Plan. "All you have to do is show up to see her grandpa a few times, and she'll probably 'help' you by making the entire collage herself," he reasoned. "Win-win."

"It went fine, I guess," I tell him now. "I still feel a little weird about lying to him, though."

"Yeah, but sometimes that's just how it is with Asian families." Rollo rips open a mini matcha Kit Kat and takes a bite, crunching down on both sticks at the same time. He's been eating a lot of candy since Rollos and More closed up shop—probably way more than he should. "Personally, as the oldest son of an oldest son, I face a *lot* of expectations. I have to tell my a yèh stuff he wants to hear all the time."

"Like what?"

"Like how I'm gonna be the valedictorian of our class. Or how I'm waiting until after college to date."

"Isn't the second thing true by default?"

"Wow, rude."

When we get to the AP Bio classroom, Francine and Jiya are already at their seats. Francine is wearing Jiya's oversized headphones, which are plugged into the computer that sits between them, and the volume is cranked up enough that I can tell she's listening to some kind of music. She's not paying any attention to me, but just seeing her there makes me feel, strangely, as though she were.

Jiya nods at me when I sit down, which is more of a greeting than I've ever gotten from her, so I guess that means I've moved up in life. Francine, too, gives a little wave. "Hi, Ollie," she says loudly, because she can't hear herself over the music.

"Hey," I say, trying to sound casual, just as Rollo pulls his chair out with a noisy scrape.

"All right, what'd I miss?" he says, whipping out his iPad.

I watch as he diligently copies down the homework assignment from the board, and I wouldn't put it past him to have shown up primarily to have a reason to test out his new Apple Pencil. "You're really gonna start coming to class now?" I say, skeptical.

"Just trying something new."

"Isn't that a great music video?" Jiya asks Francine, who is taking off her headphones. "Love the song, too, obviously."

"Wait, are you talking about Violet Girl?" Rollo leans across me to get a better look at Jiya's screen. Another video has started auto-playing, and it features more grainy footage of the same purple-haired girl Francine was watching. In this one, she's chasing a friend down a pier, and the two of them end up cannonballing into a lake.

"Yeah, her new album just dropped this morning," says Jiya. "Total surprise." Then she seems to remember who she's talking to. "You know about Violet Girl?"

"Duh." Rollo draws himself up. "I am a man of culture."

Jiya cocks her head at him, but then pushes her lip out in an expression of respect. "Cool."

"Did you just read about her on Apple News or something?" I say, because even *I* haven't heard of Violet Girl.

"No need to be jelly, Ollie, just because you don't know what's up," Rollo retorts, which means he totally did read about her on Apple News.

Jiya, however, has already moved on and is now uncapping a fat silver marker, preparing to ink in a Jiya-style illustration of Violet Girl in her sketchbook.

"Whatever, Rollo," I grumble. "You barely know what's up."

"Um, false." Rollo wags his Apple Pencil at me. "I happen to know, for example, that Violet Girl is playing in LA the week after next."

"That *is* true," Francine confirms. "Jiya and I looked it up earlier."

Rollo glances over at Jiya and then down at the illustration in her sketchbook. Suddenly—and I can tell by the way his eyebrows jump halfway up his forehead—inspiration strikes him.

"Hey, Jiya," he says, "have you thought any more about my offer lately?"

"Hmm." She pauses, her marker slowing on the page. "You mean to be my agent?"

"Yeah, exactly!"

She turns back to the drawing. "No."

"Hold up," says Rollo. "Before you make any hasty decisions that might cost you the chance of a lifetime, you've gotta at least listen to my idea."

A grin sneaks up on Jiya, but it's definitely the is-this-guy-for-real variety. "All right, hit me with it."

"Three words, Jiya." Rollo half sprawls across the desk dramatically, holding up a trio of fingers. "Violet Girl swag."

Jiya laughs, which is frankly the only reasonable reaction to Rollo right now.

"I'm serious! Picture that"—he points at her illustration—"on a T-shirt."

Francine peers over Jiya's shoulder to examine the open sketchbook. "Maybe he's onto something, Jiya."

"Thank you, Francine," says Rollo. "I always knew you had a great eye for quality." He smirks at me meaningfully, and I kind of want to punch him in the face.

"Okay, fine." Jiya rests her chin on her hands. "Tell me more."

"I know a guy who can get the shirts printed for a great price." Rollo has entered full business mode now. "We get those made, we go to the concert—"

"We can't because tickets are already sold out," interrupts Jiya. "They were gone in, like, a minute. I tried."

"Don't worry," Rollo assures her. "I know a guy who can help us out with that, too."

Jiya gives him a long, appraising look. Then she breaks out into another grin. "You are *so* sketch, Rollo."

"Trust me, Jee, this is the one of the least sketch things I've done," he declares, and I see Francine tilt her head side to side, as if weighing the truth of this, before conceding the point.

"All right, *Roll*," says Jiya. "You get us into that concert, and I'm in."

"No problem!" Rollo swipes at his screen. "Four tickets to Violet Girl, coming up."

It's so like Rollo to rope me into something like this. I mean, I still haven't even heard a Violet Girl song and he's already signing me up to go to a concert—when, again, I'm not even sure *he's* a real fan. I glance at Francine and wonder how she feels about getting caught up in a Rollo scheme.

She looks, as a matter of fact, puzzled. "Four tickets?"

Rollo gestures at her, Jiya, and me. "Yeah, one for each of us."

"Oh, but I don't need one," she says.

"Stop it, of course you do." Jiya sets her marker down. "You obviously have to come."

"I want to." Francine twists her gold bracelet thoughtfully. "But I can't."

Jiya frowns at me like it's somehow my fault, but I'm even more surprised by Francine's reaction than she is. "Because your grandpa's sick?" I ask.

"I just don't think I'll be allowed to go to LA on a Friday night," she replies. Like it's that simple, and she doesn't have any feelings about it.

"What about a Saturday night?" Rollo is already checking his iPad.

Francine shakes her head. "I think it's the 'night' part that's the problem."

"Overprotective parents," Jiya explains to us in an aside.

"Well, I *am* an only child." Francine looks apologetic. "Being a girl doesn't really help either. And my grandparents would have to know where I was going, so they'd worry about me, too."

"Thank god my sister was such a hot mess." Jiya sighs in relief. "Now everything I do seems totally tame."

"Yeah," Francine agrees. "I wish I had a sister!"

Her voice is cheerful, like always, but when she glances in my direction, I notice a glimmer of something wistful before she looks away.

"Have you ever been to a concert?" I say suddenly.

The force of my question surprises her. "No, I haven't," she answers, and her hesitation only makes me barrel on.

"You should at least ask your parents," I suggest. "Maybe they'll let you go."

"It's pretty unlikely," she says. "Given everything that's been going on, I'm sure they would prefer I stay home and spend time with my grandpa." When she notices how soberly Rollo and Jiya are nodding, she puts on a smile. "Don't mind me, though. You all should go and have fun!"

If I hadn't been at Francine's house over the weekend, I might have dropped it there. But I saw the way Francine is so focused on her a gūng, and I think it might be good for her to get a break. Besides, it's not like he's going to be awake after nine p.m. anyway.

"I really think you should at least give it a shot," I press on. "Asking your parents, I mean."

Rollo looks at me like he doesn't recognize me. And maybe there's a part of me I don't recognize either. Since when did I care that much what Francine does with her Saturday night?

"Only if you want to, of course," I add quickly.

Francine is quiet at first. "I don't know," she says in a rare moment of uncertainty. But it doesn't last, because her voice grows sure again almost immediately. "It's not a big deal, though."

"Well, let me know if you change your mind," Rollo tells her, slipping his Apple Pencil behind his ear.

"Sure, will do," says Francine, sounding a lot like she won't.

Ms. Abdi walks in then, and the conversation ends there. Inexplicably, I feel irritated by the fact that Francine, despite clearly wanting to go to the Violet Girl concert with us, refuses to even try to get permission from her parents. Why won't she push back on them? It's just a concert—what kind of trouble could *Francine* get into? She's honest-to-goodness the most responsible seventeen-year-old I know. In fact, I think she could stand to be a little less responsible.

I have to stop myself there, though, because all of a sudden, my thoughts are getting jumbled in a way that's hard to ignore. What exactly do I *want* from Francine? I'm already going to her house this weekend, and the next, and probably the one after that. I can't possibly be disappointed by the prospect of spending less time with her.

I study her now, as she opens her notebook and proceeds to jot down today's date in neat, round handwriting. The same handwriting she's had since at least fifth grade. Because she's still Francine, I remind myself. The same old Francine.

What I'm not sure about? Whether I'm the one who's changed.

14

Francine

AFTER SCHOOL, I WAIT IN THE PARKING LOT FOR Ollie, watching people head out to their cars. The afternoon sun has settled over the sea of shiny metal, reflecting heat back into the air, and the asphalt is warm beneath my sneakers. It feels a little unnecessary to wait for a ride home when I could just as easily walk—but at the same time, I admit that's also kind of why I'm looking forward to it.

I spot Ollie in the distance, and my stomach tells me *he* may be another reason, but then it squeezes in a different way because I notice that he looks less than excited.

"Hey," he says as he approaches. "I'm sorry, I know I said I'd give you a ride, but can we maybe rain check?"

"Sure." I shade my eyes, because maybe all the sunshine is getting to be a bit much anyway. It might be nice to just get going on my usual route home. "No worries."

"It's just—" Ollie stumbles and starts over. "It's dumb, but I have to go get, like, a poster board thing." He gestures at his phone. "Amanda Moreno has called a special meeting to preview everyone's Global Gala booths tomorrow."

"Right, of course." I shift my backpack from one shoulder to the other. "I'll just see you later then?"

"Okay, yeah, I'll see you later. Or tomorrow, probably. Or, I mean . . ." Ollie scratches behind his ear, color rising up in his cheeks. "Unless you want to come?"

I pause. A Gūng has a doctor's appointment today, so no one would know whether I got home until later. Normally, I would've just gone straight there regardless and finished my homework, but watching Ollie tug nervously at his T-shirt as he waits for my answer, I find myself saying, "Why not?"

We listen to the rest of *Wait Wait . . . Don't Tell Me!* on the way to this place called the Artist Warehouse, which I've convinced Ollie is the best place to get supplies for his booth. "I've been here a few times with Jiya," I say as we pull into the lot. "They'll have everything you need."

The store is cavernous, with aisles crammed full of everything from easels to paints to gift wrap. The poster boards are in the back, so we have to meander through a few aisles to get there, and when we get to the photography section, Ollie suddenly stops. "Hey, they sell photo albums here."

I backtrack so I can check out what he's looking at. "Oh, yeah! I didn't even realize."

"You should get one." Ollie grabs an album off the shelf and hands it to me. "These are nice."

Inside, the pages are crisp and cream-colored because they're supposed to be, not because they're old, and the cover, too, feels nice to the touch—the linen has just enough texture to feel expensive. When I check the back, however, there's a price tag to match.

"It's a bit pricy," I say, holding it out in front of me. But then I remember how much A Gūng enjoyed looking through the photos with us, and I decide that finally getting them organized could be worth it. "I've got some money saved from Lunar New Year, though. Maybe I should go for it."

Ollie pulls down a few more albums, each a different color. "Which one would you get?"

"Teal, definitely," I reply, reaching for it. "That's my favorite color." At the last second, though, I hesitate. "Actually, maybe I'll just go with red."

"How come?" Ollie watches me place the other colors back on the shelf.

"I just think everyone else in my family would like red better." I hug the album to my chest. "My mom is always saying how it's a lucky color."

Ollie is contemplative as he follows me toward the poster board section. "Do you ever wish you didn't have to think about what your family wanted?" he asks as we round a corner.

I almost say no without thinking, but then I walk right into a tower of masking tape, and I have to scramble to the floor to corral the runaway rolls. Ollie gets down on his knees to help, his fingers skimming my wrist when we reach for the same roll, and I feel a zap that sends something tumbling inside of *me*. It makes me stop to reconsider his question more seriously.

"Sometimes," I acknowledge. Since we learned about A Gūng's diagnosis, I've been so occupied with helping him that I haven't asked myself . . . well, much of anything at all. I get back to my feet and pick up the photo album, which is bulkier and heavier than I realized. Maybe there's a small part of me that *is* tired. But doesn't being part of a family mean you can't—or shouldn't—shut them out whenever you want?

Ollie doesn't say anything else, so I feel a need to fill the silence. "I don't mind most of the time, though. I like it when I can do stuff to make them happy."

"Have you always been like that?"

"Probably?" I adjust a tape roll at the top of the pile we've rebuilt. "I'm pretty sure the first time I remember thinking about it was when I was really little, like maybe three or four."

My cousin Sandy and I, unusually, were at a pool party. It was at a family friend's house—I still don't know whose. I had never seen a pool before and remember thinking it looked so pretty, almost like turquoise Jell-O. Neither Sandy nor I knew how to swim, so we sat on the edge and dangled our feet in the water while the other kids had a blast splashing around. Mom had specifically told me I couldn't join in, so I stayed where I was, only kicking now and then to watch the sun glinting off the sprays of water. Even though what I *really* wanted to do, of course, was jump in. Sandy, too, apparently had the same impulse, but what she did was the opposite—she jumped.

What happened next was a blur: Sandy flailing and wailing and swallowing water, someone's older brother rushing over to pull her to safety, my aunt wrapping her in towel after towel, me feeling soaked through and shivering even though I wasn't the one who'd almost drowned. At some point, Mom grabbed me, dragging me away from the pool edge. "Thank heaven you listen," she said, her nose pressed into my hair like she could keep me sitting there forever, safe in her arms. "I'm so happy I don't have to worry about you like that." Her relief, the way it washed warm over both of us, made me feel like I'd been responsible for something precious. I've felt responsible for it ever since.

"And now you make sure she never worries," says Ollie when I've finished the story. "That's why you're always thinking of her, and the rest of your family, without being asked."

"You could say that." I tuck the photo album under my arm and resume walking. "But now it also just feels good to take care of others."

"Sometimes, though, doesn't it also feel good to take care of yourself?" Ollie gives me a look when he says this, immediately sending my insides back into free fall. When he offers to carry the album for me, I am too surprised to protest, so I let him.

We end up choosing a couple of black foamcore boards for the Global Gala booth. Some gold Sharpies, a few packages of photo paper, and one can of spray adhesive later, we're ready to check out. The cashier, who is thin and blond with a name tag that reads Harper (they/them), greets us with a big smile. "Did y'all have a chance to check out today's artist-led activity?" they say, aiming the scanner gun at Ollie's boards.

"No, what's that?" I ask, intrigued.

Harper points at a long table in the corner, where a guy wearing perfect-circle glasses waves at us. "Pablo can show you how to do blind contour portraits. You should totally check it out!"

"Ah," I say, thinking it's too bad Jiya isn't here because she would love this kind of thing. "I'm not any good at drawing, though."

"That's okay!" Harper rips off the receipt and hands it to Ollie. "It's just about trying out a different part of your brain."

"I think we should do it." Ollie swings his shopping bag toward the table. "What do you say?"

I check my phone to see if Mom has texted me. "Do we have time—"

"Come on, Francine." Ollie is already hauling his foamcore boards over. "It'll be fun." He looks back at me with a grin, and I've never found those words more convincing.

"Okay." I run a little to catch up to him. "Sure."

Ollie and I sit down on opposite sides of the table, as instructed by Pablo. The foamcore boards themselves take up two whole seats, but since no one else is around, Pablo doesn't seem to mind. It's a snug little nook over here, I decide, though I don't realize *how* snug until I notice Ollie's sneakers squeaking underneath my chair.

I glance at the drawings pinned to the wall behind Ollie, the paint stains on the tabletop between us, the jars of markers and pens lining the top edge of my drawing paper—basically, everything but Ollie. Sitting here this way, face-to-face, is suddenly more than I can handle.

"Okay, friends," says Pablo, "the idea behind a blind contour drawing is to keep your focus on your subject the whole time." To illustrate, he points at Ollie's face, indicating his forehead, nose, and chin. "Move your eyes over each feature and let your hand recreate what you see. The trick, though, is you can't lift your pen and you can't look down at your paper until you're done. Got it?"

I finally let my gaze fall on Ollie, and our eyes lock. "Got it," he says, and I manage a nod.

Pablo starts the timer for two minutes, and we begin. I start with Ollie's hair, the way it fluffs up a little at the front, and then it's a curved line down the middle of his forehead to his eyebrows, which arch over his eyes in their natural boy way, followed by the gentle slope of his nose and, eventually, his parted lips, which look like they could use some water, or maybe a—

I lift my pen without meaning to, breaking off my contour line. Ollie, though, is still concentrating on me, his eyes lingering on places I never knew could be interesting. The slow, careful motion of his pen, along with his occasional half smile, makes me feel exposed, but willingly—like I'd reveal more in a heartbeat if he asked.

The chime from Pablo's phone snaps me back into my seat, and Ollie sets down his pen with a grin. "How'd you do?" asks Pablo, gesturing for us to share our drawings.

Ollie's is actually pretty good—you can tell it's my face, because those are my eyes staring right back at us. Sure, they're a bit crooked and wider set than they are in real life, my hair is just a shock of scribbles by each ear, and my jaw is too round and lopsided, but the overall effect is cool. I look like a surrealist masterpiece, and funnily, it makes me feel important enough to be the subject of one.

My drawing, on the other hand, isn't quite finished, and when I hold it up, it's embarrassingly clear where I got distracted because the line ends abruptly at his mouth. Ollie, though, is pretty tickled. "I think it's great." He reaches for the portrait. "Can I have it?"

"Yeah, of course," I say, laughing because the whole thing is kind of silly. But when Ollie asks me to sign it, insisting I place my signature prominently in the corner, I do it with a flourish.

15

Ollie

"THAT *WAS* FUN," SAYS FRANCINE AS WE LEAVE the Artist Warehouse. She's not just saying it, either—she's almost skipping through the parking lot, she's so happy. It makes me feel light, too, and maybe because that drawing exercise was strangely exhilarating, I find myself thinking about how I can keep up whatever this is that's now buzzing around us.

"Should we grab a coffee or something?" I say.

This time, she doesn't hesitate at all. "Sure!"

We stop at a Nguyen's Bakery, which is nestled in a long, narrow strip mall a few blocks from the Artist Warehouse. In terms of excellent banh mi, it's a toss-up between Nguyen's and this other place, Phan's, but Nguyen's has a better selection of other foods, both sweet, like chè puddings, and also savory, like bánh cuốn rice noodle rolls. I get my usual Vietnamese iced coffee before I realize I don't need the extra caffeine—but then again, maybe I do.

The shop has just one dining table, which is technically big enough for four people, but I grab a seat there anyway because the afternoon seems slow. Plus, there are only two chairs, both pushed up against the wall. Before I can decide whether to move one so they're not side-by-side, Francine walks over and sets a slice of strawberry cake in front of me. She'd insisted on paying for her own taro milk tea, and I guess this is why. "My treat," she says, sitting down.

"What's the occasion?" I grin and reach for a fork. I've always been a fan of the Asian bakery strawberry cake, which has a light sponge and fresh berries mixed in with whipped cream frosting. I haven't had it in ages, so half the slice is gone in about thirty seconds.

Francine takes a sip of her tea. "Just wanted to say thank you, I guess. You've been really nice."

My chest feels kind of funny, and I can't tell if it's because I'm pleased by what she said or embarassed by how mistaken she is. "I'm not sure I was nice enough for *this*," I quip, pushing the plastic cake container toward her. "You better have some now before I inhale the rest."

"No, you should have it all," Francine urges. Then she eyes the cake and adds, "Also, I don't like the toasted almonds on the sides."

I laugh and pop one into my mouth. "The truth comes out."

Francine twirls her straw in her drink, knocking the ice around. "But seriously, Ollie, I do appreciate your help. I know you still think the whole situation with my a gūng is kind of odd."

She's not wrong, but agreeing somehow doesn't feel right. I take another bite of cake and gulp it down before answering. "Well, who knows? Maybe I'd do the same for my grandpa."

This sets off a spark in Francine's eye, and I hope she's not concocting *another* zany scheme when I've only just barely accepted this one. "Are your other grandparents still around?" she asks. "Besides your a yèh, I mean."

"Yeah, both of my grandmas are." I drag a napkin along the side of my coffee, wicking away the condensation. "I don't really talk to them though."

"You don't?" Francine looks scandalized, like I've just confessed to occasionally forgetting to feed Dexter. "How come?"

"I don't know." Even though I don't want it to, I feel a familiar guilt closing me up. I wish Francine would understand that not everybody can be BFFs with their grandparents. "I don't speak Chinese or Vietnamese that well, for one," I tell her. "As you've seen."

"But calling one of your grandmas would be a way to get better," Francine insists.

"It's not that easy," I say, and hope she'll drop it.

"Have you tried, though?"

"No, not really."

She goes quiet, biting her lip, and I'm relieved. But then she comes back with, "What are the other reasons?"

"Hmm?"

"You said one reason is that you don't speak Chinese or

Vietnamese well. What else is stopping you?"

For a while there, I'd almost forgotten about Francine's tendency to be a walking self-help book. I shovel the last of the cake into my mouth and chew it silently. It's still good, but I wonder if I've eaten too much.

"I've met my a pòh like three times in my life," I say, sounding petulant. "I'm not even sure she remembers which grandkid I am—she's always mixing me up with Isaac."

Francine clearly doesn't think that's a legitimate excuse, but she lets it go. "What about your a mā?"

I push the empty cake container away. "I guess I've seen her more recently."

"You could try her," Francine suggests. When I don't answer, she leans forward suddenly, her straw grazing her cheek. "Would you want to?"

I roll my shoulders a few times, because all of a sudden, they feel stiff. I've never talked about this to anybody before, but Francine is sitting there very still, just waiting for an answer, and the next sentence kind of spills out on its own.

"Yeah," I say, "but I guess it feels like too much, somehow, to do something different."

Francine nudges my fork so that the frosted tips don't touch the table. "You mean like, it's too much effort?"

"No, not exactly." I struggle to find a way to explain. "It's just . . . let's say I call her, right? After all these years of never doing it once. And I talk to her in my paltry Cantonese, not even saying anything besides "A Mā hóu" when she picks up and "hóu" when she asks me how I'm doing."

"That would be fine. Old people don't mind conversations like that."

"Yeah, sure, it would be fine." I think back to the day I dropped A Mā off at the Vietnamese bus stop, her dry fingertips light on my face. "More than fine, honestly. My a mā would be super happy. Except that's part of it—I feel like shit that she'd be overjoyed by such a lousy little thing."

Francine's silence is thoughtful, and for once I wish she'd interject something annoying so I wouldn't have to keep talking. But all she does is cup her chin in her hands.

"And I guess . . ." This part makes my voice stick, and I swallow to dislodge the words. "I guess I haven't wanted to face the fact that I could've been doing this lousy thing—that I could've been doing something different—all along."

"It's not too late, though." Francine looks at the tabletop instead of me, scratching at a smudge that's past any chance of being removed. "It's never too late."

She *would* say that. But I'm not sure I believe her.

Her eyes fall on my phone, which sits on the table next to my coffee, and suddenly, she reaches over and grabs it.

"Hey," I say. "What are you doing?"

"Do you have your a mā's number?" Francine can't search for it because my phone is locked, but that doesn't stop her from brandishing the screen at me.

"I don't know, probably. Can I have my phone back now?"

"I really think you should call your a mā."

"Yeah, I can tell." I reach my hand out. "I'll consider it if you return my phone."

Francine holds up a finger. "I will, but only if you call her right now."

"No way."

"Look, I know you're worried it'll be awkward, but how *she* feels will more than make up for it. I promise."

"I'm not gonna do it, Francine."

The way I say her name makes her twist her mouth to one side, but a moment later, she slides the phone back over. I've got it almost halfway to my pocket when she stands up to gather our trash. "It's all right to be embarrassed," she says, walking toward the bin. "But that doesn't mean you can't do it anyway."

A few minutes later, after stopping in the bathroom, she sits back down across from me and fiddles with the zipper on her wristlet wallet. I clear my throat. "I didn't have the number."

She pauses mid-zip. "Ah," she says before turning back to it.

"So I texted my mom."

Francine's face splits into a grin. "I knew you wouldn't chicken out," she says, and I wonder what could have possibly given her that impression.

Sighing, I set my phone down and hover my finger over the call button. "What am I supposed to say?"

"One sec," Francine says. "I have an idea." She runs over to the counter and comes back with a handful of napkins, which she spreads out before us. From inside her wristlet, she pulls out a pen and draws a lopsided happy face. "I'll help if you get stuck," she offers, pointing at it. "How's that?"

"Okay, I guess," I say, even though the whole thing seems like a lost cause. "Here goes." And before I can convince myself it was a bad idea to let Francine talk me into this, I tap the screen.

The phone rings for a while, and I wonder if this is going to end anticlimactically with A Mā not even being home. Maybe she's out and about, living her best A Mā life, and she doesn't need a stupid phone call from me.

I'm about to give up when finally there's a click. "Hallo?" A Mā's voice is faint and a little weary.

I open my mouth but my mind goes blank. Francine gesticulates at me to go on. *Say something*, she mouths.

"Uh, hello," I manage. "A Mā, néih hóu ma?"

"Oh? Pìhng há?" Instantly, A Mā sounds different, full of surprise but also energy. "Hóu, hóu, néih géi hóu ma?"

I tell her I'm doing fine too, and then there's a silence. "Is anything the matter?" A Mā asks, still in cheerful Cantonese.

"No," I say hurriedly. "Nothing."

Francine scribbles on a napkin and holds it up: *Tell her you just wanted to see how she's doing.*

"I just wanted to see how you're doing," I say.

"Oh, thank you, Pìhng," she replies, and repeats that she's very good.

More silence. Francine picks up her pen again and writes furiously: *Ask if the weather's been warm.*

Wait, is she serious? *That's* the best she's got? I don't need a napkin to tell me I should ask about the weather. But when I make a face, Francine waves her hands impatiently. "Trust me," she whispers, so I do it.

Weirdly, though, she's right. The weather, of all things, ends up being a turning point in the conversation. A Mā tells me about the upcoming forecast for rain, warning that she thinks it'll probably hit LA a few days later, so I'd better get ready to dress in extra layers. Then she starts giving me advice about all kinds of other random stuff, too—like taking the bus in San Francisco or interacting with dogs I haven't met before—and I just listen. It's mostly boring and not particularly helpful, but as Francine smiles proudly from across the table, I get the sense that's maybe beside the point.

When I hang up the phone, Francine comes over to pat me behind the shoulder. "You did good."

I don't really deserve that because all I did was call my grandma—something I should've done a long time ago. Something I shouldn't have needed Francine to get me to do.

But it's nice to feel her hand on my back.

16

Francine

SOMEHOW, I THINK OLLIE'S DECIDED WE'RE friends after all.

It seems implausible, but there's no arguing with the evidence. On Tuesday, he offered to drive me to school again and hung around to drive me home in the afternoon, too. Then he did it again the next day. And the next. In some ways, it feels like we've always done this—and yet my chest gets all fluttery every time I see him waiting in the parking lot. That part especially doesn't make sense, because we're certainly not *more* than friends. I haven't considered that to be a possibility since probably at least eighth grade.

But now it's Saturday, and Ollie is placing chopsticks in front of my a gūng, who's sitting in his usual spot at the head of the dining table. Today's afternoon visit has somehow turned into dinner, but Ollie hasn't complained yet. When A Gūng extended the invite, Ollie said he had to go home to walk Dexter but remarkably agreed to come back, reappearing at our doorstep not twenty minutes later.

As I carry the rice pot over to the table, I watch Ollie maneuver around our chairs. He's taller than everyone in my family, even Dad, and I can't tell if he makes that enclosed space look cozy or cramped. When I catch his eye, he gives me one of his small smiles—so easily, like he's throwing it away, and I get an old impulse to hoard it like the luxury it once seemed. But then I remember I don't need to anymore because I see him smile all the time now. I'll even start taking it for granted, probably. In psychology, that's what they call habituation—once the novelty of a stimulus wears off, it stops sending that little fizz down your spine every time. So I'm pretty sure that'll happen to me. Soon.

Ollie is hovering near the dining table now, having finished with the chopstick distribution, and A Gūng motions for him to sit down. At first, Ollie hesitates over which seat to take, but of course A Gūng points to the chair right next to him—my usual seat. The pang of such a trivial thing surprises me, and I consider retreating into the kitchen to hide my discomfort. But then Ollie flashes me a helpless glance and I decide to stay for his sake.

"Pìhng," says A Gūng, curving his hands comfortably over the armrests. "Did you know that tomorrow is Qingming Festival?"

"M̀h," says Ollie, and it's clear he has no clue what Qingming Festival is. I realize, belatedly, that I should've made sure he knew about that. What kind of male heir hasn't heard of Qingming Festival?

"It's a day for honoring your ancestors," I say. "You're supposed to go to the cemetery to pay your respects and take care of their grave sites."

"Gotcha." Ollie nods soberly. The bags under his eyes are especially pronounced in the light of our fluorescent lamp, but pensive is a good look for him—and when my heart does its weird little skip, I'm struck once again by how strange it is to see him here.

"Tomorrow, we are going to visit A Jóu," says A Gūng, meaning his mother, my great-grandma. She passed away before I was born, almost twenty years ago now, but I've been to her grave many times. A Gūng, who obviously takes his ancestral worship responsibilities very seriously, insists that we go visit every few months. I assumed, however, that with everything going on, we wouldn't be making a trip anytime soon. I certainly hadn't anticipated that Ollie would need to get involved.

"Would you like Pìhng to come?" I ask, even though I know the answer.

"Of course," A Gūng answers. "He *must*."

"Where does he want me to go?" Ollie asks in English. He looks a bit confused, and the warmth that had been creeping up my neck takes on a slightly more unpleasant charge. I find myself feeling impatient about having to explain yet another thing to Ollie—which is weird, because normally I love explaining things. But it's not really Ollie's fault that he's so clueless. He's not actually part of the family, after all. Not like me.

"Grove View Memorial Park," I tell him. "That's where my a jóu is buried. It's in Westminster, near Little Saigon." Then I realize I sounded a little snippy, so I try to dial it back. "It would be great if you could come—only if you're free, though."

"Oh," says Ollie. "Yeah, sure." His face contains a question, but I avert my eyes.

"Very good." A Gūng looks pleased. "How lucky we are that Pìhng is such a good boy."

"It's time to eat!" A Pòh shouts just then, her voice cutting like a lifeline through the kitchen din. I hop up in a hurry to help her bring out all the food.

A Pòh always makes too many dishes when we have company, and that's certainly true tonight. There's tilapia, steamed in soy sauce and topped with chopped green onion; pork stir-fried with glistening sesame oil and ginger; lotus root and spare rib soup, cooked long enough so the meat is falling off the bone; and of course, lots of boiled choy sum for A Gūng. Once everything is laid out, I take a seat next to Ollie, across from Mom and Dad.

A Pòh, however, doesn't sit. Instead, she walks over to A Gūng to tuck a paper towel into the front collar of his shirt, like a bib, and then scoops a portion of fish for him onto a small plate. Without any fanfare, he starts in with his chopsticks. "Everybody eat," he says, gesturing at the spread.

The rest of us take this as our cue to start—except A Pòh, who disappears again into the kitchen. Shortly after, we hear the microwave start up, its hum mixing with the whirring of the range hood. "Ma," Mom calls out. "Are you ready to eat?"

"Yes, yes," she yells back over the cacophony. "I'm coming now." But still, she doesn't return to the table.

Ollie, who has loaded his rice bowl with pork, pauses before taking a bite. "Should we wait for your A Pòh?" he asks me.

"Don't worry about her," A Gūng interrupts. "You go ahead and eat, Pìhng."

"Yes, go ahead and eat first," A Pòh echoes from the kitchen.

Ollie is still waiting to see what I'll do, so I pick up my chopsticks. But I hesitate, too. Mom glances at Dad, who shrugs, like he wants to stay out of it. "I guess you'd better," she tells us, sighing. "Everything will get cold otherwise."

"Your a pòh is always like this," A Gūng complains as he takes a sip of the lotus root soup. "I really don't know what she does that takes so long."

It's true that A Pòh is often late coming to the table, but I don't really like it when A Gūng criticizes her for stuff like that. She just spent a couple hours cooking for us—what's wrong with letting her wrap up at her own pace, even if means she can't eat right away? Really, we ought to wait for *her.* Yet she never lets us, and we never do.

A Gūng, however, doesn't notice any of this. "Pìhng, make sure to eat a little more," he urges, his hand shaking as he spoons more pork into Ollie's already full bowl.

I stand up suddenly, my chair scraping against the laminate floor. "I'm going to see if A Pòh needs more help."

I don't get very far, though, before A Pòh appears in front of me. She's holding a plate of leftover tofu and tomato stir-fry from last night, the plastic wrap peeled back halfway. "No, no, no," she orders. "You sit down."

Reluctantly, I obey, and A Pòh sets the dish down next to A Gūng. Dad is sitting next to the rice pot, so he begins to fill a bowl for her, but she hurries over to wrestle it from him. "I will do it," she chides. Then, instead of taking the last open seat—the one at the other end of the table—she drags over a metal folding chair and squeezes it between A Gūng and Mom.

"A Pòh, why don't you sit over there?" I point at the real dining chair. To be fair, we almost never use it because there are only five of us normally, and right now there's a pile of mail on the seat that no one remembered to toss out. But that's easily fixed—I jump up to do it now, ignoring A Pòh's protests.

It's strange, because sometimes she can be so vocal and forceful, her presence dominating everything around her . . . and then other times, she's like this. In fact, right now she is being vocal and forceful *about* this.

"Aiyah!" A Pòh cries so vigorously, you'd think we were telling her to dump her bowl of rice in the trash. "I'm fine!"

A Gūng shakes his head. "This a pòh," he says, setting his rice bowl down. "So troublesome."

On the one hand, I *do* kind of wish A Pòh would just take her seat at the table—I don't understand why she's so stubborn about refusing. Can't she see that her desire to avoid a fuss is creating a more complicated situation? Yet A Gūng's remark—like his other one—digs an awful lot.

"Here, A Pòh," I implore, pulling out the chair. "I cleared it off for you."

She's about to shut me down again, but then Ollie, who looks partly embarrassed and partly sympathetic, gets to his feet. "I'll sit there," he offers. "Because I took A Pòh's normal seat, right?"

That is so far from the reason for this whole kerfuffle, I can hardly believe Ollie is bringing it up. A Pòh isn't acting like this because she misses her usual chair. She couldn't care *less* about that.

But amazingly, this is what causes A Pòh to spring into action.

"No, Pìhng, it's bad luck to change seats once you've started eating!" She pushes him down by the shoulder, and the look Ollie slips me is the closest thing to sly that has ever crossed his face. I nearly drop a piece of choy sum in my lap.

A Pòh walks over to perch on the chair cushion. "Okay, everyone," she says. "You want me to sit here? I'll sit here."

"That's better," A Gūng declares. "Your rightful spot."

A Pòh's elbows float stiffly above the armrests as she reaches for a piece of leftover tofu with her chopsticks. When she notices that we're all watching her, she waves her chopsticks at us. "Eat!" she commands. And we do as we're told.

* * *

After dinner, when it's time for Ollie to leave, I follow him outside and we stand together on the front steps. It's just beginning to get dark, but the air, chilly and a little sharp, already smells like night.

"Thanks for coming over," I say automatically, which is just as well because I don't know what else to say. It seems like I've been feeling that way a lot lately. The evening has been somewhat disorienting, and it's made me oddly shy.

Ollie, though, seems looser than he's ever been, like he's just discovered for the first time how much room he's got to stretch out in the world. "Thanks for inviting me," he replies, leaning back against the side of the house. He bends one knee and rests his sneaker on the stucco, settling into the stance of someone who's not planning to leave anytime soon.

"Technically, A Gūng is the one who wanted you here," I joke.

"That's true," Ollie agrees, grinning. He zips up his jacket halfway, then slips his hands into his pockets. "He and your A Pòh have an interesting dynamic, don't they?"

I spy a moth landing on the wall. "What do you mean?"

"You know, like how everything revolves around him. Like how she always has to take care of him first, before herself."

"He's not feeling well right now." My voice takes on an edge of disbelief even though I have an idea of what Ollie's getting at. Because it was true before A Gūng was sick, too.

"I know," says Ollie, subdued—though only slightly. "I'm sure that's part of it. But I mean stuff like the way he talks about her. Some of that seems kind of sexist, doesn't it?"

I don't respond at first because my throat feels unusually tight. My initial reaction is to defend A Gũng, because he's my grandpa and I don't want to think about him being a terrible person. Because he's not. I know he's not. Maybe he isn't perfect, but what right does Ollie have to judge after just a couple weeks of pretending to be in our family? "It's complicated," I say eventually.

"Is it, though?" Now it's Ollie's turn to sound like he doesn't believe me. "I dunno, it doesn't seem that great."

"Well, this whole thing we're doing, The Plan, it's not great in the same way." The words come out before I can stop them.

Ollie is quiet for a moment. "We can just tell him the truth, you know. We don't have to keep doing this."

"No, we can't tell him *anything*." I turn away and squint up at the streetlamp, which casts a halo of light on Ollie's car.

"Why not? Aren't you tired of pretending that his beliefs don't bother you?"

I fling my hands in the air. "He's *old*, Ollie. You can't expect old people to understand because they won't. You're just supposed to care about them anyway." I take a dramatic step away from him, only to trip over a jade plant that A Pòh had recently placed on the porch. Flustered, I jump forward and almost land on his toes.

Ollie, however, doesn't move, and I flashback to the blind contour exercise as my gaze travels up from his shoes, taking in many things at once: that his jacket zipper is missing its tab, that his shirt isn't black but navy, that his bottom lip is slightly more pronounced than his top. Once again, I get tripped up, in particular, by that lip.

"Fōng?" A Pòh appears behind the metal screen door, and suddenly the glow filtering out from the living room is much too bright. Only when Ollie and I spring apart does it register in my mind that he'd been leaning forward, too.

"Coming," I reply, my voice crackly with something hard to pin down.

"Sorry," says Ollie, his hand going to the back of his head. His eyes are on the ground. "About . . . I mean, if I upset you." He drops one foot to the lower step, as if preparing to leave, but then he pauses. "I'll still help with The Plan as long as you want me to."

I open my mouth but only manage to say, "I'm not upset."

"Okay." Both Ollie's hands go back into his pockets. "See you soon, then?"

I nod and then watch him cut across our driveway to his car. My questions begin chasing after him: Was he right about A Gūng? Was he right about me? What was that just now, between him and me?

All of a sudden, there's so much I want to know, and I wish he'd come back so I could find it all out. The answers—or some of them, at least—seem hidden in the angles of his shoulders and his long-legged gait. As he reaches the edge of our lawn, I surprise myself by calling out, "Can you give me a ride tomorrow?"

He turns around, his grin slowly returning. “Sure.” He gives me a salute as he backs away, and I finally have to admit I’m hurtling down a road I’ve definitely been down before.

17

Ollie

LAST NIGHT, I HAD A CONFUSING DREAM ABOUT Francine. It wasn't a *bad* dream, exactly—just unexpected. Although if I'm being honest, it actually didn't seem weird right up to the point that it did, which was when I woke up in a sweat, throwing off the covers because they suddenly felt too heavy. I was relieved, of course, to have been interrupted, but as I lay there in the solitary quiet of the dark, I did wonder how the dream might have ended.

Not gonna lie, it wasn't easy falling back asleep.

In the morning, I try to forget about the whole thing, because that's what I've always done with stuff like this, and anyway, it was just a dream. But as I pull up to the curb in front of her house, I'm all jittery, like Francine isn't the girl I've known for over a decade, the one I've been offering rides to without a second thought. Like she's not quirky and meddlesome and full of wacky ideas. Like maybe . . . I *like* her.

The realization hits me at the worst possible moment, just

as Francine opens the door and slides into the passenger seat. Her hair is freshly damp and the scent of her shower comes off her in waves, filling the car in a way that makes me grip the steering wheel a little tighter.

"Hi, Ollie," she says, buckling her seat belt. "Ready?"

"Yup," I say. My voice cracks, coming out like a squeak.

Francine, thankfully, doesn't seem to notice. "Do you need directions?" She taps on her phone screen. "I can text them to you."

As she busies herself with typing in the address, however, something occurs to me, and I stop avoiding her eyes long enough to realize she might also be avoiding mine.

Yesterday, after I left Francine's house, I'd convinced myself I'd imagined everything in that moment when we stood together outside her front door. I thought I was just coming around to her, as a friend, and I was totally off-base when I sensed, in the vague but pleasant haze between us, that she wanted me to kiss her. Francine didn't like me anymore, I reminded myself—at least, not in that way she used to. No, the look she gave me last night . . . that wasn't anything I'd ever seen from her before.

Now, as I hand her my phone so that she can open the maps app, I wonder if she's spent any time thinking about yesterday, too. She keeps her gaze fixed on the screen, her lashes still. The weirdness from my dream is back, but out here, in reality, it solidifies into a kind of wall that neither of us knows how to climb over.

"Starting route to Grove View Memorial Park and Mortuary," interrupts the voice from my phone. "Head south on Citrus Lane, then turn right on Monterey Avenue."

Our eyes snap to each other, and the sobering reminder of where we're going is, ironically, what makes things feel normal again. At least for now.

"We can put on *Wait Wait . . . Don't Tell Me!* if you want," I say as I drive away from her house.

"Ah." Francine links her fingers together and looks down at them. "I already listened to the new episode."

"Okay, you can choose something else, then."

"Anything?"

"Yeah, of course."

Francine scrolls on my phone for a few minutes and then, finding something that she likes, puts it on. Cheerful banjo music spills out of the speakers.

"What *is* this?" I ask, laughing.

"*The Best of Car Talk.*" Francine sets my phone in the drink holder.

I shake my head as the squawky voices of two old guys start wisecracking about April Fool's Day. "You listen to *Car Talk*?" I can't keep it together.

"You *don't*?" Now Francine is laughing, too.

"I didn't even know it was still on!"

"It's not, but the reruns get reissued as podcast episodes," explains Francine. "For a while, they were still broadcast on the radio, too. I used to love listening to the show every

Saturday morning on my way to piano lessons." She leans her elbow on the door and grins at me through her side-eye. "I don't even care about cars."

Francine is seriously the strangest girl I've ever met, but her smile—man, now it gets me every time.

I have no idea how this happened, and even *less* idea how I feel about it.

Fortunately, Click and Clack of *Car Talk* are more than up to the task of padding air that you'd rather not fill yourself, so I let them chatter on for the whole drive. Francine, too, doesn't say very much, and she only turns the volume down when we pull into the memorial park driveway and see that there's a security guard booth up ahead. I hesitate, hoping Francine knows what we're supposed to tell the man sitting inside. But when I drive up, he just waves us through without a word, like we're regulars.

It's a gloomy day, gray and heavy with the chance of rain, which I guess is appropriate weather for visiting a cemetery. At first glance, Grove View seems like it could be a regular park—only when you look more closely do you notice that the large expanses of green are crisscrossed with paved roads and, occasionally, interrupted by mausoleums.

"Turn right." Francine is directing me now, because the GPS obviously doesn't know where her great-grandma's actual plot is. She tells me to park halfway down one of the roads and then hops out as soon as I cut the engine.

"I don't know the last time I was in a cemetery," I say, getting out of the car. I lean back against the door, wrapping my arms around my chest. The wind isn't strong, but it's got a bitterness to it, the kind that makes you shiver and sweat simultaneously inside your jacket.

Francine walks over and settles next to me—not too close, but not too far either. She also hugs her arms against the cold, stretching the sleeves of her turtleneck down over her hands. "It's not the most happening place," she says, and I kind of laugh, because what a thing to say about a cemetery!

Her phone buzzes, and she hides the notification without really looking at it. "They're almost here," she says, meaning her a gūng and a pòh, who are riding with her parents. It crosses my mind that she could've just come with them, and I could've driven myself. Instead, she'd specifically asked me for a ride. Of course we spent it listening to *Car Talk*.

She's studying the ground now, looking like she wants to say more. But then her parents' car pulls up behind us, and she bounds forward like a spooked squirrel—leaving me to wonder what exactly it was she might've said.

Qingming Festival, I learn, apparently calls for a lot of stuff. I help Francine unload tightly packed plastic bags out of her parents' trunk, and I'm about to step onto the grass when her a pòh stops me. "Pìhng, be careful of the neighbors!"

The bags dangle from my hands as I teeter in place, unsure of what to do next. Francine's a pòh brushes ahead of me, meticulously threading between the flat tombstones—all the while nodding and mumbling to each one, like she's making her way through a crowded bus.

I stare after her until Francine comes up behind me. "A Pòh believes we need be respectful of other people's graves," she explains. "She doesn't want us to step on them."

"Oh," I say, shifting the bags a little. "I wasn't going to walk on anyone's headstone."

"Well . . ." Francine looks embarrassed now. "You're not supposed to step on the grassy part in front of the headstone either."

I glance down at the graves in front of me, which are laid out roughly in a grid, with not that much space in between each one. "Okay," I say.

"And, um, she also thinks you should apologize if you do step on anyone."

"Okay," I say again, because what other response is there?

I begin to pick my way between the graves, trying to keep my feet away from each plot's perimeter, but it's hard. Especially because the grid starts to get a little messy, so you really can't tell if you're stepping on anyone or not.

Ahead of me, Francine whispers, "Sorry," to everybody she passes.

Francine's a pòh is a few yards away, already crouched down where the grave of Francine's a jóu must be. She kneels in the grass and digs into a bag for some gardening gloves, which she unceremoniously slips on. Then she begins to yank at the grass overgrowing the headstone.

I turn to Francine to ask whether her grandma should really be on her hands and knees like that, but she's already on *her* hands and knees, getting in on the grass removal. I set the bags on the ground and stoop down next to them, but as soon as I do, Francine's a pòh swipes my hand away. "You don't have to do this," she scolds.

I don't really have much else to do, though, so I just stand there beneath a nearby oak, watching. In the distance, there are empty chairs set up under a white canopy, and I realize they're for a funeral that's either already happened or about to. On the other side of the lawn, there's a strawberry field, the plants forming long, thick rows.

"When I was a kid," Francine says, noticing where I'm looking, "my cousin used to say we shouldn't buy strawberries from there because the field was haunted."

That sounds a lot like something Isaac would make up to freak me out. "So were you afraid to?"

"No, that's so illogical," replies Francine. "What could ghosts possibly do to strawberries?"

Together with her a pòh, Francine and her mom work on cleaning the headstone, scrubbing away the dirt with a brush and then rinsing it with water from a nearby tap. Francine's dad gets involved only when her mom struggles to wrench a vase out of the dirt. Otherwise, he waits next to me, along with Francine's a gūng, who stands grimly, hands clasped behind his back. Francine's a gūng doesn't take any part in the flurry of activity, despite the fact that this whole visit seemed to be his idea. I wonder what it's like to be in a cemetery when you know you're about to die.

I'm beginning to feel pretty useless until Francine hands me a fistful of incense sticks, the pungent smoke swirling from the crumbling tips. "These are for the other graves," she says. When I look at her blankly, she separates out a few of the sticks, the bottom ends leaving red dye on her fingers. "Put one or two in the dirt above each headstone until you run out."

"What for?"

Francine crinkles her forehead. "I'm not sure, actually. We've always just done it because A Pòh said we should." She turns back toward her a pòh, who is too busy positioning a pot of yellow chrysanthemums to explain. "Maybe it's about respect. Like we're saying thank you for letting us disturb their peace in order to visit A Jóu."

I'm still not totally sold on this neighborly spirits thing, and I think it shows on my face.

"It's all right if you don't want to," Francine says quickly, lowering the sticks.

I reach out without really thinking and almost grab her hand. At the last second, I close my fingers around the bushel of sticks instead. "No, I'll do it."

Gingerly, I take the incense around to the other graves. The neighbors, I find out, are surprisingly diverse. Some of them died years ago, their headstones now faded almost to the point of illegibility. Others are shiny, the etchings sharp, almost too fresh to look at. Most are mothers and fathers and grandmothers and grandfathers, which I guess isn't surprising. But then I see one that's different—the years engraved in the stone don't span very long at all. When I do the math, I realize the person was basically a kid. Younger than me, even.

A hand touches my elbow. "Are you all right, Ollie?" asks Francine. Her fingers flutter back down to her side when I glance at her.

I hold the incense away from me because the fragrance is starting to give me a headache. "Have you seen this one?"

Francine looks down at the headstone. "You mean Billy?"

I'm not sure whether to laugh or what. "You know him?"

She takes an incense stick from me and plants it in the dirt of Billy's grave. "What you're doing with these is normally my job," she says. "Over the years, I've gotten to know all the tombstones."

I watch her dust the specks of ash off her jeans. "Weird to think how we're already older than he'll ever be."

"That's true." Francine pauses mid-wipe. "I haven't thought about it like that before."

We both study Billy's red granite tombstone, which stands out among the grays and blacks. "Do you know how he died?" I ask.

"Car accident." Francine shudders a little. "I looked it up online. His friend fell asleep at the wheel."

"Geez."

"She survived, though."

"Geez."

"It's been a while, so I wonder if that's why I've never seen anyone visit Billy."

"Not once?"

"No, not in all these years."

This has got to be one of the most depressing things I've ever heard. "That's why, when I die, I wouldn't want to be buried." I follow Francine back toward her a jóu's headstone. "Because someday, at some point, nobody's gonna be around to care."

Francine stops abruptly, and I almost step on somebody else's grave when she spins around to face me. "Your family will care."

"But eventually, there might be nobody left."

A few yards away, Francine's a gūng is now standing over her a jóu's grave, palms pressed together and moving in prayer.

"Well, that's the whole thing with A Gūng, remember?" Francine tugs on her bracelet. "He's worried there won't be anyone to do for him what we're doing for A Jóu."

Francine's a pòh begins to pray as well, her motions brisker and more vigorous than her husband's. Francine's mom, who is preparing to join in, beckons us toward them.

"I still don't get why you're not enough," I say to Francine as we trudge over. "Even though you're a girl and not a Huynh or whatever, I could see you making your kids do all this stuff. And your kids' kids." Imagining a bunch of mini Francines is both hilarious and strange.

She sighs. "You know that old Chinese saying about how girls are raised to be part of someone else's family, not your own?"

I *don't* know that saying. But I'm not sure if it's because my parents are super progressive or because they don't have any girls. "Your a gūng really thinks it won't count if you do it?"

Francine doesn't reply, and I get frustrated all over again. Not at her, exactly . . . but maybe?

"What's the point of it all anyway? If you get cremated and maybe scattered somewhere, then it's done. You're not creating this burden for everybody who comes after you."

"It's not a burden," says Francine. "It's not *just* a burden," she tries again, seeing my look. "The rituals are supposed to bring you protection and good luck from your ancestors."

"You don't really believe that?" I lower my voice because we're back under the oak tree, waiting for our turn at her a jóu's grave.

Francine goes quiet again, though only for a moment. "No," she admits. "But it's not about whether I believe it or not." She gestures at her family as they bob their heads in worship. "I don't think all this is just about the person who's dead. It's also a way to bring the living together—a way for us to feel more connected to each other."

I think of my own family and how we don't do anything like this. I don't even know where my a yèh is buried—my dad has never said. I'm assuming somewhere in Hanoi, where I've never been.

Francine's mom and dad are done with their prayers, so Francine and I step up to take their place. Imitating Francine, I sandwich three sticks of incense between my hands and do that praying motion, too. Down below, laid out in front of the tombstone, is a tableau of offerings. Some, like the plate of apples or even the Chinese pastries, make sense. I've seen that kind of stuff in front of shrines before. But other items are a little more perplexing.

"What's the carton of milk mean?" I whisper to Francine, pointing to it with my prayer hands.

"That's one of the last things my a jóu requested before she died," replies Francine, and I decide not to ask any follow-up questions.

Francine, I discover, prays in Cantonese, and when doing so, refers to herself in the third person, using her Chinese name. Her words have the feel of a recitation more than a request. "A Jóu, please protect Fōng, ensuring good health and good grades. Please protect Mom and Dad, ensuring good health and prosperity. Please protect A Gūng and A Pòh, ensuring good health . . ."

Meanwhile, to my left, her a gūng has assumed a more conversational tone. It takes me a second before I realize he is talking about me. "Mà, Pìhng has come to visit you today. He's a part of our family now."

I glance at Francine, who's already squatting down to push her incense sticks into the dirt. She doesn't say anything, but I know she heard him, too. We'd ignored the ethics of lying to a dying person, but what about somebody who's already died? Do the dead already know the truth anyway?

I stab my incense into the ground and back away without uttering any prayers myself. From under the oak tree, I listen as Francine's a gūng continues his one-sided dialogue with his mother's headstone—quietly and deferentially, unlike the way he usually talks to the people in his family.

"Your a gūng seems different here," I say to Francine. Then I notice that Francine's a pòh, too, is still praying. In fact, she keeps it up even after her husband has finished, so she ends up being the last one remaining at the grave. "Your a pòh seems . . . her usual self," I add. "Is she worried about what future generations will do after she dies?"

Francine rubs her elbows. "I don't know," she says. "I don't think she's mentioned it."

We watch as her a pòh goes all in with the kowtowing, each time bending her knees slowly so she can lower her forehead to the grass. She's lined the grave's perimeter with incense, and as the smoke escapes in ghostly streams around her, it makes me think of a spirit freeing itself from the earth.

When all the rituals are done—the food cleaned up, the teacups and chopsticks packed away—we make our way back to where the cars are parked. I support Francine's grandpa with my arm, guiding him around the headstones. Once we've reached the curb, I open the car door, but he pauses before getting in. "Lāan," he says, over his shoulder to Francine's mom. "I'd like to get my plans in order."

She unlocks the trunk with one hand, her arms around a bag of supplies. "Right now, Bā?"

"Yes, we must," Francine's a gūng replies, and lowers himself into the front seat.

As usual, I look to Francine for an explanation, but this time, she seems lost, too. Francine's dad has to fill in the blanks for us: "He means the arrangements for his burial."

The Grove View administration offices are housed in a flat, midcentury building on the edge of the grounds, and there are plenty of parking spots when we pull into the lot. The place is old but well kept up—the automatic glass doors gleam like they've just been Windexed, and there's a newish plaque embedded in the brick façade that reads *A Monumental Group Property.* I'm not sure if it would be more or less demoralizing if the whole place were shabbier. Would you want your funeral home to mirror the dreariness of death? Or would you rather have it be as shiny and dependable as a Starbucks?

"I've seen this building a million times." Francine touches a plant by the door to see if it's real. "But I've never been inside."

Luckily, Grove View takes walk-ins, and pretty soon we're ushered into a wood-paneled room where a white lady in a forest-green blazer smiles at all of us. The two chairs in front of the desk are given to Francine's a gūng and a pòh (who takes hers only after arguing about it for a full thirty seconds). Francine sits on the arm of her a pòh's chair, and her parents hover behind her. Pressed up against the back wall, I get the sudden impression that there are too many people here and maybe I shouldn't be one of them.

"Hi, I'm Cathy," says the Grove View lady. Her voice is gentle but not something you really want to listen to, like elevator music. "Are we here to plan ahead? Or are we talking about a recent or imminent death?"

The rest of us turn to Francine—even me, for some reason, even though I obviously understand the question and am also capable of responding in English.

"I guess you might say it's both," she says, and explains the situation to Grove View Cathy.

"Tell her we want two plots," Francine's a gūng interrupts in Cantonese. "One for A Pòh and one for me. We want to be in the same area as A Jóu."

Francine dutifully translates the command, and Cathy nods, like she gets this type of thing all the time. "Absolutely," she says, clicking around on her computer. "I understand. Let me pull up some options."

I notice Francine is jiggling her foot a lot, like she's not sure if Cathy is going to come back with anything good, and I have this urge to put my hand on her shoulder and tell her it'll all be okay. But right as I'm considering it, Francine turns around like she sensed something was up, and I chicken out, diving my fingers into my hair instead.

"All right, here we are," says Cathy as the printer behind her desk whirs to life. "Let's take a look at what's available."

She slides over a sheet of paper filled with little sketches, each showing a different area of Grove View. On the first, she uses a highlighter to outline two faint rectangles, both squished up against the curb line. One of them is so near the edge that its right corner is slightly cut. "You're in luck," Cathy tells us. "We have just two spots left in the section you mentioned."

"Hmm." Francine leans over the map, brow furrowing. "I'm wondering if those look a bit cramped?"

"Just a trick of the drawing," says Cathy cheerfully. "There is plenty of space underground."

Francine's a gūng pulls the map closer so he can get a better look, but almost immediately shakes his head. "It's not good to be next to the street like that," he says in Cantonese. "Tell her I want them to be side by side." Then, in an unexpected move, he points at Francine's a pòh, his shoulders squaring. "Tell her I want to be next to my wife."

"Aiyah," says Francine's a pòh, like she's embarrassed. "If there isn't space, there isn't space."

Francine, again, translates as she's told, and Cathy nods, her old-lady bouffant wavering a little as she moves her head. "Absolutely, I hear that," she says. "I'll check what else we have."

Some minutes later, after a lot more clicking, she produces another printout. This time, though, she doesn't highlight anything. "This is the Garden of Eternal Tranquility," she explains. "It first opened up about ten years ago to serve the local Vietnamese community. I think this is a wonderful option for your grandparents."

She swivels her computer monitor around to show us photos of the garden. I'm surprised to see they've really gone all out with it. There's an orange-and-yellow pagoda, surrounded by a man-made pond. There's a pair of bronze statues memorializing Vietnamese boat people refugees.

"That does seem nice," agrees Francine. "What's the availability there?"

Cathy traces a finger around an empty section of the map. "The garden is so popular that it's currently being expanded," she says. "You're welcome to reserve spots in this area here, which we recommend doing as soon as possible to ensure all your requirements are met. Construction will be completed in just a few months."

Francine's face falls when she hears that, and I know what she's thinking: What if her a gūng doesn't have a few months?

"You don't have anything that would be available sooner?" Francine's fingers creep over the edge of the desk and grasp it it tightly.

Cathy looks like she feels bad for us. "I'm afraid not, hon." She clasps her hands in front of her. "At least, not two plots next to each other. We've only got single spaces left."

She glances at Francine's grandparents, who don't understand what she's just said and are simply waiting, like small, patient children, to be told the truth: that they might have to go into eternity alone.

My throat burns in a familiar way, and I rub my eyes in a hurry, willing the wetness to disappear. I'm the only one not in this family—I can't be the one who cries.

Francine, in fact, is already standing up. "Thank you, Cathy, we will discuss all of this and get back to you," she says, her voice steady and her back straight.

But as we walk out of the office, I feel her hand slip into my clammy palm, and my fingers instinctively wrap around hers. It lasts for only a second before she lets go, and her wan expression, too, is gone before anybody sees—and in that moment, I really couldn't tell you if it was her comforting me or the other way around.

Back in the parking lot, when it's time to leave Grove View, I'm instructed to head over to a phở restaurant in a nearby strip mall. I don't really feel like eating, but everybody insists.

"You can't go straight home from the cemetery," says Francine, sounding not at all like we were maybe just holding hands. "You don't want the ghosts to follow you there."

We're given a circular table in the center of the restaurant, where we have a prime view of the flatscreen playing exclusively Vietnamese pop music videos. The TV's aspect ratio is off, so the singers are all stretched out as they lip-sync about some maudlin romantic drama. I couldn't tell you the details, though, because if my comprehension of spoken Vietnamese is bad, you can just forget about asking me to understand anything being *sung*.

"Pìhng likes this music," Francine's a pòh observes in Vietnamese, seeing me watch the screen. She smiles at me kindly.

"Oh, no," I say, blushing. "No, I don't."

The waiter, a kid barely older than me and Francine, arrives to take everybody's order—we all get chicken phở except for Francine's dad, who decides on the special with beef—and then clears away the menus without writing anything down. As he turns to leave, a lull settles over us, and my eyes are about to drift helplessly back up to the TV when Francine's a gūng begins to speak.

"There's something urgent we need to discuss." His voice is authoritative, but he's wearing a paper napkin as a bib, the way he did at dinner the other night, and Francine's a pòh has to readjust it when one corner slips from his collar.

"What's that, Bā?" asks Francine's mom.

I'm expecting him to mention our failure to secure a satisfactory burial spot, but instead it's a topic that's much more uncomfortable.

"I want to talk about Pìhng's inheritance."

Silence falls around the table, so the only sounds come from the oblivious families around us, slurping and clinking innocently through their own lunches.

"Inheritance?" Francine repeats the word, which her a gūng said in Cantonese, like she doesn't know it. But she does. Her real question is *What inheritance?*

Francine's a pòh apparently has the same thing on her mind. "Aiiiiyah," she says, puckering her face so that her expression gets lost in the wrinkles. "What's the point of bringing up such things now?"

"A Mā is right," Francine's mom agrees quickly. "Let's not talk about this here. We don't want other people to hear that you have money."

"He *has* no money." Francine's a pòh shakes her head. "But he likes to act like he does."

"This is important!" Francine's a gūng knocks over a chopstick, catapulting it onto the floor. Francine's dad bends over to pick it up but wisely chooses not to contribute anything else to the discussion. Personally, I want to crawl under the table. I tell myself it's not my fault Francine's grandpa is talking about stuff that wasn't part of The Plan. Francine said the lie was supposed to be about tending his grave and shit. How could I have known he would take things this far?

Even Francine seems shocked, her eyes ping-ponging from her a gūng to me, like she's hoping there's a way to stop this train wreck. In a rare attempt to override his order, she tries to speak up. "Maybe—"

"I have decided," Francine's a gūng interrupts. "The money will go to Pìhng. I would rather give it to him than Wáih, who is not filial at all."

Wait, what? Who is Wáih?

I whisper the question out the side of my mouth to Francine, who is staring down at the little tray holding chili and hoisin sauces. She rotates it slowly as she answers. "He's, um, my second cousin."

This news hits me out of nowhere. "You have a male *cousin*?"

"Well, second cousin, but yeah."

"Why isn't he . . ." My voice trails off because I don't want to expose The Plan, but seriously, why are we even *bothering* with The Plan if there's this Wáih kid somewhere who could be shouldering all of it instead?

"Wáih doesn't really like to spend time with my grandpa," Francine explains simply.

I still have a lot of questions, but Francine's a gūng doesn't give me a chance to ask them. "Wáih doesn't understand things," he says. "Not like you, Pìhng."

Me? I barely understand anything. And I don't want any money, especially not from somebody else's dying grandpa.

"You don't have to give me anything," I say as respectfully as I can manage.

"No, no," says Francine's a gūng. "Who else would I give it to?"

Everyone tries not to look at Francine, who peels off a napkin from the metal dispenser and begins to fold it into a square.

"Francine," I say suddenly. Then I remember to use her Cantonese name. "I mean, Fōng. What about Fōng?"

The table goes quiet again, just as the waiter returns with the first bowl of chicken phở. "Phở gà?" he says, setting it down when Francine's a pòh gestures wordlessly toward the spot in front of Francine's a gūng.

Finally, from behind the steam rising out of the bowl, Francine's a gūng chuckles a little. "Fōng doesn't need this money," he says, and when the waiter returns with another chicken phở, this time placing it in front of me, I lose the nerve to ask him what he means.

On the drive home, Francine and I ride in silence for a while. It has started to rain, the drops delicate but persistent as they scatter across the windshield. I turn on the wipers, and with each swoosh against the glass, they make a scraping noise that seems a lot louder than it should be. But Francine has switched off *Car Talk*, and there's nothing else to listen to—just that repeated grating of rubber on glass.

"So . . ." I watch the layer of rain build up while we're

waiting for a red light. "What's the deal with Wáih?"

Francine leans her head against the window, uncharacteristically subdued. "You mean Wesley?"

"Sure, Wesley, Wáih, whatever his name is. When were you gonna tell me about him?"

She straightens up, her eyes flicking over to me. "There's nothing to tell. He was never going to do anything for A Gūng."

"But did you ask him?"

"No, I didn't see the point."

"Um, I think the point would've been that he's a boy who's actually related to your grandpa? Which, you know, I'm not?"

Francine stretches her legs out in front of her, then half scrunches her face. "A Gūng once asked Wesley to spend Thanksgiving with us, because he's a grad student at UCLA, but his family—including his grandma, A Gūng's sister—live in Florida," she says. "Wesley said he'd come, so A Gūng made us wait for him for hours, until all the food—the roast duck and the pork belly and the seafood soup, all that fancy Chinese feast stuff—got cold. And he never showed."

I don't know what to say. "Ah."

"All my other cousins either were out of town or live too far to come anyway, so it was just my parents and me." Francine twists a strand of hair around her finger and gazes out the window. "I really hated seeing my a gūng sitting there, getting up, pacing around, and sitting back down again, all while it got darker and darker because A Pòh kept the lights low to save electricity. It probably doesn't sound like a big deal to you, but the whole thing just . . . I dunno."

"No, I know what you mean." I keep driving, and the rain begins to let up, fading into a mist. "I—I would feel that way, too." I let my shoulders drop, not realizing I'd tensed them. "It's almost like it hurts more because it's happening to someone else."

Francine studies me, like she's looking for some detail that she missed before, and it feels different from last night on her front steps—gentler, maybe, and more sentimental. But there's some of last night, too.

"Yeah," she says eventually, glancing back out the window. "So I didn't really want A Gūng to be let down again."

We're back in our neighborhood now, and Francine's street is empty as usual, though wet. Rainwater has already started to form a puddle in the intersection, and we make a bit of a splash as I drive through it.

"What made you so sure I wouldn't let him down?" I say. "Not sure I have a great track record for that kind of thing." I'm kidding, but also not.

"I don't know," Francine admits. "I guess I felt like you could be different." She doesn't look at me as I pull to a stop in front of her house. "But maybe that's just because I like you."

I kill the car engine just as she says this, and we're left with the truth between us, cradled by silence. My ears go pink, prickling from the heat. It's my turn to say something, I know, but my mouth is dry and can't wrap itself around the words.

I take too long and Francine reaches for the door. "Well,

thanks again for coming today," she says, fingers gripping the handle. "It meant a lot to my a gūng." Then she lets herself out in a hurry.

"Wait." I slide out of the car and round the front of it, slamming the door behind me. Francine stops at the edge of her lawn, gazing up at me expectantly, but once again, I struggle. "I need to tell you . . ." I begin. The sentence, however, ends somewhere else because I'm not sure where I wanted it to go. "I wouldn't take any money from your grandpa."

"Yeah." Francine traces the toe of her sneaker through the grass. "But my a pòh was right—there really isn't any money anyway. Especially with all the medical bills and everything. My mom says she doesn't want to tell A Gūng that, and maybe she's right. Maybe it's better that he doesn't know."

"No." The word, loud and decisive, slips out unexpectedly, and I can't help careening forward into the things I was afraid to say. "He *should* know, Francine. He should know about that and all the stuff you've done for him, and it's shitty he can't see how much you're a goddamn *paragon* of everything he's ever wanted." I take a deep breath, faltering a little on the inhale. "I think . . . he should have realized that a long time ago."

The rain has picked back up, the droplets falling faster and harder, almost catching up to my sped-up heart. We'll be soaked through if we don't get inside soon. But Francine, her hair already glistening from the drizzle, doesn't make any move to escape the downpour. Instead, she just stands there, again looking at me like she needs something from me, and I have this wild urge to give her my jacket, or throw an arm around her shoulders, or—

“Francine,” I say, my voice hoarse. “Can I—”

“Yes,” she says.

So I kiss her.

18

Francine

I'D BE LYING IF I SAID I DIDN'T USED TO WONDER what it'd be like to kiss Ollie. Because I did think about it—a lot. There was a period when I daydreamed about it constantly, imagining his smile close to mine, his hair falling over his forehead while he looked at me the way they do in K-dramas.

But I didn't have an actual frame of reference for that kind of thing until the end of last year, when Jared Morales-Smith, who I knew from orchestra class, asked if I wanted to see a movie with him. I was over Ollie by then, and Jared really was a very good flautist, so I said yes. We watched a Marvel movie that I thought was pretty funny but turned out wasn't supposed to be, and afterward, Jared kissed me, his mouth tasting of popcorn and Altoids. The situation was sloppier than I expected, and I was not at all impressed, especially for someone as handsome as Jared. If that's all kissing was, I thought, I didn't need Ollie to kiss me.

I was wrong.

Ollie's kiss—I felt that all the way down my spine. I didn't understand how something so soft could become electric by the time it reached the places I haven't spent much time thinking about. Unlike Jared, Ollie was more tentative, like he wasn't really sure what he was doing, but I liked that. I got the sense that he wouldn't mind if I did what I wanted—and as I stood there, pressed up against him in the rain, I realized I wanted a *lot*.

"Francine?" Mom is standing at the door, and I snap to attention. I'm sitting cross-legged on the bed with my laptop, and I reach out to slap it shut before I notice the screen has already dimmed. The room is almost totally dark except for the weak glow of a tiny lamp clipped onto the bed frame. "What are you doing still awake?" Mom asks.

"Just some homework," I say, pushing my computer away. "I'm going to bed now, though."

"Okay, good." Mom leans against the doorframe. "If A Gūng knew you were still up working, I wouldn't hear the last of it."

"I know." I tuck my feet under the covers and make a big show of settling in—even though I feel anything *but* settled. Normally, I'd want Mom to stay and chat for a bit, but tonight, it's weird. . . . I kind of just feel like being alone.

My phone buzzes, and it's a text from Ollie. All of my insides do a somersault and land in a heap somewhere below my stomach.

Maybe *alone* isn't exactly the word I'm looking for.

"Are you okay, Francine?" Mom comes in and sits on the edge of the bed, her forehead wrinkling with concern. "You seem anxious."

"I'm okay." I turn on my side so she can't see my face. "Just tired, I think." I try not to look at the unread notification on my phone.

"You aren't still thinking about Ollie, are you?" says Mom, and I freeze. How did she know? Did she see us kissing? She's never really said much about boys one way or another, but then again, she hasn't had to. I knew what was expected. I never even told her about Jared—she wouldn't understand that I was mostly just curious—and there hasn't been anyone else since then.

Until now, of course.

"What about Ollie?" I hedge.

"Try not to let what A Gūng said about the inheritance bother you," says Mom. "You have to understand, he will always care a lot about you. Even if it seems like he prefers Ollie, that's not really true."

It was almost possible to forget about those details, given how distracted I've been, but Mom's comment drags me back. I think of what Ollie said about A Gūng being sexist—what he's been saying for a while—and I want to ask Mom whether she really believes what she's telling me.

But when I prop myself up on my elbows, I notice Mom's face is more drawn than usual, the shadows magnifying the hollows of her cheeks, and I lie back down. "A Gūng will always care about you, too."

Mom's smile is wistful but confident at the same time. "Of course. Fuh móuh will always love their children. That's how family works." She leans over to kiss my forehead. "I am also lucky to have a daughter who is so haau seuhn."

As she closes the door behind her, however, all thoughts of haau sehn—or filial piety—follow her right out. I'm surprised at how easy it is to let them go. How nice, too. I grab my phone and roll over on my side. Here in the dark, I can pretend that Ollie and I are the only two people in the world.

Well, two people . . . and a dog. Ollie's message is a picture of Dexter looking up into the camera, his eyes hopeful. It's goofy and a little melancholy. **Dexter says he misses you**, Ollie wrote.

This new thing we have now, it's still a little surreal. I don't quite know how to make sense of everything, to pinpoint the before and the after, but there definitely *was* a before and this is definitely the after. Every text from Ollie, no matter how mundane, sends me down the plunge of a roller coaster—the drop of my stomach is simultaneously alarming and also exactly what I hoped for. Even more strange is how it keeps happening, over and over, because Ollie seems to want to talk to me all the time now. Thirteen-year-old me would fall flat on her face if she could see this. If I'm being really honest, maybe seventeen-year-old me can't quite believe it either.

I reread Ollie's message a few more times before I decide to tell him that I, too, miss Dexter. But in the intervening minutes, I get another text.

I just told him not to worry because he'll be seeing you soon.

That makes me smile. **I'd like that,** I type back. **Is tomorrow early enough for him?**

Yeah, I think so, replies Ollie, playful in the expected way, and I relax into the comfort of our rapport. Already, the warmth is beginning to feel familiar.

But then the ellipsis bubble pops up again, then disappears and reappears several times. Finally, another message arrives.

Not for me, though.

My heart starts beating faster, and I drop my phone to the comforter. What was he trying to say? It's just past twelve—if we saw each other any sooner, it'd be tonight. It'd be . . . now. Less than ten hours since our kiss.

I can't help thinking, though, that he's right. Because all of a sudden, it feels like an eternity.

Turning onto my back again, I leave my phone facedown and tell myself to chill out. Maybe if I fall asleep, I can just respond in the morning, which will give me time to come up with a good reply. Because what are you supposed to say to something like that? *Good night?*

The problem is, I don't feel the least bit tired. When I close my eyes, all I can think of is Ollie. Ollie, who's always asking me about *me*. Ollie, whose hands and lips were curious about *me*.

I place my own hand on my stomach and consider, for a moment, whether I should move it lower. I know it's totally normal to want to, but I'm not really sure about the how.

Personally, I've only ever tried a handful of times, and on those other occasions, it had been more because I was bored than anything else.

Today, though, I am definitely something else. Lots and *lots* of something else.

So I decide to go for it. I breathe in slowly and play back the kiss in my head, remembering the way it felt to be pulled in by Ollie, his bottom lip slipping over mine, and the wetness of everything as the rain came down around us. I think, too, of my palms spreading over the long muscles in his back and the surprising heat under his jacket, and how quickly his fingers lost their shyness to find my waist. In real life, that's where they stopped—though even then, I was very much aware of where else they could go.

All this feels good, of course, and yet I can't help the sensation that something is eluding me, like a word that's right on the tip of my tongue. After a while, I find myself lying there, flushed and a little too warm, still wound up enough to know there's a lot left to figure out.

Casting my blanket to the side, I curl up and think about what might happen when I see Ollie next. I pick up my phone and reply to his message.

Me neither.

Because tomorrow can't come soon enough.

"Hey, Francine! Earth to Francine!"

Jiya stands in front of me, waving her French horn case over my head. She looks like she's been laughing a long time.

"Ah, sorry!" I glance around the orchestra room to see if anyone else has arrived without my noticing, but it's just the two of us. "Did you say something?

It's Monday morning, and I'm sitting on the piano bench with my AP Bio textbook open in my lap. I got here early even though I didn't sleep that well last night, which is negatively impacting my ability to concentrate.

"I was just asking if you did the bio homework yet." Jiya drops her stuff on the floor and leans over the piano lid. "Now, though, I'd rather know what's turned you into a space cadet."

I hesitate, but Jiya is still waiting, so I shut my book and hug it to my chest. "Can I get some advice?"

Jiya pulls up a chair and plops herself down into it. "Shoot."

"What do you know about orgasms?"

A whistle escapes Jiya, whose amazement throws her against the seat back with a loud thwack. "Francine," she says, her voice low. "Are you and Ollie having sex?"

"What? No." My cheeks heat up way more than I thought they would. Whenever Jiya and I have discussed relationships, they've mostly been hers, so I confess I feel a little awkward bringing this up. We've also never talked about masturbation specifically—I don't know why. On the one hand, everything I've ever read suggests that plenty of people do it, lots of them discover it pretty early, and it's perfectly healthy. On the other hand, everyone in real life makes the topic seem somehow more taboo than sex itself. *Especially* when it comes to girls doing it. I've never even heard Mom tell me it's wrong, not even in the guarded Chinese terms she uses to hint that I should be "careful" with boys. It's almost like I'm not even supposed to know what it is.

But I do, obviously. And I kind of want to know more.

"This isn't about Ollie," I tell Jiya, and then pause. "Or, I mean, not exactly."

Jiya's wide-eyed astonishment shrinks slowly into smugness when I tell her about the kiss and then my dilemma. By the end of my explanation, she can hardly contain herself. "First of all," she says, "I knew it. I *knew* it." I let her freak out for a few solid minutes before she's ready to move on. "And second of all, good for you, Francine. You *should* learn how to take care of yourself first, especially when you're hooking up with boys. You really have to teach them what to do."

I haven't even thought that far ahead. "You mean, like, in the middle of it?"

"Sure, in the middle of it, or before, or before the next time. Whenever. The point is, they're not gonna magically know, even if you're super into them."

"Is it different if you're hooking up with girls?"

Jiya thinks for a second. "You do have to talk about it with them, too," she says. "But at least in my experience, there's a higher chance they'll already be familiar with what's going on down there."

I set my textbook down on the piano and study the cover photograph, which features a mesmerizing nautilus shell.

"That's the thing, though," I say. "I *am* aware of what's there, anatomically speaking. But I'm not sure it's been that helpful so far?"

"Maybe you should try thinking about it less scientifically." Jiya pulls the textbook away from me and searches through the pages. "It's more like an art, really. You have to try a bunch of different things to see what works. And the same thing doesn't even necessarily work every time."

"This all sounds very complicated." I find where I'd stuck my completed worksheet and hand it over to Jiya. "How does anyone ever get the hang of it?"

Jiya uncaps a pen and chews on the end. "I think the most important piece is how you're feeling. It's a physical thing for sure, but a lot also depends on what's going on in your head. If you're feeling good and not too pressured about the whole situation, and the right image pops into your mind, then *bam*. You've probably got it."

"So you're saying I should relax."

"I'm saying relax, yeah, and if you can, get out of your own way."

I watch her copy the answers from my homework. "I see." I still feel like I have a lot of questions, but it's hard to single out what else to ask.

Noticing my silence, Jiya glances up from her worksheet. "You could also try using a pillow?" she offers. "That's how I figured it out accidentally."

"Okay," I say, mulling over this suggestion. "Thanks."

"Of course," replies Jiya, giving me a kind smile. Then she returns my homework, folds her own in half before stuffing it into her bag, and fishes out her sketchbook. Without missing a beat, she begins to draw.

"How's the Violet Girl project going?" I ask.

"All right, I guess." Jiya stops for a second. "Want to take a look at the concepts I'm working on?"

"Sure," I say, and she turns the sketchbook around so I can see. There are pages and pages of sketches, along with various Violet Girl lyrics written in all different lettering styles.

"These are great," I tell her. "Will you turn all of them into T-shirts?"

"No, I'm only picking one," Jiya replies. "I have no idea what will sell, though. Maybe this one?" She points at a simpler drawing of Violet Girl's smiling face. It's good, of course, though lacking the fantastical detailing I usually associate with Jiya's best artwork.

"Cool!" I say, because I don't want to seem like I'm down on anything she does. "Is that your favorite?"

"No, my fave is actually this one." Jiya flips back a few pages and shows me another drawing. This one features Violet Girl looking in the mirror while the contours of her reflection intermingle with her actual face—definitely more unusual and a little bit disturbing, but also much more Jiya.

"I think you should go with that," I say.

"Really?" She examines it again. "My cousin saw me sketching and said it creeped her out."

"What did Rollo say?"

"He said my cousin is probably into hotel art."

I laugh, because Jiya's cousin is a management consultant who does, in fact, spend a lot of time in hotels. "Well, there you go. You have Rollo's full support."

"Yeah, but the jury's still out on Rollo's judgment, isn't it?"

"He's right, though. Your opinion is the most important one! Pick the drawing that means the most to you because I think that'll come through." I tap the sketch with my finger. "Maybe it won't sell, but maybe it will."

Jiya retraces a line in the drawing. "So what you're saying is . . . I should *also* relax."

"Yeah," I reply, grinning. "Relax, and trust your agent."

She smiles and shakes her head. "Did Rollo put you up to this?"

The door opens, and some other orchestra kids start to file in. There are only a few minutes left before class, so Jiya snaps her sketchbook closed. "This may be a hot take," I say, watching her gather up the rest of her things, "but I actually really like Rollo."

"Yeah, I know." Jiya slings her bag over her shoulder. "Just not as much as you like Ollie."

I blush as she heads over to the brass section. "How come you were always so sure about him, anyway?"

Jiya's smirk takes up half her face. "Is that a serious question?"

* * *

Ollie's still driving me home from school every day, but now what this means is we end up making out in his car. A lot. I'm secretly glad for all that room in his SUV and it feels pleasantly blasphemous to think so. Suddenly, the hours seem to dissolve—for three afternoons in a row, I'm nearly late to everything. On Wednesday, I don't get home in time to help A Pòh make the rice, which is my usual job, and when I show up just as the cooker beeps to signal that it's already done, Mom seems concerned.

"A Pòh says you've been really busy lately," she tells me, wiping down the table—another thing I normally do before anyone asks.

"Oh, yeah," I say, thinking fast. "I've been at school." This is not strictly a lie. Whenever Ollie has asked if I wanted to go over to his house, I've demurred because I didn't want to commit to a whole afternoon thing when I could be spending the time with A Gūng instead. But of course we just put off leaving, because neither of us wants to start the too-short ride, and only once we've hung around the parking lot for too long do we finally get in the car, and, well, I've already said what happens after that.

As if she could tell he was on my mind, Mom says, "A Gūng has been asking about Ollie a lot since Sunday." Her voice is low as she wrings out the washcloth in the sink. "Are you two really going to carry on with The Plan?"

Guilt streams over me like cold water because I haven't thought about The Plan very much. In fact, Ollie and I haven't talked about A Gūng at all, really, since we got back from

Grove View. My first instinct is to tell Mom I'll ask Ollie to visit tomorrow, but then I realize, with unsettling clarity, that I don't want him to. Or rather, I don't want him to come over and hang out with A Gũng—I want him to come over and hang out with *me*.

This isn't a feeling I'm used to, and a voice inside me points out how immature I sound. But aloud, all I say is, "Yeah, we are."

The next day, I suggest to Ollie that he should leave his car at home so we can walk instead. "We've been driving too much," I tell him that afternoon as we make our way down the sidewalk. What I don't mention is I'm hoping that no car means no getting distracted and therefore no losing track of time.

"You didn't seem to mind yesterday. Or the day before." He grins at me, his dimple deep. "You haven't seemed to mind very much at all lately."

"I'm just *saying*." I skip ahead to hide my blush, waving at the blue sky above us. "This is nice, isn't it?"

Ollie catches my hand and falls into step with me. "It is," he agrees.

We stroll along like that for a few minutes, fingers intertwined, but then I let go to retuck my hair behind my ear. "How's the Global Gala stuff going?" I ask, because that seems like a safe topic. "You're still planning to bring egg rolls?"

"Yeah," Ollie replies, stretching his arms over his head. "They're easy to transport, and everybody loves them."

"Well, your mom always made the best ones," I say, remembering.

"I'm actually just gonna buy them." Ollie's hands drop back down to his sides. "My mom doesn't really cook anymore."

I'm surprised because Mom or Dad would certainly have made me egg rolls for a situation like this, and neither of them ever had the flair for cooking that Ollie's mom did. I think again of the old gatherings at their house, and it strikes me that although Ollie and I have been spending a lot of time together, the last time I really saw his parents was at one of those parties.

At the next corner, Ollie pauses at the curb and lets the tips of his sneakers hang over. "So you're going straight home today?" He studies a black spot of gum on the sidewalk.

Now I kind of wish we were still holding hands, but instead, I just say, "Yeah, my a pòh could probably use my help."

Ollie puts two fists in his pockets and nods. "And your a gūng," he adds.

He doesn't sound annoyed, but it reminds me of what he said about A Gūng being sexist, and I adjust a strand of hair behind my other ear. "I know what you're thinking."

Ollie kicks his leg out at nothing in particular. "What's that?"

"That I shouldn't be worrying so much about A Gūng. Or that he doesn't deserve all this effort."

Ollie glances at his shoes and kneels down to retie one of them. "I do think your grandparents are fine without you for a few afternoons," he concedes after a while. "Mostly, though, I just want what you want." He finishes with his laces and stands up again. "I feel strongly that you should get to make decisions for yourself."

"I see," I say as we resume walking.

"But maybe that's just because I like the ones you've been making."

That makes me laugh, and I'm startled to find that, in all these years, I never realized Ollie was funny.

We've reached the edge of a small park next to our old elementary school, a grassy field that spans the entire block. In this corner, there's a playground set with monkey bars, and Ollie slows down in front of it. "This used to seem a lot taller." He reaches up to touch the bars. "Remember it used to be a thing to dare people to walk across the top?"

"Yeah," I say, rapping on the steel posts. "I never did, though."

"Dared anyone or walked across?"

"Neither." I cross my arms instinctively. "It was against school rules."

"True, but *after* school, the rules didn't apply."

"Still, it seemed kind of unnecessary."

Now Ollie laughs. "Maybe, but it felt pretty good once you got up there."

"*You* tried it?"

"Well, Isaac dared me once, and I wasn't going to hear the end of it if I didn't." He gives me a mischievous look, a challenge and a joke rolled into one, and climbs up the ladder.

"What are you doing?" I try to keep the concern out of my voice.

"It sounded like you didn't believe me."

"I believe you!" I watch him place both feet on the side rails, then slowly unfold himself—awkwardly at first, and then with more confidence. "You do know your center of gravity is higher than it used to be, right?"

But Ollie doesn't seem fazed now that he's standing, and he moves across with the calm of a tightrope walker, rebalancing a little with each step. At the other end, he stops and takes a bow.

"How's the view from there?" I ask, hiding a smile.

"Pretty nice," he replies, grinning back down at me. His hair is ruffling in the breeze, his cheeks are rosy from the sun, and I feel a new piece of my heart wake up.

"I'd like to see." I move toward the ladder. "Do you think I could make it up there?"

"Yeah, of course." Ollie drops down to sit on a bar. "Need a boost?"

"No, it's all right." I want to climb up on my own.

I'm a bit clumsy maneuvering up the rungs, but with careful steps and a little patience, I do manage to reach the top. Just as Ollie had, I bend down to grab the nearest bar and focus on planting one shoe on each side rail. Once I've made sure my footing is solid, I'm ready to stand up—all I have to do is let go.

That, however, is when I notice a piece of mulch fall off my shoe and topple to the ground. Suddenly, the rails seem awfully narrow, my sneakers seem awfully slippery, and this is a *lot* higher than I want to be.

"Hey, you can do this," says Ollie, leaning over. He's not chewing any gum right now, but the lingering scent of his usual peppermint calms me. "Just take one hand off, and then the other. There's no rush."

"Okay," I say, even though I'm still tense. *It's just adrenaline*, I remind myself. An overreaction, though a normal one. So I do what Ollie says and peel my fingers back from the bar. Then, very deliberately, I straighten my knees, one joint at a time, until I finally stand up straight.

"Look at you!" says Ollie, and I feel weightless, like I belong at this height, or maybe that this height belongs to me. From here, I can see the tops of the same houses and trees I've passed by a thousand times, but now they are unrecognizable, as if the sunlight at this angle makes everything brand-new. I understand for the first time why a kid might want to climb all the way up here for no reason—the world feels so much bigger at the same time that you do.

"You were right," I tell Ollie, stepping toward him. "It *is* nice up here. I—"

My foot slips then, and the entire view kaleidoscopes in on itself right before I make a frantic grab for the rungs. I feel my heart pounding so hard in my ears, I wonder if I'll even hear my bones crack when I full-body slam into the cold metal.

But I don't. Instead, when I stop blinking, I realize that I'm clutching Ollie's shoulders, my knees rammed up against his chest while he holds my hips steady. Though my one foot is waving in the air, the other is still, blessedly, flat on the rail.

"Here." He helps me sit down. "I got you."

Shakily, I settle on the bars next to him, and we let our feet dangle in the silence, his shoe occasionally hitting mine.

"Are you okay?" Ollie asks after a moment.

I'm still feeling unsteady from the whole thing, but when I turn to look up into his eyes, the way I get lost in them makes me realize I don't mind the spinning at all.

19

Ollie

I DIDN'T THINK I'D FEEL ONE WAY OR ANOTHER about how I got to and from school, but turns out walking is pretty great. Turns out, our neighborhood is pretty great. That old park with the monkey bars? Great. This sidewalk that we're strolling down? Great.

And Francine? *Really* great.

I still wonder sometimes how she snuck up on me like this, but maybe I also care less and less. Most of the time, I'm so full of this new elation that there's no space left in me to care. After I walk Francine the rest of the way to her house, I head home even though I'm still way too jazzed up. Maybe I'll take Dexter for a run or something—that could be good. I never want to go for a run, but right now, I could probably finish a marathon if I had to.

I even start jogging a little bit now, because it's like my feet can't stay on the ground, but when I get to my block, I see Francine's grandpa at the corner.

That's weird. Is he supposed to be out here alone? I slow down as I approach him. "A Gūng hóu," I say.

When he looks up, his face becomes way happier than it should be, considering I'm just me. "Pìhng a?" he says in his usual Cantonese. "What a nice surprise."

"Are you taking a walk?" I ask, because of course I do, despite the fact that he clearly is. Like my A Mā, he always seems to be dressed for colder weather than it is, and today a sweater peeks out from under his windbreaker. He seems almost lost underneath all those layers.

"Yes, A Pòh sent me out to get some air," he replies. "I think she was getting tired of me being a grump."

"Ah," I say. And then I'm at a loss because it feels awkward to just leave, but I have no idea what to do instead. Although my Cantonese has gotten a lot better, my conversation skills have not.

Francine's a gūng lifts his hat and wipes his brow. "Looks like I may have wandered farther than she wanted." He laughs a little. "I should head back."

"Do you need help getting home?" That's something I can do at least.

"Hóu," he agrees as I take his arm. "Sorry to trouble you, Pìhng."

I tell him it's no big deal, and we head down the street back to Francine's house. Her grandpa's steps are slow and tentative, and though he manages all right, I feel these few blocks much more than I ever have.

"How are you doing in school?" he asks after a few minutes. "Very well, I'm sure."

I agree without elaboration because that's the only possible response to a question like that. In reality, of course, I haven't been paying much attention to school at all lately—except as a place where I see Francine. Thinking of her makes me wonder if she's worried about where her grandpa is. Probably, knowing her. When I take out my phone to text her, however, I notice Francine's a gūng is still smiling at me generously, and I'm bothered that she's not on his mind at all.

"Francine—I mean, Fōng—is doing even better than me, though," I say suddenly. "She's probably the best student in our science class."

"Fōng?" Francine's a gūng nods. "Oh, yes, she is a very smart girl."

He almost sounds proud, which isn't the reaction I was expecting. "Yeah," I reply, "she wants to be a doctor, right?"

Francine's a gūng reminisces as he trudges along. "Yes, she's said that since she was a small child," he says. "I'd take her around to all my friends' houses, and she'd announce it to everyone."

I kind of chuckle to myself, because I could totally see Francine doing that. Especially since it was likely something she thought would please her grandpa. In fact, now that I think about it, maybe that *was* why.

"A Gūng," I say, cautious about changing the subject but curious about what he'll say. "Why do you think it's so important to have a male heir?"

His response is matter-of-fact. "As the eldest in my family, and the only son, it's my responsibility." He looks out at the street for a moment. "Although, you know, it wasn't always that way."

I feel his pace slackening even more, so mine does, too. All of a sudden, he seems very far away.

"I had a brother who was two years older than me," Francine's a gūng explains. "One year, however, when I was very small and we still lived in the village where I was born, all the children got sick, including my brother. Everyone was poor. No one knew of any cure, and besides me, only one other child, another baby, survived. These scars are from that time." He raises a hand to his cheek, and I realized I never would've thought they were remnants from a faded trauma—I thought they were just symptoms of old age. "That was how I became an eldest son."

"Wow." I want to tell him I'm sorry, but I'm not sure it means the right thing in Chinese, so I don't say anything else.

"I had other siblings, too, who were born later," says Francine's a gūng, turning thoughtful. "All girls, and some were given away because there wasn't enough money to raise them. That was common then." He strokes his chin. "My father was a tailor, but he had an opium habit—that was the trouble. Even if one had all the money in the world, there would never be enough for that."

We're back on Francine's street, but now I'm sucked into her grandpa's story, so I actually hope we don't get to her house just yet.

"My mother said he used to make the most beautiful cheongsam," Francine's a gūng continues, reaching for a hibiscus flower that has grown over the sidewalk. "Maybe the best in all of Hanoi. Which wasn't easy, either, because those dresses are so unforgiving." The shaking of his hand knocks the petals off, and they slip away in the breeze. "There was a time when it seemed maybe he could've done well for himself. Except all the money he made—more and more of it—went into the opium. One day, I came home from school and realized he'd sold the sewing machine. That's when I knew it was over."

I rub my nose hard with the back of my arm. I'm definitely not tearing up, but my sinuses sure are acting like I am.

"When I was fourteen, we had to spend the night in a church after we were evicted," says Francine's a gūng. "The next day, I went and got a job at the textile factory. If I didn't, who would?"

He shrugs, and I watch the weight of his jacket rise and fall with his shoulders.

"A man is responsible for his family, Pìhng," Francine's a gūng tells me. "A man needs to make sure his family has a future."

His words feel heavy, like stones that he's handed me to carry, and I want more than anything to put them down. I wish, suddenly, that Francine were here in this conversation with me. Or better yet, if she were here *instead* of me.

"Wouldn't you rather have an heir who's already in your family, though? Like Fōng?" I know this is a futile argument, but I need to make it. "Isn't blood thicker than water?"

Francine's a gūng shakes his head. "Fōng is in our family, yes. But she is not a relation anyway."

"How could you say that?" I let go of his arm in disbelief. "She's your granddaughter. Would you really disown her just because she's a girl?"

"You misunderstand me, Pìhng." Francine's a gūng sounds flustered. "I'm not disowning her at all. It's simply the truth—we are not related by blood."

I'm debating how I should tell Francine that The Plan is over—because this is honestly all too much for me—when the meaning of what he said sinks in. "Wait." I pull down on a hibiscus branch. "Fōng is not actually your granddaughter?"

Francine's a gūng sighs. "My daughter, Lāan, has raised Fōng as her own child, but she is not her birth mother. Fōng is her father's daughter from a previous marriage. He was a widower before he met Lāan."

I stagger backward, reeling from his words. The shock of it all reverberates deep into my chest, and that's where the sadness takes over, so thick and painful I could suffocate.

"She didn't tell me that," I sputter, even though that's the last thing that matters. But it earns me an even more surprising response.

"She doesn't know, Pìhng." Francine's a gūng looks exhausted. "Her parents wanted to protect her from the tragedy until she was older."

Holy shit. Holy *shit*. As far as family secrets go, this makes The Plan seem like an effing amateur hour. I'd been so worried about Francine wanting us to lie to her grandpa, but this whole time, it was him—and the rest of her family—lying to *her*.

"I should not have told you," Francine's a gūng is saying now, as he watches me. "I've made a mistake."

He sounds concerned, but I'm still too shaken up to reassure him. "Does anybody else know?"

"No, other than some people in our family," says Francine's a gūng. "You mustn't say anything to Fōng. It would be very hard for her."

Up ahead, the front door to Francine's house opens, and she pops her head out. "Oh, good," she calls to us. "You found A Gūng!"

"Don't worry, Pìhng." Francine's a gūng reaches for my arm again. "She will know when the time is right. But until then, it is a kindness to carry the burden for her."

Francine bounds down the steps and flashes us a giant smile. "Everything okay?" she asks me in English. And I swear, her eyes are goddamn sparkling from the sight of me and her grandpa together, all buddy-buddy.

"Yeah," I tell her. "Everything's great."

I'm still thinking about the whole situation later that night as I lie on the couch with my laptop on my chest, ostensibly cropping photos to use in my Global Gala booth. It's been at least half an hour, though, and I've only gotten through two photos.

Because this revelation about Francine is some serious shit.

I should just tell her, right? I mean, how could I not? How could her parents not? She obviously deserves to know. She'd *want* to know.

Or would she?

It would be very hard for her, Francine's a gūng had said. That much is true. Her family is everything to her, and I really don't want to be the one to ruin that. Besides, she's already having trouble dealing with her grandpa's terminal diagnosis—can she really handle another major tragedy right now? When is the truth worth the hurt it would cause?

Never, I hear Francine's voice in my head. *It's never worth it.* That's absolutely what she'd say. She thought it was a good idea to lie to her dying grandpa to make him happy. Maybe she would want to be protected the same way.

My stomach is all twisted up, so I reach down for a bag of Oreos I left on the floor. I'm not in the mood for cookies, but once I pop one into my mouth, it seems like I need another. Then another. I tell myself the answer I'm looking for will get more obvious with each successive cookie, so I end up downing the entire package. When I finally brush off the last crumbs and fall back on the couch, I realize I was right—the answer *has* become clear, but I feel sicker than ever.

I pull a pillow over my face and groan. This is too big not to tell Francine, and at some point, I'm just gonna have to do it. But as I lie there, nose pressed into the dusty linen, I wish it weren't up to me. I wish I could brush all this off the way I used to—because it's not *really* my business. If I hadn't gotten myself so tangled up in Francine's bizarro life, I could finish this stupid Global Gala stuff and go back to reading basketball Reddit. I wouldn't have to care so much about anything. Especially not Francine.

Except I do. And it's really fucking hard.

The hum of the garage door opening interrupts my thoughts, and Dexter, curled up on the floor, lifts a lazy head. I check the time in the corner of my screen: 10:51 p.m. It's a later than usual night for Dad.

"Is your mom asleep?" he asks when he comes through the door. His shirt is wrinkled, and his coffee cup, dribbled down the side with an hours-old stain, is a little crumpled in his grip.

"Yeah, she said she had a headache." I sit up and make room for him on the couch even though I can't tell if he's planning to take a seat or not.

"I don't blame her." Dad lets out a huge sigh and drops himself onto the chaise section. I think maybe he's going to elaborate, but he doesn't. Instead, he gestures at the TV, which is tuned to a replay of a basketball game from earlier tonight. The sound is on low because I wasn't really paying any attention. "Who's winning?"

"The Clippers," I say, and Dad makes a disgusted sound that's something between *ugh* and *aiyah*. He's ride-or-die for the Lakers.

We watch the game in silence, and I wish, not for the first time, that Dad was the kind of dad I could talk to. Like, what would he suggest I do about Francine? Would he have advice on how to break the news to her? I glance at his argyle socks, which are made of merino wool or some shit that's the complete opposite of what I would wear, and I wonder if he would tell me the truth if we weren't related. It definitely feels sometimes like we're not, but I guess there's no overlooking those ears. As I study him more closely, I notice that the creases around his eyes are more pronounced than they once were, and his jawline softer. Although it never seems that way, I'm reminded that I'm actually taller than him these days.

"How's work?" I ask, because I feel like I should say something to him.

"Busy." Dad yawns. "I think the contract with the Germans is finally going through."

"Which contract?"

Dad looks surprised because I usually never ask questions like that. I'm kind of surprised, too. Maybe Francine is rubbing off on me—she's the one who'd inquire all about it and then some, even if she didn't personally care.

"The one with the new cosmetics firm," replies Dad, spreading his arms across the top of the couch. "They want to source extracts for their new skincare line."

That really does sound boring as hell, but I nod. "Cool."

"Yeah, it's a big deal for the company. It's twice the size of any other account we have."

"Sounds like a lot of money."

Dad chuckles. "That's the point, right?"

He *would* say that. It's the type of comment that used to

make me want to immediately leave any conversation with Dad. But then I think of the story Francine's grandpa told me this afternoon, and instead, I just say, "I guess so."

"How about you?" Dad motions at my computer. "What are you working on?"

I can't imagine he really wants to know, but I explain about the Global Gala booth anyway. "I'm using a bunch of Francine's old family photos for the display," I say. "She let me digitize them."

"You're friends with Francine now?" Dad says this like he's asking something else, and my face burns. Since when has he ever been with it enough to know whether Francine and I were friends? I decide to ignore his question.

"These pictures are interesting." I tilt my computer to show him. Currently up on the screen is a photo of Francine's grandparents on their wedding day, the two of them in a sea of family and well-wishers from the neighborhood. I don't know what color they're actually wearing, but in the sepia cast, they seem light and radiant—otherworldly even, like stars.

"That's a nice one," agrees Dad. From his polite tone, I expect that to be the end of it, but then he examines the photo a bit longer and adds, almost in spite of himself, "I remember that street."

"Really?" I zoom in closer to look at the background, but it's pretty blurry. "You can tell where this is?"

Dad points to a doorway that's visible in the corner. "That was the building where we lived."

I wish, suddenly, that I could clear out the crowd and move

the camera down the street, refocusing it on that nondescript spot Dad's talking about. But of course I'm stuck forever on this side of the lens, decades too late.

"You don't know where our family photos are, do you?" I ask Dad, even though I can already guess the answer.

"Somewhere, I'm sure." Dad waves a noncommittal hand around. He has no idea.

"When's the last time you saw them?"

"Years ago, probably." He gets up from the couch but stands there for a second, watching me cycle through the other photos. "Is Francine's grandpa doing any better?"

I consider making a snide comment about how pancreatic cancer doesn't work that way, but I don't. "He's the same," I tell Dad, turning back to my computer. "But you can see for yourself soon, I guess."

"Oh, are you having him over?"

I pause mid-click, wanting to give Dad the benefit of the doubt, but already I feel another rush to my face—this time, though, it's anger.

"No," I say irritably. "Francine's been planning a dinner party at their house. Remember I told you he wanted to see you? She sent the invite over a week ago."

"Did she?" Dad looks totally innocent, and I don't know what would be worse—if he's lying or if he actually has no recollection of what we're talking about. "Are you sure?"

"Yes." My jaw clenches because the likelihood of Francine forgetting to invite him is close to nil. I'm positive he got the email—he must have. And if I can't bring myself to tell

Francine about her family yet, then the least I can do is follow through with this.

Dad pulls out his phone. "When did you say it was?"

"Next Saturday." I'm shutting down, but I don't try to stop myself.

A few scrolls later, Dad sighs at his screen. "It looks like I'm going to be in Berlin."

"Okay." I sit forward stiffly. "Should we reschedule, then?"

"There's a lot going on right now, so it might be tough—"

I slam down on the lid of my laptop, my rage completely boiled over. "You said you were gonna do this."

"It's an important partnership, Ollie. You know that."

"I already *told* her you were gonna do it."

Dad looks tired but unruffled. "I'm sorry, Ollie, but you really can't get this worked up over a girl."

I leap to my feet, so agitated that Dexter, too, launches himself up and races around in a circle. "I am *not* getting worked up over a girl!"

Dad's voice stays calm, but he switches from English to Vietnamese, which usually means he's not happy. "Your mom is sleeping," he says. "Show some respect." In response, I shut up, but sullenly, and he shakes his head. "Life isn't just fun and games, Ollie. The work I'm doing is necessary for our family. If you don't understand that's a bigger deal than indulging some girl you like, then you need to grow up."

"This isn't about *indulging* her." I keep my voice low, but I'm fuming. "This is about doing one crummy thing for her grandpa, who took care of you when A Yèh died. Who fed you when you were *starving*. Which you don't seem to remember because you don't want to remember a goddamn thing."

I don't know why the hell I'm defending Francine's family, because they're clearly a shitshow in their own way, but for some reason it's Dad who's really getting to me, and I can't stop the words from escaping my mouth.

"Oliver." Dad has switched back to English—which means I'm *really* in trouble—but I blow past him anyway, Dexter on my heels.

"And she's *not* just some girl I like!" I grab Dexter's leash and head for the front door, resisting the urge to wrench the stupid foyer mirror off the wall and shatter it to pieces on the floor. Instead, I run outside, corralling Dexter alongside me, and slam the door behind us.

The night is chilly and I forgot my jacket, but I obviously can't go back for it. I walk around the block several times, but my heart is still pounding for a fight, so I peel off and keep going down another street, and another, until I'm in front of the abandoned Victorian. The one across from Francine's house.

I take my phone from my pocket and call Francine. As I listen to the sound of the rings, each one drawn out like a slow exhale, I realize I've only ever texted her, never called, and I have no clue what I'm going to say now. I can't even explain to myself why I'm so mad.

"Ollie?" Francine's voice is quiet when she picks up, like she's whispering in my ear, and for a second, I *can't* speak. I just stand there and hold the phone still, recovering from the rush to my head. "Are you there, Ollie?" she tries again, and I manage to string together a sentence.

"Can you come outside?" I croak. "I'm . . . across the street."

There's a pause, and all of a sudden I feel kind of stupid. "It's late, isn't it?" She sounds like she's trying not to let anybody else hear.

"Yeah," I say. "Yeah, you're right."

Another pause. Then: "One sec."

A few minutes later, her front door opens, the rectangle of living room light flashing in the dark before she closes it, and I see her glancing around as she comes down the steps. I wave and move closer, but it's the jangle of Dexter's collar that catches her attention and sends her running toward us.

"Hi," she says, a little out of breath, kneeling to pet Dexter but grinning up at me. Her hair is tied up all the way, and the curve of her neck is smooth under the glow of the streetlamp.

"Hi," I say, unearthing the word from the back of my throat.

"I can't stay long," she says. "I had to tell my mom I was getting some plant specimens for a science project."

That is such a Francine lie, I can't help but laugh out loud in spite of everything. Although Francine has no idea why, she smiles at me anyway, and I pull her in, just to feel her close—but then she's kissing me, and I'm kissing her, and maybe I'm getting too into it for being out on the sidewalk because she breaks it off, saying, "Hold on, Ollie." She studies my face. "Are you okay?"

I drop my hands and watch Dexter immerse himself in the tall weeds. The secret about her family, obviously, is what weighs on me most, but when I try to put together the words, nothing comes out. So instead, I just say, "My dad says he can't see your grandpa anytime soon."

"Oh." Francine looks disappointed, though not as disappointed as I thought she would. "That's all right."

"Not really." I walk away from her, cutting across the barren lawn. On the left side of the house, farther from the light, there's enough darkness to wallow in, and I plop myself down on the ground.

Francine comes over and settles next to me. After a minute, she says, "What's really wrong, Ollie?"

"Nothing." I pick at a hole in the knee of my jeans. "I mean, besides the fact that my dad's a jerk."

"Is he really a jerk or—"

"Yeah."

"Everything about him?"

I sigh, leaning against the side of the house. "I mean, it's never everything."

Francine sits back, too, and folds her hands over her knees. "Maybe you should cut him some slack."

Given how devoted she's been to The Plan, this reaction surprises me. "*You* think so?"

She stretches her legs out in front of her. "He probably just doesn't feel like he has time."

Her generosity only makes me more pissed off at Dad. "He doesn't have time for anything that isn't money." I pluck a huge handful of grass and toss it, the yellowed blades flying everywhere. "But we have money. We already have enough."

"Except you didn't always, right? And he *really* didn't."

I try to imagine Dad as a little kid, running down the street in the background of that photo of the wedding, disappearing through that doorway you can barely see. I can kind of piece together his world, based on Francine's other old family photos, but it's hard to truly picture what it must have been like—to be poor even among the poor.

"I think," says Francine in my silence, "sometimes that makes you feel like the only amount of money that's ever enough is more."

She's probably right, and a bit of sympathy for Dad creeps up on me. Then I remember the way he talked about her, and I'm upset all over again. "It's not just that, though. He makes these assumptions, and he's so sure he's right—" I hesitate because I don't want to tell her exactly what he said. "But he doesn't get it," I finish vaguely. "He doesn't get anything."

"Did you try to explain?" says Francine. "About why you're mad?"

I look over at her, unsure if she's being serious. "What good would that do?"

"You never know." She shrugs and begins to knock her toes together absently. "The truth can help sometimes. You should tell him."

My irritation overtakes me before I even realize it. "You mean the way you and your family always tell each other everything?"

Francine's feet stop moving. "What do you mean?"

Shit, that's *definitely* not what I wanted to say. "Never mind."

Luckily, she has no idea what I was talking about. "But I'm

not mad at them," she says, not looking at me. "I'm fine."

I consider spilling everything right there, but as she glances back toward her house, I wimp out. "Sorry, I'm just being a shithead."

Her phone buzzes then, and a second later, mine does, too. It's a group text from Rollo to me, Francine, and Jiya:

Violet Girl tickets about to be secured!

Francine, this is your last chance . . . you sure you don't want to come?

You're only gonna miss out on PROBABLY the best night of your life . . .

"Hey," I say as Francine studies her phone, which is lying flat in her lap. I reach for her hand. "You can ignore him. He's just being Rollo."

There's another double buzz and a follow-up message:

(Ollie told me to say that.)

"I didn't," I clarify, blushing. "Obviously." This is what happens when you tell Rollo *anything*.

Francine's fingers curl around mine, though she's still contemplating Rollo's messages. "What would I tell my parents?" she murmurs, almost to herself.

"Another school project?" I joke. "For orchestra class?"

Francine throws me a side glance and then one of her slow-growing smiles. "Guess I'm pretty busy these days, huh?"

"You are," I say, laughing. "It's true."

"Okay." Francine gets up on her knees and leans over me. My heart speeds up as she places a careful hand in the grass, just by my hip.

"Okay?" I repeat, because it's the only word that comes to mind.

"Okay, I'll go," she says, touching her lips to mine, and then a lot more than just our lips are touching before we hear her mom's voice split the air.

"Francine?" Her apprehension is palpable even through the distance. "Francine!"

"Shoot, I have to go." Francine jumps up and brushes off the grass from her legs, and Dexter, seeing her movement, scampers over from the shrubbery a few feet away. "I'll see you later, Ollie," she says, stopping to pet Dexter again, and turns to run toward her house.

"Wait." I scramble to my feet and scan around. "Here," I say, tugging a fistful of flowering weeds from the ground. "Your specimens."

Francine beams at the bouquet. "Thank you," she replies, taking it with both hands. Then, without any warning, she lunges in to kiss me one more time. For a split second, I think about stopping her and trying again to broach the topic of the secret. But then I'm not thinking about anything at all, and by the time she pulls away, it's too late.

I will just have to tell her another day, I decide, and bend over to pick up Dexter's leash. I notice my palms are stinging slightly from where I grabbed hold of the weeds—but as I watch Francine dash back across the street, every thorn feels worth it.

20

Francine

I AM AFRAID THAT SPINNING THE VIOLET GIRL concert as a "school project for orchestra class" might be a hard sell, and it is.

"You have to go at night?" Mom asks from behind my old computer. I've had it since elementary school, so basically every click requires a wait time of about fifteen seconds, but Mom uses it so infrequently that she doesn't mind. Right now, she's trying to log on to some site to pay the bills for A Gūng's latest lab tests, and I'm concerned that the delays might give her a little too much time to think critically about what I'm telling her.

"Concerts are often at night," I say, hoping that I sound convincing.

Mom peers down at the paper statement that had come in the mail, trying to locate the account number that she's supposed to type in. "You have to go to LA?"

I take the page from her and scan the line items until I find what she's looking for, then pivot the keyboard toward me so I can input it for her. "Yeah, but I'll be getting a ride from Jiya."

That part isn't a lie. Rollo had offered to chauffeur us, but Jiya refused. "I just get the sense Rollo would be a bad driver," she said to me. "Don't you?" So we're all going in her car instead.

"What does Jiya play again?" Mom squints her eyes into the distance. "Trumpet?"

"French horn," I say.

"I see." It's clear she doesn't remember what a French horn is. "Well, if it's going to be fifteen percent of your grade . . ."

This detail had been a contribution from Rollo, though he'd suggested claiming it was fifty percent. "That line always works," he claimed. When I told him I was going to lower the stakes a bit to make it sound more realistic, he shrugged. "Hey, I'm gonna trust you know your audience."

Apparently, however, I knew it less than I thought because I didn't expect it to be this easy to get Mom on board. I think it's because I never lie for stuff like this. Mom probably believed me because I've literally never given her a single reason why she shouldn't. Which kind of makes me feel guilty. Because lying for The Plan is one thing, but this—lying just because I want to do something for myself—seems different.

Still, I'm also aware that knowing the truth would make Mom worry unnecessarily, and I obviously don't want that. Given everything she's already got to be anxious about, I figure not telling her is really doing her a favor. Besides, I'm sure

I'll be fine—other kids go to concerts all the time, and nothing bad happens.

Yet as we zoom along the freeway, Violet Girl blasting from the car speakers, I admit there *is* something that feels a little dangerous about the whole situation—something that feels both more real and less real than A Gūng being sick. Secretly, that's part of the reason I wanted to go. In the same way, Ollie seems a little dangerous now, too. At any given moment, I'm never quite sure what could happen next, or what I might uncover about him—and myself.

The two of us are sitting in the back seat of Jiya's car, with crumpled In-N-Out bags between us, because Rollo had called shotgun. "You're welcome," he says to us, smirking, and it's hard to tell how selfless he was really being.

"All right, Rollo, what's the game plan?" Jiya signals and looks over her shoulder before changing lanes, none of which interferes with her ability to continuously ingest french fries, and I am very impressed.

"Well, once we get there, you should drop us off outside the theater first so we can unload the shirts, and then you can find parking," says Rollo. "If you want, go to one of the paid lots—we'll expense the cost."

"Is it coming out of your cut or mine?" Jiya teases.

"Jee, I'm so confident in your potential, I'm gonna say mine."

Jiya rolls her eyes, but you can tell she appreciates Rollo's comment. He showed us the shirts earlier, which are made from a fuchsia jersey and screen-printed in gold with Jiya's artwork. The design is based on the sketch she'd liked best, and it was definitely the right choice—her intricate lines really pop against the dark fabric. I might be biased, but the shirts look legit.

"We're going to set up on the sidewalk?" says Ollie, sipping from a strawberry milkshake. He's leaning up against the door, but his legs are stretched all the way across the floor of the car, and when no one's looking, he slides his ankle playfully under mine.

"Don't worry, we'll find a good spot," says Rollo. He turns around to dig through the bags for extra ketchup and then raises his eyebrows at us. "Are you two keeping it PG-13 back here or what?"

"It's G," says Ollie, laughing. "Just G." But he doesn't pull his leg back, and he doesn't take his eyes off me, and the way I suddenly feel the need to fumble for the air conditioner vent . . . well, I'm not so sure that's true.

"I love this part!" Jiya squeals from the front seat, turning the volume all the way up. She starts singing along, her voice blending in with Violet Girl's fuzzy crooning, and then Rollo, to our amazement, joins in, too. It's not clear what's more sensational—the fact that Rollo knows the words to a Violet Girl song after all, or that he can harmonize like nobody's business.

I look out the window at the sunset, all gauzy with pink and purple like fancy cotton candy, and watch as the familiar landmarks fly by: the old Santa Fe Springs drive-in theater, the outlet mall shaped like an Assyrian castle, the overpasses that crisscross over silhouettes of palm trees. I've seen it all before, of course, again and again, driving with Mom and Dad up this same freeway to A Gūng and A Pòh's house. But as I sit here, surrounded by the dreamy sounds of Violet Girl, just inches from Ollie and his drowsy smile, everything seems like it's finally alive.

The Tangram Theater is downtown, on the same block as an art gallery and a bodega, just down the street from a slightly seedy historic hotel and—as Rollo expected—several parking lots enclosed by chain-link fences. It's a squat, slate-blue building that I would never have guessed was a concert venue except for the massive marquee. When Jiya pulls up to the curb I hop out of the car and immediately notice that the sidewalks smell faintly of cigarettes and urine.

Still, there's already an energy in the air that I don't recognize, a briskness to the night that's buzzy around the edges. Like I'm someone else and the universe is thrilled.

A few feet away, Rollo is assembling a clothing ladder that he'd unloaded from Jiya's trunk ("My mom won't miss it," he assured us), while Ollie carries over the box of T-shirts. I help him unpack them and drape each one over a rung on the ladder.

"Perfect, Francine," says Rollo as he unfolds a TV tray table next to me. With a flourish, he covers it with a large square of sparkly geometric fabric. Then, next to his trusty iPad, he sets down a white paper lantern. "Lighting," he explains, dropping a flashlight inside, "can make or break the retail experience."

And it's true, the little gleaming orb is what pulls together the whole setup, making us look like a mini pop-up shop instead of just some kids trying to hustle T-shirts on the sidewalk.

Even Ollie seems to think Rollo's done a good job. "This is pretty nice, man."

"Obviously." Rollo sounds smug. But then, feeling magnanimous, he reveals, "The execution of the details was mostly Jiya."

Jiya herself appears now, jaywalking from across the street, her keys jingling in her hand. "Wow, you guys work fast," she says, surveying our handiwork. "We look ready for business."

"We are," I agree, pulling out my wallet. "In fact, I'll be the first customer."

"That'll be twenty-five dollars, please," Rollo informs me as he unlocks his iPad. "Accepted forms of payment include cash, Apple Pay, and all major credit cards."

Jiya swats at him. "Don't make *Francine* pay," she says. "Just give her a shirt."

"No, I said I'd pay," I remind her. "You're a professional now, Jiya! Your work is worth real money."

Rollo's hand hovers over a shirt on the ladder, waiting for Jiya's response as she considers what I'm saying. She's the picture of cool—her hair freshly streaked with blue violet and her jeans baggy in a cut that's so unfashionable, it's probably going to be the thing to wear in five years—and yet she looks so unsure. But then she straightens up. "All right," she says. "If you *insist*."

I give her an encouraging smile. "Great," I say, putting on the T-shirt that Rollo hands me. It's loose enough to fit over my existing top. "How's it look?"

"Gorgeous." Jiya grins, and I'm about to pay Rollo in cash when Ollie reaches into his pocket.

"I got it." He holds his phone up to Rollo's card reader, and when he smiles at me, I realize I've never appreciated how beautiful the chime of contactless payment could be.

Doors to the Tangram haven't opened yet, but people have already started to line up alongside the building. Most of them look like they shop at the same thrift stores as Jiya, who relaxes a little as she checks out the crowd. Before long, one girl—dressed in purple coveralls embellished with a heart-shaped Pride flag—ducks under the velvet rope to approach the table. "Hi," she says, waving her phone at us. "I'm here to pick up."

Jiya, Ollie, and I are totally confused, but Rollo doesn't bat an eyelid.

"Let's see your confirmation email," he tells her, and she shows him something on her screen. "Wonderful, Emily." He lifts a T-shirt from the box. "Here you go. Oh, and by the way, this is the one and only Jiya herself!"

"Really?" The girl is ecstatic. "Oh my god, you're so talented!"

To her credit, Jiya responds as if she is treated like a celebrity every day. "Thank you," she says serenely.

"What was that?" asks Ollie when the girl walks away.

Rollo looks at us like it should be self-evident. "Preorders," he says. "These days, the key to successful conversion is having an in-person touchpoint"—here, he waves a hand over the T-shirt display—"that complements your online presence." At that, he wiggles his phone.

As it turns out, he must be right because the whole scheme is a wild success. So much so that Rollo eventually forgets to act like he was predicting it all along.

"Are you seeing this?" he whoops, holding up the half-empty box. "Can you believe we're almost out?"

We've only been there for about thirty minutes—the opening act, a band called Tidal Squeegee that Jiya says is overrated, has just started their set—but between the preorders and the extra interest generated from being right by the line, the shirts are flying off Rollo's clothing ladder.

"I didn't think you were gonna be able to pull this off," says Ollie as Rollo hands a shirt to another customer.

"Bro," retorts Rollo, "you gotta learn to believe."

When it's almost time for Violet Girl to go on, Jiya, Ollie, and I head inside without Rollo, who insists—even after our cajoling—on keeping the pop-up open until after the concert.

"Why would he want to miss out?" says Jiya while we get our IDs checked. "It seemed as though he actually liked Violet Girl."

"I think he does," says Ollie, "only he loves money more."

The lobby of the Tangram is small and dimly lit, but the walls, covered in a dazzling pattern of blue and navy tiles, are immediately impressive. Off to the left side is a bar, outfitted with old-fashioned stools and wood paneling, but we're not allowed over there because we don't have the wristbands that say we're old enough.

"It's fine." Jiya dismisses all of that with a wave of her hand. "We don't need to get wasted for Violet Girl anyway."

We move instead through the double doors that lead to the main room, which is even darker and packed full of people. The ceiling curves high above the glossy black floor, and at the far end is the stage, which is currently empty. The only music playing right now is blasting from speakers on the walls.

"I'll be back!" Jiya has to shout to be heard. "Bathroom!" Then she glances at me. "Do you need to go, Francine?" When I shake my head, she smiles and squeezes my shoulder before disappearing, leaving me with Ollie.

It's funny how you can know a boy for so long and then spend almost a whole week *really* getting to know him—and still, every time, in those first few thrilling moments of finding yourself alone together, feel like you've only just met him.

Ollie, too, seems suddenly shy again. "There's water," he says, nodding at the back of the room. He blushes for no reason, the way he often does, and it's cute.

I turn to see another bar, only this one has a large dispenser of water on the counter next to a tall stack of paper cups. I'm about to tell Ollie that I don't need a drink when I realize there's an awful lot of old white people on their phones hanging around there. This confuses me until I see a girl—maybe my age or a bit younger—run up to one of the women, hand her a sweater, and then scamper off to join a group of friends. That's when I realize the woman is her mom.

"Wait, do other kids' parents take them to concerts?" I say to Ollie.

He glances back at the middle-aged crowd. "I guess so," he replies, chuckling. "*Mine* definitely wouldn't."

"Neither would mine!" Part of me wishes they would because I've never gone with them anywhere this fun. In fact, despite having lived in Orange County all these years and visited A Gūng and A Pòh so many times, I don't think my parents have been to very many places in LA at all. I picture them now at home—maybe watching a Chinese drama on TV, while A Pòh finishes up the dishes and A Gūng gargles in the bathroom—and everything about their existence suddenly feels small, like a diorama I might've made in elementary school. I couldn't imagine them in a place like this, where the air is too dank, the music too loud, and the lighting too dark.

Then I notice Ollie again, and another part of me—the part that's expanding so fast now I could burst—is relieved my parents aren't here. "I'm glad I came with you," I say, reaching for his hand.

"I'm glad you did, too." He smiles a little, catching my fingers, and the space between us dissolves.

Onstage, a few people dressed in black are moving things around, and a few minutes later, some familiar figures begin to take their places among the instruments. One of them, her trademark purple hair flowing in mermaid waves, picks up a guitar and settles herself in a wide-legged stance before the center mic. Cheers erupt from a few corners of the audience, gradually mounting into a full-on roar as the spotlights flick on and Violet Girl, with no preamble, launches into a song.

Jiya, pushing her way back to us through the crowd, is already dancing, her head bobbing to the rhythm. Behind her is a girl we don't know, her eyelashes very long and her hair buzzed close to her scalp. "This is Ana," yells Jiya.

"Hi," says Ana, blissfully contributing a ring of weed smoke to the fog that surrounds us. I want to tell her that research has shown teenage brains are much more susceptible to the effects of marijuana than adult brains, and also, contrary to popular belief, the smoke itself *can* cause respiratory issues, just like tobacco—but Jiya grabs my hands and starts swinging them wildly, and before I know it, I'm laughing and dancing, too. Violet Girl's music isn't complicated like a fugue or a sonata, where the technique is sometimes part of the beauty. Her songs hit me differently, in a place deep inside, like I've drunk a soda way too fast and my lungs feel fizzy enough to float.

Jiya is still bouncing up and down, singing along with the crowd, but on the latest beat, she grins and releases me to reach for Ana instead. I find myself spinning away, totally off-balance but not even realizing it until I run into Ollie, who catches me with his arm around my waist. As Violet Girl's voice soars over us, he says something I can't make out, the words nothing but hot breaths in my ear, and I know then that I will never, ever hear music the same way again.

About halfway through Violet Girl's set, Rollo appears behind us. "Hi, friends," he says, sipping water from a paper cup.

Jiya, still dancing with Ana, shakes her head to indicate that she can't hear him. "What?" she yells back.

"Hi!" Rollo repeats, waving exaggeratedly.

"What are you doing in here?" Ollie shouts. "Weren't you going to keep selling shirts?"

Rollo shrugs, as if everything is totally chill, but his shoulder has a suspicious twitch. "Something came up," he hollers. "I'll explain later, but I've got it under control."

Jiya, however, immediately stops moving and studies Rollo's face. Then she takes his arm and pulls him toward the patio.

"We'll be right back," I tell Ana, before Ollie and I follow them outside.

The main room opens out onto a large outdoor area, where small groups of people are hanging out under the white string lights. The night air is refreshing even though I hadn't necessarily minded the sweat and noise of the crowd indoors.

Rollo, however, looks uncomfortable as soon as we're outside. "Isn't this the smoking area?" he says, pretending to cough. He gestures to the far corner, where there are, in fact, a couple of smokers sharing a cigarette. "I really don't think it's a good idea to be breathing in all this secondhand smoke."

I want to ask Rollo if he didn't notice the weed situation inside, but Jiya cuts to the chase. "Then make it quick," she says. "What happened?"

"All right." Rollo glances at Ollie, who puts up two hands as if to say *You're on your own, dude.* "Well, the good news is we sold out of the shirts."

"And the bad news?" Jiya cranes her neck impatiently.

"The bad news is . . . we don't get to keep any of the money."

"What?" Jiya blinks in confusion. "Why?"

"Violet Girl's people came out and told me I wasn't allowed to sell unofficial merch," Rollo says. "They told me I can't use Violet Girl's name without her permission and what I was doing was serious enough to warrant legal action."

Jiya is horrified. "What?"

"I mean, it probably wasn't. They were just trying to threaten us because our shirts were doing so well. I bet we were undercutting the official merch sales." Rollo pats Jiya on the back. "Seriously, they should hire you."

"Rollo, I'm not trying to undercut Violet Girl!" Jiya looks like she could shake him. "Did you know something like this could happen?"

Rollo stuffs his hands in the pockets of his sweater. "I can't honestly say I expected this outcome, no."

Jiya seems to have run out of words, so she turns to me helplessly.

"What happens now?" I jump in. "You've already sold the shirts."

"It was obviously a sticky situation, so I had to do something." Rollo rubs the back of his head. "So . . . I kind of told them we were going to donate a hundred percent of the proceeds to the HRC."

"HRC," Jiya repeats, incredulous.

"Yeah, the Human Rights Campaign," says Rollo. "Hope that's okay?" He sounds chipper but raises his arm over his face, like he's afraid she might hit him.

At this point, Jiya bursts out laughing. "Rollo," she says between breaths. "You couldn't make this stuff up, could you?"

Relieved by her reaction, Rollo visibly relaxes. "You should still feel great, Jee. People *were* paying for your art! They didn't know their money was actually going to a good cause."

Inside, the music has stopped, and it sounds like Violet Girl is talking to the audience. "We'll finish discussing this later," Jiya says, linking her arm through mine, and leads us back through the double doors. "Let's see what's going on."

On the stage, Violet Girl is holding a homemade poster that reads *Keisha will you go to prom with Megan?*

"What do you say, Keisha?" Violet Girl asks into the mic. "Will you go with Megan?"

"Yes!" Keisha screams from below, hugging the person who is probably Megan, and the whole audience cheers.

Now Violet Girl is being handed a huge pile of friendship bracelets, which she pulls apart somewhat clumsily but excitedly, slipping on every last one until her arm is a rainbow of embroidery floss. "Oh, my god, you're amazing. Look at these." The stagehand keeps bringing her more, and she continues to gush. "Wow, I love you so much. I'll add all of these to my collection. Did you know I have a big box under my bed of things you've given me? Seriously, it fills me with so much joy."

Just as Violet Girl seems like she's about to wrap up this interlude, she gets one more gift: a fuchsia T-shirt screen-printed with a familiar drawing. Next to me, Jiya has clenched my arm and gone totally still. Ollie and I look at Rollo. "I had one shirt left, so I told them we'd saved it for her," he whispers, shrugging.

"This is so cool!" Violet Girl says, showing it to the audience. "Look, that's me!" Then, to our astonishment, she unloops her guitar and *pulls the shirt over her head*. Jiya's grip on me gets even stronger.

"Thank you again, lovelies. Thank you for being part of this. You are all beautiful." Violet Girl picks up her guitar again. "This one's for you."

While the opening riff of Violet Girl's next song begins its slow crescendo, Jiya throws her arms around Rollo. "How is it that one minute I want to punch you in the face, and the next, I could hug you *forever*?"

"That about sums up how I feel, too," says Ollie.

Rollo, only somewhat stunned to be the subject of Jiya's embrace, grins. "I told you I had it under control."

* * *

After the concert, Jiya takes Rollo home first, then drops Ollie and me off on my street because Ollie says he can just walk home.

"Have a nice *walk*," Jiya says to Ollie before winking at me and driving off.

Once her car disappears around the corner, the night becomes silent again under the streetlamps. The old Victorian is completely dark, but there's one light on in the bathroom window at my house.

"How'd you like your first concert?" Ollie asks, fiddling with the zipper of his jacket. He pulls it up halfway, and I have this irrational desire to reach over and yank it back down. "Was it what you expected?"

"Better," I say, grinning at him. "I'd go to a hundred more." I don't add *with you*, but I think he hears it anyway because his cheeks turn a little bit pink when he smiles back. Suddenly, overcome with a sensation that's much bigger than adrenaline, I stride forward and kiss him.

"I should go home, shouldn't I?" Ollie murmurs several minutes later, but he doesn't stop kissing me back.

I check my phone. I'm supposed to be home by midnight, but there's still almost an hour before then.

"Can I come over?"

Ollie is surprised. "Can you?" His eyes travel over to my house and the lit-up window.

"Sure." I grin at him again. "What my mom doesn't know can't hurt her, right?"

I might be imagining things, but Ollie seems to tense up at that. A second later, though, when I give him a curious look, he relaxes into a reassuring smile. "Right. Sure."

I sidle away from him, down the sidewalk. "But just in case," I say, "we should probably hurry!"

We run the whole way to his house, our hands clasped together, laughing because we're rushing and tripping over nothing. When we get there, I am out of breath, but feel like I could go another five miles. Even though the lights are all off, we sneak in through the back door, skipping around a delighted Dexter, trying not to giggle as we slip and slide across the marble floor to Ollie's room.

Kissing here feels different. It's not like when we're outside, when any moment someone could see us, and it's not like when we're in the car, when every move means hitting an elbow or a knee. Here, on a real bed—*Ollie's* bed—there are no more limits. Even time seems like it's stopped. Yet the kissing feels more urgent than ever, and still, somehow, not enough.

Eventually, we lie side by side on our backs, neither of us sure what ought to come next.

"You used to have those glow-in-the-dark stars," I say, pointing at the ceiling.

"Yeah, I took them down when my dad made me get this new furniture." Ollie gestures around the room at all the dark wood.

"Your bed is a lot bigger now."

Ollie laughs, blushing again. "It is."

I tilt my head back to study the ceiling, which is smooth and white, without a crack in sight. "I kind of liked the stars," I say, almost to myself.

Ollie stares up at the emptiness and is quiet for a moment. "I did, too." He shifts onto his side, and I can feel his eyes falling on me.

"I liked you for a long time, Ollie." I swallow, and my stomach tightens, but not quite in the same way it had only a few minutes before. This time, the wooziness has a bit of a sting.

There's a long pause before Ollie answers. "I know." He flips onto his back again. "I don't know why you did, though. I was pretty awful."

"You weren't always." I think back to that day we played Life together, the day his smile felt like a secret I'd uncovered for the first time. "You just seemed afraid to be yourself. Like you felt as if you couldn't be nice. But it was the times when you didn't worry about that . . ." The familiar feeling seeps through me, like warmed honey. "I don't know, that's when I couldn't help it."

Ollie half-closes his eyes, exhaling slowly. "I think I know when you decided you didn't like me anymore," he says. "It was the thing with Mr. Marchand, wasn't it?"

I look down at the duvet cover and pull at a thread.

"I couldn't even tell you why I was such a dick. I knew Corey and them were assholes. It didn't really matter what they thought. Except I couldn't be okay with that because I didn't know how." Ollie sits up partway, his voice sounding scratchy. "But you did. You *did* know."

Now it's my turn to stay quiet for a while before answering. "I didn't realize you still thought about that."

"I do. And every time, I wish I'd been more like you. I wish I hadn't been so hung up on trying to be one of the guys. Because deep down I've always wanted to tell you I'm sorry about what I said that day and what I did—and didn't do—all the days after that." He sucks in another breath. "I'm sorry I spent all those years pretending I didn't care about you, because it's not true."

I let Ollie's words—everything I'd ever wanted to hear, everything I didn't know I wanted to hear—fill my heart.

"It wasn't the Mr. Marchand thing," I say suddenly. "That wasn't when I stopped liking you." My heart beats faster as Ollie looks uncertain, and then a little glum. "Because really . . . I never stopped."

Ollie searches my eyes, his melancholy blurring into something else, and even before he leans down to kiss me, I know that it's going to be different yet again. As his lips trail from my mouth down to my neck, I feel fragile inside and out, like the lightest touch could break me. But I *want* to break apart. I want it almost more than he does.

And yet, it doesn't quite happen right away. Even after the Violet Girl shirt finds its way to the floor, along with Ollie's jacket and several other layers. Even after I feel Ollie through his jeans, and he's fumbled through the zipper on mine.

I remember what Jiya said, about how it wouldn't automatically work just because I was into Ollie, that I'd have to show him what to do. So I think back to what I've been discovering over the past week—what I did to finally manage it on my own—and I tell Ollie to roll over. Then I climb on top of him, like I would a pillow.

"This is good?" he whispers as I bring his fingers to where I want them to go.

"Yes," I say, kissing him, and even though I have to keep my hand over his, it *is* good.

It is very, very good. All the way to the end.

I'm still trying to catch my breath as I pull down at Ollie's jeans, already curious about what could happen next, when his phone goes off.

"Ignore it," says Ollie, kicking off one leg and then the other.

But the buzzing continues, and finally, he reaches for it on the nightstand. "Fuck." He flashes me an anguished look.

"What?" I say. "What time is it?"

Ollie shakes his head and shows me the screen. "It's Jiya," he says.

I grab the phone, but my eyes can't make any sense of what Jiya's written, and I only understand because I hear Ollie explaining it to me:

"Your mom called her because you weren't picking up. They had to take your grandpa to the hospital."

21

Ollie

FRANCINE IS SILENT THE WHOLE WAY TO THE hospital, curled up all the way against the window. She seems so closed up it's hard to imagine that she was in my room barely half an hour ago, sitting on top of me, opening up in a way that nearly sent me over the edge. I didn't think I could forget that—ever, maybe—but seeing her now, her face calm as stone, it already feels like a long time ago.

At first, she had been more frantic, both of us scrambling to retrieve our clothes from the floor, and she hardly even registered when Dad, probably woken up by the noise, appeared in the foyer.

"Where are you going?" he called after me as I ran past him, my arms barely in my jacket.

"Francine's grandpa is in the hospital," I snapped, grabbing my keys and then her hand, and we were out the door before he could ask any more questions.

Once we got in the car, Francine didn't look at me, and when

I asked if she was all right, the only thing she said was, "I'm okay." I wondered if she would cry, but she didn't—and I was struck by the fact that in all these years, I've never seen her cry.

When we get to the ER waiting room, I try to take her hand again, forgetting that nobody should see us together like that, and she pulls it away gently. There's nothing necessarily awful about the way she does it, except that somebody probably *should* hold her hand, and I can't.

"Francine!" Her mom emerges from the corridor, and her face is ashen. "Where were you? I thought you said you'd be home by twelve. I called you over and over, and you didn't answer!"

"I was at Jiya's house," Francine lies, because that's what Jiya had told her to say. "I'm sorry—we went there after the concert, and I lost track of time."

"We were so worried! We thought something had happened to you." Francine's mom is speaking in hushed Cantonese, but it's clear she's upset. "We thought you were still out, and it was so late. You know that's dangerous, especially for girls."

This is the first time I've run into Francine's mom since I found out about their secret, and it makes me consider her differently. I notice things I never did before—the white in her pulled-back hair, for instance, and the smudges on her glasses that she probably can't see. I wish she'd take a moment to wipe them off.

"I'm sorry," Francine says again, almost like she's memorized a script. "My phone was on silent, and I just didn't hear it."

"That was so thoughtless, to worry your grandpa like that. And now he's here in the hospital." Her mom's voice climbs a little, the anxiety hardening into an accusation. "Honestly, what's gotten into you, Francine? You're usually never like this."

"She didn't know," I say, because I can't stand to hear anybody, even her mom, calling Francine *thoughtless*. "She came as soon as she could."

Francine's mom looks at me then and understanding seems to pass over her face for the first time. I realize suddenly that I'm wearing my shirt inside-out, and I kick myself for not having made sure to put it on the right way.

"I asked Ollie to give me a ride," Francine says, though it's really unclear whether that explanation helps things or not.

But curiously, her mom lets it go, despite what seems to me like pretty obvious evidence that Francine is lying—something I thought *would've* warranted being chewed out for. Instead, she just reaches for Francine and sighs, squeezing her tight.

"You're a good girl." She sounds so sure it's almost willful. "I know you'll always be."

Over her mom's shoulder, Francine looks pained.

Suddenly, I wish everybody could just tell each other the truth—Francine, her mom, her grandpa. Me. But this is definitely not a great time for that, so I stay silent. "It's nice of you to come," Francine's mom says to me. "My dad will be glad you're here." She starts to lead us toward the admitted patients' area, and when Francine trails after her, so do I.

Francine's a gūng, it seems, had been experiencing unexplained nausea, which escalated into vomiting that they couldn't stop. They gave him some antinausea medication but were waiting to decide what to do next.

As we approach, Francine's dad draws back the curtain divider to let us in. A Pòh is sitting in the corner, her puffer coat bunched in her lap. She looks exhausted but manages a weak smile for us. "Pìhng and Fōng are here," she says to nobody in particular.

Francine's a gūng, however, is wordless as he lies there, his arm taped up with IV tubing. Asleep, he looks small and already ghostly, like he might crumble away if he so much as opens his eyes. It's weird the way hospital beds can have that effect—the only other time I've been in the ER, when Isaac broke his arm playing basketball a few years ago, he too had seemed shrunken against the sterile pillows. Maybe it's all the equipment that's crowded around, or the unfamiliar proportions of the mattresses. Or maybe it's just the sense that getting into one of those beds means, inevitably, having to embrace mortality itself.

"When was the nurse last here?" Francine asks, her voice quiet but brisk. She glances at the screen showing A Gūng's vitals, and I have this vision of her, ten years from now, as a medical resident in some hospital, taking charge the way she's doing here. It suits her, I realize. The more I think about it, the more I see how she *would* be a good doctor—she's smart, kind, and not afraid to boss you if she thought it would save your life.

"Just a few minutes ago," Francine's dad tells her. "She said the doctor will check back in soon."

Francine's a gūng rouses himself on the bed, and she goes over to kneel by his side. "How are you, A Gūng?" she asks. "Are you still feeling nauseous?" The sound of her talking seems to wake him up a little more.

"Fōng a?" he says. He does seem happy to see her, and for a second, I fill up with warmth, watching them together. But then he adds, "Where's Pìhng?"

Everybody else turns to look at me, except Francine, who keeps her eyes on her grandpa and her expression unchanged. "Pìhng is visiting you, too," she says. "Come over here, Ollie."

I walk up to the bed and stand next to her. "A Gūng hóu," I say, feeling stupid because he obviously isn't good at all. "I hope you feel better soon."

"Thank you, Pìhng," Francine's a gūng says. "Please, sit down. It's good to see you."

Francine backs away from the bed to give me space, except the last thing I want to do is take her place. I almost turn around and slip back into the hallway that very moment.

But then Francine's a gūng smiles at me, and it's softer and sadder without his dentures, like time is already reclaiming the lines that define him. So when Francine says, "Go on, Ollie, sit," her eyes needing me for the first time since we got to this goddamn ER, I feel like I have no choice but to go along with it, and sit.

* * *

The thing about being in a hospital is that it involves a lot of waiting. We wait and wait for the doctor to come talk to us, and once she says that Francine's a gūng will be moved to another room for overnight observation, we wait and wait for the team to get it all set up. Then we wait for them to transfer him, and then we wait for the doctor to check in again.

In the middle of all this waiting, some of Francine's extended family arrive. Most of them I haven't seen in ages, including Sandy, Francine's cousin, who is now a senior in high school. Francine says Sandy isn't that close to her grandpa because she only sees him a couple of times a year—she's really into tennis now and is away most weekends.

"Are you guys, like, dating or something?" Sandy asks, intrigued. The three of us have been sent back into the waiting room, as if the adults imagined there was a kids' table out there.

I hesitate before responding, but Francine has a ready answer. "Ollie is pretending to be A Gūng's honorary male heir," she explains. When Sandy looks utterly befuddled, I wish we could just tell people we're together.

The real surprise of the night, though, is that Wáih, aka Wesley, shows up. "You drove all the way here from LA?" Francine asks, sounding more incredulous than Wesley seems to like.

"I would've," he says. "Obviously." He tugs his beanie over his hair. "But I was already meeting some friends in Irvine," he admits.

"Oh, that makes more sense," says Francine, and based on what she's told me about Wesley, it does. But based on *his* reaction, she maybe could've laid off a little on the matter-of-factness.

"I need a coffee." Sandy hops to her feet. "I'm going to see if the cafeteria is open. Anyone want to come?"

"I will," says Francine. "Ollie, Wesley, do you want anything?" When we shake our heads, Sandy slings her purse over her shoulder, and they disappear around the corner.

"Ugh, she is *such* a drag," says Wesley.

I tense up. "Um . . . you mean Francine?"

"Yeah." Wesley slouches in his chair. "She's always martyring herself and then making you feel bad for not doing the same."

My initial reaction is that I want to shove this guy—who does he think he is anyway? He's been completely useless all this time, so much so that *I* had to be involved, and now he's bagging on Francine for just trying her best?

Yet there's also a part of me—no matter how hard I push it down—that does know what he means. The part that remembers how I might have said the same thing once. The part that's stirring in a way I don't like.

"She's not trying to make you feel bad," I snap.

"Wait." Wesley arches his eyebrows. "You know Francine?"

That he can't seem to believe this only irritates me more. "Yeah, I do."

"I totally thought you were with Sandy." He leans forward

to get a better look at me. "I didn't know Francine had any normal friends." He seems to reconsider whether or not the description fits me.

"I'm helping her with something," I reply testily, and before I can think better of it, I'm telling him about The Plan, too.

Wesley stares at me like he thinks I'm a clown, but not the funny kind. "You're joking."

"I know it all sounds over-the-top, but it seemed important to your a gūng—"

"He's not my a gūng," Wesley points out. "He's my a pòh's brother, so that makes him my káuh gūng, technically."

"Okay, well he's not *my* anything, but Francine asked me to do this, so I'm here." I get up and stalk over to the window, wishing I'd just gone to the cafeteria after all. Wesley seems like he sucks.

He's squinting at me now. "But you don't think the whole thing is . . . kind of weird."

"I mean, I do, but—" I stop. But what? How do I tell him the weirdness is beside the point? "I think she just didn't want him to feel so depressed."

Wesley, clearly over this conversation, puts on his headphones. "Maybe it would help if he got over some of his old-school ideas."

It's odd—I don't even disagree with that, and yet somehow I still feel like I'm in an argument.

"Maybe it would also help if you visit when you say you will," I retort.

This makes Wesley pause, but only for a second. "I don't know what Francine told you," he says, "but it's definitely not the whole story."

We hear footsteps in the distance, which means Francine and Sandy are probably coming back, but now I'm curious about what he means. "How so?"

Wesley tugs down again on his hat so that it almost reaches his eyes. "Look, I know I should've showed up for Thanksgiving, okay?" He slides lower in his chair. "My boyfriend had just dumped me, so I was dealing with some stuff."

"Oh." I wasn't expecting this. "I'm sorry." I feel awkward for having brought up the topic. "Maybe you could've told them that?"

"No way," says Wesley. "My own grandma doesn't even know I'm gay. And it's not like Francine's grandpa would've been sympathetic. He's always asking me when I'm going to get a girlfriend."

I obviously haven't discussed the topic with Francine's a gūng, but Wesley is probably right.

"Anyway, all I'm saying is, sometimes you gotta take care of yourself," Wesley continues. "Francine could learn a thing or two about that—she's always trying way too hard to be a devoted granddaughter." He turns his attention back to his screen. "But you know she's not even *related* to her grandpa?"

I freeze. What the actual fuck—Wesley knows? "Isn't that supposed to be a secret?"

Wesley shrugs. "Yeah, but my grandma accidentally let it

slip once. Apparently Francine's mom isn't really her mom. Isn't that wild?" Then he seems to realize something and turns down his music. "Wait, how did *you* know?"

The sound of something crinkly hitting the floor makes us both look toward the hallway, where Francine has reappeared with Sandy.

"What are you guys talking about?" Her face is stricken, and it's clear she heard everything.

"Nothing," I say quickly, but she's backing away, like she's in a horror movie and I'm the monster. "Francine, wait!"

"This was for you." Sandy scoops up a package of strawberry Pop-Tarts from the floor, and I snatch them from her as I run after Francine.

I catch up to her at the end of the hallway, but she keeps on walking. "Why would Wesley say that stuff?" Her voice is small and packed tight, as though it might implode any second.

At this point, I know I just have to tell her. But once again, I can't seem to find the right words. When my silence becomes ugly and bloated between us, she walks even faster.

"I don't believe him," she says.

I finally pull myself together to answer. "It's true, Francine."

"*No.*" She balls her hands into fists at her sides. "That doesn't make any sense."

"Don't worry about it right now," I suggest, grappling for anything that might sound comforting. "You can ask your parents—"

I mean to add *later*, but she's already marching purposefully toward her a gūng's room.

"Hold on," I call out, following her. "Maybe you should take a breather first. You know, figure out how you should bring it up. I don't want you to—"

She spins around abruptly, and the look in her eye stops me. "You're the one who said I should make decisions for myself, right?"

I'm taken aback, but I manage a nod. "Right."

"Well, I want to know the truth. Now."

I don't try to argue with her any further, and soon we see Francine's parents standing in the hallway, speaking to each other softly.

"What's the matter, bǎo bǎo?" asks her mom, picking up instantly that something isn't right. She holds an arm out, but Francine stands firm, a few feet out of reach.

"Wesley told me that Mom and I aren't related," Francine says to her parents, and it's like an explosion you can see before you're overcome by the roar. They both look stunned.

"Of course I'm your mom, Francine." Her mom recovers first. "I'll always be."

But this response only riles up Francine even more.

"Is Wesley telling the truth?" she asks outright.

Francine's dad clears his throat. "Francine," he says, and his tone tells her everything she didn't want to hear.

Once again, she takes off, this time sprinting so hard, I can barely keep up. She doesn't stop running until we're outside the hospital, the harsh lights of the entrance casting the parking lot into darkness.

"Why didn't you tell me?" Her voice is sharp, and she bends over like she's got a side cramp. She doesn't look at me.

"I wanted to." The words come out pleading and stupidly inadequate. "I was going to, I swear. But your a gūng said not to—"

"A Gūng?" Francine glances up at me now, only her face is more twisted up than ever. "That's how you know—he told you?" She stumbles backward and almost trips over the curb. "He told *you*?"

"I don't think he meant to," I try to explain. "No one was supposed to know. Not Wesley, not me."

"But *I* should have known," she says. "Shouldn't I?"

My shoulders slump. "I'm really sorry, Francine."

"I don't understand why you didn't say anything." She drops down to sit on the curb, burying her face in her hands. "This whole time, I thought we were—" She stops, hesitating over what to call us, and the fact that she's unsure makes me feel like a complete dirtbag. Because I'm the reason she's unsure.

I squeeze my eyes shut. "I know I should've told you," I say. "But every time I tried, I couldn't do it. I was afraid it would make you upset."

"*You* were afraid?" Francine shakes her head like she can't believe it. "Ollie, when are you going to realize that you can't always be thinking of yourself?"

My chest tightens when she says that. "I'm not."

"You are," Francine says, and it's a distracted observation, almost careless. "You're always so worried about feeling uncomfortable. Except sometimes people need you to do things that are hard, and you can't always take the easy way out." She rubs at her eyes. "But you—you never want to do the hard thing, do you?"

"That's not true," I argue even though she's kind of right. But how do I explain that this time, the reason I couldn't do the hard thing wasn't me? That ultimately, it *was* because I was thinking of somebody else—and that somebody was her? Because that's the thing: I didn't want to crush her. I didn't want her to feel sad and angry and alone.

All the things I've probably made her feel now.

"Maybe you should just go," she says.

I sigh, because everything seems wrong and I wish we could reset somehow. "I can take you home," I offer. "Or somewhere else. Wherever you want to go." Maybe if we get away from here, where we're alone again, I can make her understand.

But when I reach for her arm, she pulls it away. "Don't, Ollie," she says, the words catching in her throat.

"Francine, just hear me out—"

"I'll see you later."

I still don't move. "Tomorrow?" The way my voice breaks, though, I already know the answer.

"I'm not sure," she says and turns to go. "I'll have to see how my a gūng is doing."

She sounds totally calm, as though she's folded up all her feelings like laundry to be put away, and I'm kind of surprised. Her grandpa, after all, was in on the secret. Why isn't she angry at him? Come to think of it, why am I the only one she's shutting out? Maybe if it wasn't so late or if I wasn't so tired, I would understand her reasoning better. But this whole conversation, I've felt like my insides were crumpling into a ball, so tiny that I've become almost nothing, and now there's no chance for any kind of understanding at all.

"Are you gonna ask why *he* didn't tell you?" I say, and she pauses at the entrance. The doors open automatically, but she doesn't step through them.

"Maybe," she answers after a moment.

"I don't think you are," I say to her back. "No, you're gonna walk right back in there and act like everything is okay, just because you think that's what your family expects you to do. Because your grandpa's sick, so nothing that's important to you—even if it's something as huge as this—could possibly take precedence."

"I didn't say that." She sounds pained, but I'm too wound up to stop.

"And yeah, I should've told you about your mom as soon as I found out. But you know who's been keeping it from you for *years*? Your family. Every last one of them. I bet that hurts a lot more than what I've done, only you won't acknowledge it because you're constantly trying so fucking hard to be there for *them*. Instead, you'd rather take it all out on me, when I just wanted to protect you in the same messed up way all of you are always doing."

"Ollie," says Francine, shooting a glare over her shoulder. Her voice is low with anger. "I told you to *go*."

"Okay, sure, if that's what you really want, I'll go." I shrug, and my shoulders are so tight, I can barely move them. "But you can decide to never talk to me again—you can keep ignoring all the feelings you don't like, all the ones you can't do anything about—except you're going to find out life isn't only about *doing* the hard things. Sometimes, it *is* about feeling them. And maybe I'm one to talk because I barely have a handle on any of it, but it seems to me if you don't let yourself feel the bad stuff, you're not gonna let yourself have the good stuff either. And the worst part is, you'll be too busy lying to yourself to notice."

I regret saying all that as soon as I do, but once you spew that kind of shit, there's no taking it back. Francine is staring at me, her expression impossible to read, and I start to second-guess whether she's actually heard me until she opens her mouth.

"I was wrong, Ollie," she says, her lips dry. "You *are* awful."

This time, I'm the one who turns around to run.

22

Francine

A GŪNG IS RELEASED FROM THE HOSPITAL THE next morning, which means that the doctors don't find any further reason for him to stay. It also means, however, that they're not sure why he needed to go in the first place, either. I grilled the resident who was responsible for discharging him, but she didn't really have the answers I wanted.

"It could have just been side effects from the chemo," she told me, standing with her hands clasped in that way that doctors have—deferential but still closed off. "It could've been the cancer itself. At his age, there are so many different factors at play. We're just glad he's well enough to go home."

I try to keep the conversation going a little longer, maybe because I've refused to talk to anyone else all night, but eventually, Dad stops me. "We should go, Francine," he says gently, and I retreat into silence again.

At home, I head straight to bed because I'm suddenly so tired, I want to throw up. I doze fitfully until noon and wake up with the imprint of my bracelet on my cheek, but somehow, I feel as if I hadn't slept at all. The anger that I didn't know what to do with last night is still there, and as I stare up at the ceiling, I feel it burning away the box I've put it in.

Because Ollie was wrong—I *do* feel angry. I *am* feeling the bad stuff. Maybe I haven't always wanted to before, it's true, but I am now, and it's both unfamiliar and overwhelming. Ever since I can remember, my family has been the one thing I was sure I knew inside and out. I saw so much of myself reflected in them and our relationship. But as it turns out, there's this huge piece of my past that I had no idea about. That even *Wesley* knew about before me. What does it mean about who I was if I didn't know where I came from? And what does it mean that not a single person cared to tell me?

Someone, probably Mom, came in earlier and covered me with a blanket, but I fling it off now and roll out of bed.

When I stumble into the living room, Mom and Dad are at the dining table together, and it strikes me as unusual for some reason I can't immediately pinpoint. Then I realize it's because I've never seen them this *still*, both doing nothing other than sitting there, an open package of pineapple cake biscuits between them. Dad isn't supposed to have them—he's trying to keep his cholesterol levels low—but I'm pretty sure he's the one who's eaten almost all of them.

"How did you sleep, Francine?" asks Mom. Her face is sallow, the same shade as the one biscuit left in the plastic tray.

I don't answer and instead pull out a chair at the other end of the table. Then I fold my hands, which feel dry and cold. "I'd like to know the whole story."

Mom looks to Dad, who finishes the pineapple cake and clears his throat.

Dad used to live in Florida, which I did actually know—I was born in Tampa, a biographical quirk that always felt random until now—but back then, he was married to the mom I never met. While he was studying to become a mechanic, he worked at a Chinese restaurant that was owned by her uncle. It was in a tiny strip mall off Route 19, the lone highway running down the coast, and the only customers they ever got were white people. My mom was a waitress while she was pregnant with me, and Dad says she used to joke that I helped her earn extra tips.

It's striking how vivid these details still are for Dad, especially given that I've literally never heard him talk about this before, and that makes my throat bunch up in a funny way. Involuntarily, I think of how Ollie would probably be crying already—but I don't know why that matters because I won't be seeing him anytime soon.

Dad, however, gets quiet when he tells me how she died. He doesn't say much, only that it was an aneurysm and it was sudden and there wasn't anything they could do. Sometimes, Dad says, things happen for no good reason at all.

I swallow and nod.

Dad remarried, this time to Mom—the one I do know—because a friend of a relative knew her family back in China.

Mom wanted to come to America, and marriage was the fastest way. Did she mind if her new husband already had a four-month-old? No, she says, she didn't. Not in the slightest. Two years later, Mom came to Florida, too, and shortly after, they moved to California, where the rest of her family was—and where no one knew about what had happened to Dad and me. Then Mom found out she couldn't have any kids of her own, so I became the baby she might never have had, and it felt like fate had taken care of all three of us.

"How come you never told me any of this before?" I look down at my hands, mulling over these revelations.

Dad slides the empty pineapple cake tray back into its packaging and takes a minute to answer. "You have to understand, Francine," he says, "we only ever wanted what was best for you."

"You were so young." Mom's eyes glisten over, though she doesn't actually cry. "At the time, it seemed like the right thing to do. We hoped to shoulder the burden of tragedy for you as long as possible."

"I'm old enough now, though." I lean forward and grip onto the table. "I've been old enough for a while."

Dad takes a deep breath. "I see now that we should have done things differently," he says. "But I thought that moving forward was the way for me to shield you from the pain I was feeling. Maybe I hoped that protecting you would protect me, too."

His sadness seems heavy, like he hasn't set it down for years, and only then do I begin to grasp the weight of what he and Mom have carried.

"I didn't need you to do that," I say. "I could've handled the truth. I could've helped you work through it."

"No, bǎo bǎo," says Mom. "Right now, it's our job to take care of you, not the other way around."

A Pòh appears in the kitchen doorway with a bowl of steaming ramen, which she walks over and places in front of me. The familiar aroma of the chicken flavor envelops me, just the way it always has, and I feel my head clear up.

Mom and Dad shouldn't have kept the past a secret from me for so long, and I still have a lot of questions—about my biological mother, about the parts of my childhood I don't remember. They didn't need to lie to me, even though I understand why they did. But they're still my parents, and A Pòh and A Gūng are still my grandparents. In that sense, nothing about my family, and how I relate to them, has changed.

Unless, that is, I want it to.

I think again of the argument I had with Ollie, and I wonder if maybe all lies, even the ones you tell because you care, are more complicated than you expect. Maybe the lying takes more away from yourself than I realized. And maybe that's a good enough reason to stop doing it.

"Is A Gūng up yet?" I say.

"He probably will be in a little bit," Mom replies, looking at the clock.

I slurp up some of the ramen and chew thoughtfully. "I

think I'd like to tell him about The Plan."

Everyone pauses when I say that, even A Pòh, who's standing at the sink. When I repeat it for her in Cantonese, she nods and picks up the washcloth. "Yes," she says. "That is a good idea."

Dad gets up to toss out the pineapple cake packaging, but Mom stays seated, watching me. "Did you and Ollie have a fight?"

I answer honestly. "Yes, but not about that."

"He seems like a nice boy," Mom observes.

It's hard to tell the difference between this rush of anger and the exhilaration I used to feel not even twenty-four hours ago—they spring from the same soft place, where I've never allowed anyone but Ollie. Where I've never *wanted* to allow anyone but Ollie. I think about the way I let him kiss me, and everywhere I let him touch, and I feel sick enough to curl back up in bed for another six hours. He couldn't tell me the truth when it mattered, but then had no trouble hurling all those awful words at me last night. I'm embarrassed by how much I hoped he was something other than what he was. I believed in him so long because I wanted, desperately, for him to be nice.

In reality, he's just Ollie.

"Not as nice as you'd think," I say to Mom.

She reaches over to push a lock of my hair behind my ear. "Sometimes, I forget you're growing up," she says. "I wish we could still protect you from every kind of pain."

I stir my chopsticks in the ramen broth, watching the little bits of green onion swirl around. "It's all right, Mom," I reassure her. "I'm done with Ollie."

And it's not even a lie, because I am.

On Tuesday, Ms. Abdi decides to assign a four-person lab, which I find a bit excessive because I'm perfectly capable of measuring the anerobic respiration of yeast cells alone. Still, there's really no good way out of it.

"Let's keep it simple, loves," she says. "Go ahead and group up with the table immediately next to you."

Jiya glances at me to her right and Ollie to her left, and then bends all the way forward so she can cut through our cold front to make eye contact with Rollo. He gives her a sympathetic shrug.

"I guess I'll go get the materials," I say, standing up.

Jiya's eyes track me as I walk all the way around the table so I won't have to pass Ollie's seat. "I'll come with you," she says, and hops to her feet.

"What's up?" I ask as she follows me to the side of the room.

"I should be asking you that." Jiya leans back against the cabinet, her elbows resting on the counter. "This whole year, I've never seen you *not* volunteer to pass out the lab worksheets."

"Oh." I place five beakers on our tray. "That's probably an exaggeration."

Jiya grabs a fistful of balloons and tosses them next to the beakers. "Hey." She sounds more serious now. "Are you sure you don't want to talk to Ollie?"

Yesterday, Jiya had come over with a tub of chocolate chip ice cream, and I'd told her about everything that happened on Saturday night. She was, understandably, dumbfounded by the revelation about Mom and agreed that Ollie had been completely in the wrong when he kept it from me. She did not seem to agree that I should stop speaking to him, but it's fine if we have different opinions.

I check the worksheet and put back one of the balloons. "We only need five," I point out. "And yes."

"Rollo says Ollie feels really shitty about the whole thing." Jiya isn't giving up easily.

"Well, it's a good thing he has Rollo, isn't it?"

When I've gathered the rest of the lab supplies, Jiya helps me carry everything back to our table. Rollo is whispering urgently to Ollie, who looks sullen sitting low in his chair, but falls silent as soon as we approach.

"Thanks, France," says Rollo, like he thinks a new nickname will somehow cheer me up. "You're the best, as always. Isn't that right, Ollie?"

Ollie looks like he might murder Rollo and doesn't reply.

"Okay, Francine," says Jiya quickly. "What's the first step?"

I fill the beakers according to the instructions: 100 mL of water, 4 mL of yeast, and then increasing amounts of glucose in each one. It's soothing to go through the motions, to measure out each substance and pour it into the appropriate receptacle. I don't have to even look at Ollie, though he's sitting right there. He's not helpful—the whole time, he's just scraping something into the apron of the table with a ballpoint pen—but it's whatever, because I don't need him anyway.

Rollo and Jiya, however, are unusually gung-ho about participating, despite having spent the last eight months not showing an ounce of interest in even the more exciting labs we've done. I mean, *I* think fermentation is cool, but I wouldn't have expected them to.

"Allow me," says Rollo, nabbing an orange balloon from our tray. He stretches it out a few times with finesse, like he does this professionally, and then inflates it with one efficient breath. Apparently, Rollo is a trove of hidden talents.

Just not particularly useful ones. "Thanks, Rollo." I swipe the balloon from his mouth and let it deflate with a hiss. "But these are for the beakers, not you."

Everyone watches me cap off each beaker with a different colored balloon, and then swirl the solution inside to activate the yeast. Next, I punch five minutes into the timer on my phone and set it down in front of me.

"What now?" Jiya asks.

"We wait," I say.

In the silence, Rollo gets an idea. "Jiya, we should discuss your next art project. But over there. In the corner." He tilts his head and inches away from the table.

Jiya squints at Rollo's pantomiming for a second. "All right, this is getting ridiculous." She grabs his arm and pulls him along. "We're going to give you two some space to talk," she says to Ollie and me. "Just *consider* it," she adds when I start to protest.

"Actually, I did want to tell you about my new idea—" I hear Rollo say as they walk away.

Then it's just the two of us, separated by Jiya's empty seat.

Ollie stares up at the clock on the wall, I focus on the changing numbers on my phone screen, and neither of us speaks as the seconds tick by. Other groups chatter around us as usual, but the only thing I hear is the thumping of my heart in my ears.

"Francine." Ollie taps his fingers on the table. "Look, I—"

"We're supposed to be doing this lab." I gesture at the beakers. "We have to pay attention."

Ollie stops talking and we watch the yeast in silence. The balloons remain totally still.

"Are they supposed to—"

"It takes a few minutes for enough carbon dioxide to release," I interrupt. "The balloons will eventually fill up. I think." I pretend to verify this on the worksheet even though it's obvious that's what'll happen.

Eventually, Ollie coughs a little. "How's your a gūng doing?"

"He's been better."

"What about you?"

"Could be worse."

"Francine, will you just let me say I'm sorry?" Ollie leans over the table, his arm outstretched so that his fingers can almost touch my hand. He looks so sad and handsome, I have to turn away. But I don't say anything.

"I fucked up, Francine." Ollie sighs and sits forward. "If I could do it all over again, I would."

I want to keep ignoring him, but I can't help the words that spill out of my mouth. "You made me feel like I didn't matter, Ollie. Like how I felt didn't matter. Even though you're the one who's always going off about how I need to focus more on what *I* want."

"I know," says Ollie, "and I'm sorry."

"But I guess it's no big deal, right? Because I'm just lying to myself anyway."

Ollie rubs his forehead and forces his eyes shut. "I shouldn't have said that," he says. "I really didn't mean it."

"It's fine, Ollie. If you ask me, it's worse when you *don't* say what's on your mind." That makes him wince, but I barrel on. "In fact, if there's anything else you haven't told me, go ahead. I'm listening."

"There is," he almost shouts, and I'm surprised by how agitated he seems. "I've been trying to explain, but I keep screwing it up." His hands find their way into his hair. "The thing is, Francine, it kills me that I hurt you so much because that's exactly what I *didn't* want. Because the truth is . . . the real truth is . . . I think I—"

The timer goes off then, and I struggle to find the right button to stop it. If I thought my heart was beating loudly earlier, now it's *really* going. When I finally manage to cut off the beeping, I see Rollo and Jiya coming back our way, escorted by a disapproving Ms. Abdi.

"She caught us shirking our lab duties," says Jiya, thoroughly untroubled.

"We weren't *shirking* per se—" Rollo tries.

"It's been nice seeing you in class, Rollo," Ms. Abdi interjects before heading to her desk. "But it'd be nice if you actually learned something, too."

"I learn a ton from you, Ms. Abdi," he calls after her.

I glance over at Ollie, but he seems to have withdrawn into himself again, and I'm guessing I won't be hearing what he meant to say after all. I pick up some string to measure the circumference of the first balloon, trying to focus on the miracle of yeast producing energy without oxygen—and not on my own sudden inability to breathe.

23

Ollie

FUCK, DID I JUST ALMOST TELL FRANCINE I LOVE her?

I spend the rest of the period too spooked to say anything else—not when Jiya and Rollo pitch in to help measure balloons and read out the measurements, and not when Francine hands me her worksheet so I can numbly copy down her answers to questions like *What are the variables in this experiment?*

My mind's too muddled to know.

When the bell rings, I bolt out of the classroom without so much as a wave, and I avoid even Rollo all day, willing myself to not think about anything. Only after school is over and I've shut myself into my car, my hands clutching the steering wheel, do I let the truth settle over me.

I glance over at the empty passenger seat, where I'd gotten used to Francine sitting.

Fuck.

I don't know what I was expecting it to be like. What it *is* like is having a hole in your heart that keeps getting bigger the more you fill it. Except the clincher is, you *want* the hole. The hole is the beauty of it—making space for somebody else is the only way to fill up yourself. I didn't understand that before, not with any of the other girls I thought I liked in the past, and maybe I wasn't really ready to. Now, of course, I get it. But I wonder if it's too late.

The old me would've been glad that I wasn't able to risk making a fool of myself today. My apology didn't mean shit to Francine—why would she want to hear that I loved her? Plus, doesn't it seem way, way too soon? I'd have to be desperate to bare it all like that so fast.

But I also can't *not* tell her. Not after everything that's just happened. Not unless I want Francine to be right about my sad-sack inability to get out of my own way whenever I need to do a hard but important thing.

Is she right?

My stomach is still churning when I get home, and I don't notice that the house isn't empty until I walk right into my brother in the kitchen.

"Hey, dude," he says, chowing down on some shrimp chips. "What's up with you?"

"Isaac?" I blink at him. "What are you doing here?"

"Didn't you see my texts in the family convo?" He tosses the last chip into his mouth and then wads the empty bag into a ball. "I have an internship interview in LA tomorrow."

I forgot I'd shut off notifications on that thread.

"Oh, okay, cool." I start to inch away, except Isaac gestures at me to open the trash can in the corner, so I step down on the lever for him. He throws the chip bag and sinks the shot.

"Still got it," he says, grinning.

I give him an exaggerated double thumbs-up and turn toward the door, hoping the conversation will end there, but he calls after me.

"Hey, really, though," he says. "Are you okay?"

"Yeah," I reply, brushing him off. "I'm fine."

He leans against the island counter, studying me. "Are you sure?"

Isaac sounds weirdly genuine, which makes me wonder if maybe talking to him could be okay, since he *is* marginally better than Dad. I'm also clearly flailing here, so that may be impairing my judgment. Whatever it is, I decide to take the chance.

"Have you ever *really* liked a girl?" I ask. "Like . . . a lot?"

Isaac straightens up, still mostly chill, but there's a bit of stiffness to his shoulders that means he wasn't prepared enough for the question to lie. "Sure," he says.

I shift the weight of my backpack from one side to the other. "How did you, like, tell her?"

Isaac frowns. "Do you mean like . . . saying the L-word?"

"Um, yeah. I guess."

For one whole second, I think he might actually answer seriously, but then a stupid smirk stretches across his face.

"Hold up," he says. "Who's the girl?"

Goddamn Isaac. "Does it matter?"

"Of course it matters. I wanna know who's got you whipped."

"Just . . . forget I said anything."

Isaac follows me as I hurry out of the kitchen. "Come on, lil bro!" he teases. "You can tell me."

"Yeah, no."

He's still laughing, and I'm sure he's trying to remember the names of girls I know so he can keep making fun of me. Fortunately, I haven't mentioned anybody to him in years. Unfortunately, that means the girl he comes up with is—

"Francine." He snaps his fingers at me. "It's Francine, isn't it?"

"Fuck off, Isaac."

"Wow, I can't believe you finally caved. She was such a weirdo." He snickers, then pauses, like a thought has just occurred to him. "Wait, did she get hot or something?"

I whirl around and ram into him hard even though I know he's stronger than me. "I *said* fuck off!"

Isaac is so startled by my reaction that he doesn't even shove me back. He just stands there. "Oh man," he marvels. "It *is* Francine."

I'm about to storm off to my room and shut the door in his face, but then I stop. Why does it upset me so much that he knows it's Francine? I *do* like her. And I'm sick of him making me feel like that's some big joke.

So I take a deep breath instead.

"Yeah," I say calmly. "It is Francine. And you know what? Maybe I do love her. I thought you'd have some helpful advice, but it's fine that you don't. Just don't talk about her like she doesn't matter, and don't act like caring about somebody is embarrassing when it's probably the best fucking thing that could ever happen to you."

As Isaac stares at me, the door to Dad's office opens, and he emerges with his roller suitcase. I didn't even realize he was still in town. We haven't really talked since our last argument—in general, he's acted like it didn't happen, which is his MO.

"What's going on out here?" he says, tapping at his phone.

Before I can answer, Isaac—still dumbfounded—explains, "Ollie is in love with Francine."

Great. Exactly what I wanted to avoid—getting Dad involved. He's looking at me like he wants to know if Isaac is kidding, and I brace myself for the inevitable piling on about being too invested in "some girl."

Dad, however, surprises me. "Leave your brother alone, Isaac."

That's all he says—there's no lecture, no additional explanation—but it silences us both.

Then Dad's phone buzzes, and he swipes at the screen. "I'm heading out to catch my flight," he says. "Isaac, good luck tomorrow. And, Ollie, I'll see you on Monday."

When he's gone, I barely glance at Isaac as I head toward my room. I don't regret revealing what I did, but maybe that's enough sharing for one day.

"I never said it," Isaac says suddenly, and it takes me a moment to understand that he's decided to answer my original question after all. He appears in the doorway, crossing and then uncrossing his arms, his voice subdued. "But I wish I had."

That's when it hits me, with a clarity that makes me wonder why I never realized it before. All of these hang-ups—about feelings, about being soft—are part of the same bullshit. The more I think about it, the more I see how almost every guy I know—including Francine's grandpa and Dad and Isaac—still seems to believe in some version of "being a man" that doesn't always serve them. Even I've held on for so much longer than I realized. Even I'm having trouble letting go.

Not anymore.

"I'll be back later," I tell Isaac, and I rush past him, stopping only to refill Dexter's water bowl before I dash out the front door.

It only takes me a few minutes to get to Francine's house. I leap across her lawn in two strides and jog up the front steps, my breath jagged as I climb the steps to ring the doorbell. No one answers, so I rap on the metal screen door instead, the clangs echoing the hyped-up pounding of my heart.

Finally, the curtains in the window part, and Francine's a pòh appears. Her guarded expression transforms into happiness when she sees it's me, and I bend over awkwardly to wave at her.

"Pìhng a?" Her voice is muffled as she undoes the locks one by one. "Come in, come in!"

There doesn't seem to be any sign of Francine, but when her a pòh directs me to sit on the couch, I do it anyway. The first thing I'm asked is whether I've eaten.

"Yes," I lie, because I don't want anybody to go through the trouble of serving me a plate of fruit right now. "I've actually just come to see Fōng."

"She is at the library today, volunteering," says Francine's a pòh. "I can let her know you were here."

Francine's a gūng shuffles in from the hallway and seems surprised to find me here. "Pìhng, you are visiting?"

I haven't seen him since that night in the hospital, and he looks frail, but actually, not any more than usual. He must know that Francine found out about the secret, and I wonder if he thinks I'm the one who told her. As far as possible culprits go, I do seem pretty likely, especially if he wasn't aware that Wesley knew, and for a second I'm worried he's going to chew me out.

Instead, however, he gestures at the hand-knit beanie he's wearing. It's striped with navy and red, the colors absurdly bold.

"A Pòh just made this," he tells me. "It's nice, isn't it?"

He says that playfully, but the hat does look good. "I like it," I tell him as he sits down in the armchair across from me.

Francine's a pòh, who had gone into the kitchen, reemerges with the expected tray of oranges and sets them on the coffee table.

Francine's a gūng smiles at me. "I thought you would not be

coming by anymore," he says. "Fōng told me about The Plan."

Ugh, she must *really* not want to see me.

My hand drops to my lap, and suddenly my stomach feels sour. Maybe it would be better to skip the oranges after all.

Francine's a gūng must notice how distressed I look because he leans toward me. "Is something the matter, Pìhng?"

That's when I register how chill he seems, despite knowing the truth. "You're not upset that we lied?" I ask, somewhat shocked.

He chuckles a little, which turns into a sigh. "I can see that you and Fōng had good intentions, and I don't blame you." He takes off his hat and examines it, feeling the texture of the knit. "Perhaps I myself am responsible. Maybe I knew it could not really be true, but I wanted to believe."

"I'm sorry," I say, feeling ashamed anyway.

"No, it has made me think, and this is what I have come to terms with, Pìhng. Every life, you understand, is finite. You only have so many days. And really, you only have each day. Whatever makes that day worthwhile is all you need." He sits back in his chair. "I do not have enough days left for everything I'd hoped for, but I appreciate now how hard Fōng has worked to make them worthwhile."

I find my throat hard to clear even though I swallow many times. "I'm glad," I say, the relief crashing over me. I hadn't realized how much I'd wanted to hear Francine's grandpa say that about her.

He looks at me curiously. "Fōng hasn't told you any of this?"

"She doesn't want to talk to me." I shake my head. "Not since she found out that I knew about her mom."

"Ah," says Francine's a gūng, sounding concerned. "I'm afraid I am responsible for that, too."

"See, this is what happens when old people talk too much." Francine's a pòh, who has situated herself on the armrest of his chair, wags her finger at him. When she turns to me, though, her face softens. "Fōng will understand, Pìhng. You just have to explain."

"I don't know," I confess. "She seems pretty upset still."

"I remember the first time A Pòh got mad at me," says Francine's a gūng. "Do you recall how I won you over, A Pòh?"

"How would I?" Francine's a pòh shrugs. "It was so long ago."

"I was teasing her and accidentally made her drop her new books into the mud," he says placidly. "This was a big deal, as she was so particular about keeping them neat."

"You would be, too, if your mother always threatened to beat you for being dirty."

Francine's a gūng shrugs off this commentary. "I used all of my savings and borrowed money from a friend to buy her a brand-new set, which I presented to her in front of our whole class," he continues. "Everyone knew how sorry I was."

"What a waste of money that was!" Francine's a pòh scoffs. "I could've used the muddy ones just fine once they dried out." But she's smiling, and it's clear that she did remember all these details.

"So you see, Pìhng," Francine's a gūng concludes, "you only

have to find the right way to tell her, and she will listen."

When I leave Francine's house, I think about this story and how straightforward it was. Her grandpa was obviously just trying to make me feel better, which is ironic considering he's the one who's dying. But my problem with Francine is a lot more complicated, I decide, as I kick off my shoes at our back door and collapse onto the couch. Is there anything I could even do for her?

The photo collage boards that I'd leaned against the living room wall slide down suddenly, toppling onto the floor, and I lift my face off the upholstery.

That's when I hop up and hightail it back to Francine's house, because I've got an idea.

24

Francine

"BUT WHAT ELSE COULD YOU POSSIBLY HAVE going on tonight?"

Jiya is over at my house again, lying on the carpet with her feet up against the wall. Violet Girl is blasting from her phone, and a saree is laid out on my bed.

"Lots of things," I say. "Practicing the piano. Your AP Bio homework."

"Please, I did my own homework today."

"Let's see it."

Jiya waves me off and gets to her feet. "Come on, Francine. You've already bought a ticket."

I eye the rectangle of eggshell-colored cardstock on my desk. The words *Global Gala* are printed in a splashy script. "I guess."

"Plus," says Jiya, striding over to my closet, "don't you want an excuse to wear this?" From the very back, she pulls out a cheongsam that one of my aunts had brought over from China.

"I thought it was casual attire."

"Not since Amanda Moreno fancified the whole thing." Jiya reaches for the ticket to show me. "Now it's 'cocktail or traditional dress encouraged,'" she reads out loud and then tosses the cheongsam to me. "That describes this to a T."

The fabric of the dress, deep teal with a bold red floral print, feels cool when I catch it between my fingers. "What about my grandpa, though?"

I'd been nervous to come clean to A Gūng about The Plan, but I'd done it as soon as I could. The afternoon I made up my mind, I sat with him in the shade of our backyard orange tree, and explained everything. For a long time after I was done, A Gūng remained silent, his mouth pressed into a line I couldn't read. He didn't even seem to notice that the sun had moved the shadows off his face, and that he had to squint through the heat to see. Maybe it didn't matter because he couldn't bear to look at me anyway.

"I was wrong to mislead you like that, A Gūng," I apologized. "I shouldn't have lied." When he still didn't reply, I kept talking, as if that would somehow make the lump in my throat disappear. "I'm so sorry for upsetting you."

"No," A Gūng said finally. "No, Fōng, I . . ." He shuts his eyes. "I only regret that you felt you had to do all that for me."

A leaf fluttered down from the tree, and we watched it land in the grass before A Gūng spoke again.

"Thank you for trying to help me, Fōng. You've been a very good granddaughter." He leaned forward, and his metal folding chair creaked. "But since you will outlive me—by many years, I hope—I'm afraid I must ask of you one more thing."

"Of course," I assured him. "What is it?"

A Gūng squeezed my hand. "Don't forget to be happy."

Jiya, who is now digging around in her bag, finds a pair of earrings. "You said he was doing okay today," she says, handing them to me. They're gold with creamy teardrop opals, and even I can see that they're the perfect complement for my dress. "Didn't you?"

"All right," I say, taking the earrings. "I'll go."

The gym didn't sound like a particularly glamorous venue for a party, but Amanda and the rest of the Multicultural Club have really outdone themselves transforming it for the gala: white lights crisscross the darkened ceiling, delicate bouquets dot the tables, and the servers, though all students, are gliding around dressed in black-and-white.

"Hors d'oeuvre, ladies?"

Jiya and I turn around to find Rollo carrying a silver platter with six fried gyoza arranged in a neat row.

"I didn't know you were in the Multicultural Club," says Jiya, examining the dumplings.

"The filling is vegetarian," Rollo tells her, and she gives him a thumbs-up before spearing the nearest one with a toothpick. "And I'm not in Multicultural Club. I just happen to be helping out tonight because Ollie said they were short-staffed." He glances at me.

"That's generous of you," I say, pretending to adjust my bracelet.

Rollo brushes a speck of dust off his shoulder. "Yeah, I mean, I *was* just doing it because that's the kind of friend I am, but this turned out to be a pretty sweet event." He gobbles up one of his own dumplings, then gestures around us. "Is this better than prom, or is this better than prom?"

"You've never been to prom," Jiya observes.

"Oh, haven't I?" Rollo raises his eyebrows.

Jiya spins him around and pushes him forward. "Just show us to the rest of the food, Rolls."

We start out at the far corner of the gym, each of us grabbing a paper plate before wandering around the booths, trying foods from across the continents: pupusas, tacos, meatballs, crepes, soda bread, pierogis, and more. I purposely spend a lot of time talking to each person, getting to know their family histories in detail, partly because I am interested and partly so that it takes us a long time before we get to the Southeast Asian corner and, yes, to—

"Ollie!"

Rollo, having abandoned his server duties to follow us, waves at Ollie up ahead. When we get closer, I see that he's wearing gray slacks, a vintage-looking color-block tie, and a white shirt that's a little mussed already—like a Tony Leung character, maybe, from a Wong Kar-Wai movie.

"Hey," he says to all of us, but he's only looking at me.

I remember, viscerally, that I'm mad at him, but not what

for, because everything else has evaporated from my mind. I don't respond, thinking that either Rollo or Jiya will say something, except when I turn around, they've both disappeared.

"You look really nice," says Ollie after a moment.

"Thanks," I say. "So do you."

"I didn't have any Vietnamese or Chinese traditional clothes." Blushing, he waves his hand over his outfit. "The tie's my dad's, though, if that counts for anything."

My heart is beating faster than I want it to, so I try to deflect by checking out the booth. I have to say, Ollie's done a good job with the collages. Front and center is the picture of his a yèh with A Gūng and the motorcycle, surrounded by other photos that I'm plenty familiar with. But the way they're blown up and cropped so that unexpected corners become the focus, I do feel a bit like I'm seeing them for the first time. Like I'm seeing them through Ollie's eyes.

"I'm glad you came," he says. "I wasn't sure if you would."

I scan the table between us and zero in on the mountain of egg rolls. "These smell pretty good," I say, reaching for the tongs. "Probably not as good as your mom's, but I'll give them a chance."

Suddenly, the music that had been playing from the stage stops, and Amanda's voice takes over the speakers. She's dressed in a floor-length gown, complete with giant puff sleeves and Guatemalan-inspired embroidery, and I'm immediately grateful that everyone, including Ollie, is now looking at her.

"Thank you, Hargis Klezmer Band, for that inspiring performance." She claps one hand against the mic as they step down, then turns to smile at the audience. "And thank you, everyone, for being here. We truly appreciate all of your support for the Global Gala."

Ollie glances back at me, watching as I pile up my plate with too many egg rolls, but he stays quiet for now.

"I'd like to take this time to thank each and every member of the Multicultural Club, because they're the ones who made this event happen," Amanda continues. "Let's give them each a chance to introduce themselves." She signals at Damien Figueora, who adjusts his headset and runs a mic over to Toshie Tanaka, the girl whose booth is nearest the stage.

I could walk away now, I realize. Just give Ollie an apologetic wave and skedaddle. Instead, I stand there and bite into an egg roll, chewing on it slowly.

The mic gets passed from booth to booth, and each person shares a bit about their family and the food they're serving. When it gets to Ollie, he looks tense. He holds the microphone too far away, so his voice sounds reedier than usual.

"Um, hi," he says, "I'm Ollie Tran, and my family is Chinese Vietnamese. I brought Vietnamese-style egg rolls."

I expect him to pass on the mic now that he's said the bare minimum, but then his eyes catch mine.

"I—" he falters. "I also want everybody to know that I couldn't have put my booth together without Francine Zhang."

I drop the egg roll I was eating, and little pieces of the fried wrapper flake onto the plate. A few people turn their heads to look at me, but I know as well as they do what this is about. Is Ollie trying to make some kind of grand gesture? Here, in front of everyone? That would be the *least* Ollie move ever, not to mention the last thing I want. But there's not much I can do other than gawk at him, along with the rest of the crowd, and wait.

Unfortunately, all our attention must make him freeze up, because what happens next is . . . not much. Across the room, Amanda cocks her head at the silence, and Damien looks increasingly concerned. Finally, Ollie manages to eke out a few more words: "So, thank you, Francine. For, um, all your help."

Damien starts clapping, his enthusiasm dialed way up to usher things along, and the rest of the audience complies with polite, though somewhat confused, applause.

Personally, I'm relieved—though of course Ollie wouldn't make a big public speech about anything if he could help it, so I really shouldn't have worried.

Why, then, do I also feel a little disappointed?

I hold my plate close and squeeze my way through the crowd, not bothering to look back at Ollie or anyone, and I don't stop even when I hear the clumsy thumps of the mic being nearly dropped. By the time I slip outside, someone else's voice has come over the loudspeaker, and Ollie's moment is presumably over.

A few minutes later, however, I hear the gym's double doors

open and close, and then Ollie's footsteps. "Francine," he calls out, "wait up!"

But I ignore him and keep walking, and when I pass a trash can, I dump my plate of egg rolls into the bin. They hit the bottom with a thud, and I admit that wasting all that food makes me feel both like a triumph and a terrible person at the same time.

The problem is, it also gives Ollie a chance to catch up to me, and as he jogs over, I notice that he's carrying something wrapped neatly in brown paper. In spite of myself, I wonder what it could be.

"I'm sorry," he says, out of breath. "I—I keep making a mess of everything somehow." He untucks the package from under his arm. "I know I've been pretty useless in a lot of ways. And it's true, I haven't always had the guts to do the things I should've done." For a moment, he hesitates, tapping the sides of the mystery parcel with his fingertips. Then, somewhat abruptly, he extends it to me. "But I don't want that to be true anymore."

The gift is bulkier than I expected, and heavier, too. I unwrap it uncertainly, peeling back the paper one corner at a time. To my surprise, it's a photo album. The teal one, from the Artist Warehouse.

"Thanks," I say, hoping my confusion doesn't make me sound ungrateful. "But I already got the red one, remember?"

Ollie nods. "Yeah, I do. Except I also remember that this is the one you really wanted."

It's a totally unnecessary gesture, frivolous even—and yet, as I run my hands over the blue linen, the knot that's been pinching my chest all week starts to loosen. "This is really nice," I say, swallowing. "I'll move the photos over as soon as I get the chance."

But Ollie only shakes his head and flips open the cover. "Already done."

Stunned, I realize that Ollie has transferred all the photos from our dilapidated album over to this one, and even arranged them in chronological order. I'm struck by how meticulous he's been with it—every picture is accompanied by a little card, handwritten with the date and location. As I read each one, it occurs to me that the boyish block lettering I remember from elementary school has evolved into something much more assured.

"That pen ink is archival, too," he points out, grinning in a way that makes my cheeks flush.

I speed-flip through the pages, trying hard to focus, but my mind is more on Ollie than the photos. Warmth rushes down my throat, both sweet and tingly, like tea I've gulped down a little too fast, and I can't quite speak. All my words seem to have dissolved, and I wonder if maybe I should stop trying to grasp for them—if I should just let myself be speechless.

Then I notice a photo that I don't recognize.

"Where did you get this?" I ask, bringing the album closer.

The picture is small, about the size of something that would fit in a wallet, and it's of A Gūng and A Pòh, looking younger than I've ever seen them. A Pòh's hair is in two long braids, A

Gūng's shirt looks too big for him, and they're standing close but not touching because her hands are folded primly in front of her.

"It's from your a gūng," Ollie explains. "He said that's his favorite photo of him and your a pòh, so he's kept it with him all these years. But when I mentioned what I was doing, he wanted you to have it."

"Me?" I study the photo again, lost in how unfamiliar it seems despite the familiar faces.

"Yeah," says Ollie, his voice getting soft. "He said he knew you were the one who would take the best care of it."

He touches my shoulder, and I let his words sink in. If you'd asked me a couple of months ago, I would've told you that this was exactly everything I could've hoped for: A Gūng at peace, Ollie wanting to be with me, my family closer and more honest with each other than I even knew we could be.

What I actually feel, though, is a crushing sadness. Because it hits me then that nothing I did could chase away the sense of loss that still hangs over me like a fog I've been trying, all this time, not to breathe in.

"Whoa," Ollie says as I nearly drop the album. He dives for it just in time to catch it. "Is everything okay?"

"Yeah," I lie. "Everything's fine."

"What's wrong, Francine?" Ollie reaches for my hand.

"Nothing." I wrench away from him, but the violent swing of my arm hits my own forehead with a force that reverberates more than I expected. I grab hold of my hair, waiting out the dizziness. Then I notice my wrist is bare.

I lunge toward the ground, knocking my knees hard on the asphalt. But I don't care that it hurts like I've hit bone.

"What are you doing?" Ollie sounds apprehensive as I try to crawl around him.

"My bracelet." Frantically, I scour for it left and right. "I—I have to find it."

Ollie kneels down next to me, though he doesn't join my search. I almost dare him to tell me that it's just a bracelet, that it doesn't matter if it traveled thousands of miles and survived decades of suffering to be entrusted to me, that A Gūng and A Pòh are still alive and waiting for me back at the house—but it's his stillness that makes me bury my face into his chest and finally cry.

25

Ollie

THE DAY AFTER THE GALA, DEXTER WAKES ME UP early, as usual, demanding to be walked. I drag my blanket over my head and try to stay in bed a little longer, but soon two paws pounce on my arm, and even the layers of fabric are no match for the dank smell of Dexter's fur. When I peek outside the duvet cover, he sticks his wet snout into my eyes and I know it's over.

"You need a bath," I grumble, but it's my fault. I've been too busy to give him one—for obvious reasons.

Yesterday, I held Francine outside the gym for a long time. I didn't get a chance to tell her that I loved her, but seeing her sob that way for the first time—her shoulders drawn in sharp as she sucked in each quavering breath, over and over, until she flattened quietly into my chest—felt like something more somehow. Afterward, I drove her back to her house and she, too spent for words, only wrapped her arms around me in a hug. Then I knew to go home because I wasn't sure what else to say.

What happens now, though? Honestly, I still have no idea. I hook the leash onto Dexter's collar and let him trot toward the front door. This, at least, is something I know I have to do. Drowsily, I realize I forgot to put on socks, but it doesn't seem worth the trouble to go back and get some, so I just slip my bare feet into my sneakers, pocket my keys in my PJ pants, and open the door to find Francine.

"Hi," she says sheepishly, her hand dropping from the doorbell. She offers me a small smile. "I guess you're awake."

"I am," I say, recovering from the surprise. I point to Dexter, who's happily sniffing her knees. "Only because of this guy, though."

"Hi, boy." Francine stoops down to massage his neck, which is better treatment than he anticipated this early in the morning, and he is overjoyed. Then she kind of squints up at me. "Sorry for coming over unannounced like this," she says. "I texted, but you probably didn't see it yet, so I wasn't sure if I should."

I pat my pants and discover I also forgot my phone. It doesn't matter, though. "You always can," I say, sounding shyer than I thought I would. Out of habit, I try to gloss over it by busying myself with shutting the door. But when I glance up again, Francine is still looking at me.

"Thank you," she says.

I feel something warm grow inside me. "You wanna walk?"

The morning is gray but not heavy, the clouds thin enough that they probably could be convinced to burn off by the afternoon. We're both quiet as we make our way down the sidewalk, listening to just our footsteps and the jingling of Dexter's metal tag. Only when a neighbor's sprinklers shoot on, sending us startled and laughing into the street, does the calm feel like something we're meant to break.

After a few more minutes, Francine speaks up. "I'm sorry for getting so mad at you, Ollie," she begins, fiddling with a button on her sweater. "You didn't deserve all that."

"I think I probably did."

Her smile appears for just a second before she gets serious again. "You were right about me," she insists, "from the beginning."

Hearing her say that, deflated and certain, makes me feel like I'd rather be wrong a hundred times over. "What do you mean?"

Francine sighs. "I was so convinced that I should help my a gūng," she says. "I thought I had to make him feel better about dying. But really, the one who needed to feel better was me."

Dexter slows down to sniff a patch of grass, and I slacken his leash to let him. "Yeah," I say softly.

"I just haven't wanted to face it." Francine tears off some leaves from a nearby hedge and tosses them out in front of her. "For a long time, I hoped that pouring all my energy into everyone else—making myself smaller—would make my feelings smaller, too." Her voice loses some of its sharpness. "It didn't, though."

I want to take hold of her fingers, but I catch one of the leaves instead. "I don't know if anything does."

"No, I guess not." Francine steals a glance at me, and we keep walking until we get to the corner with Dexter's favorite fire hydrant. "You're the one who made me see how much I needed to be sad," she says. "And also how much I needed to be happy. But more than that, you made me realize it's okay to be both at the same time. Sad and also happier than I've ever been my entire life."

She smiles again, and despite the overcast sky, the sun is now bright enough behind the clouds that the whole day seems changed. The whole world, even.

"I love you, Francine," I blurt out, and though I've wanted to say it for a while, *known* that I wanted to, I still blush all the way down to my toes.

Francine slips her arms around my neck, and the coolness of her skin is a surprise and a relief. "What took you so long?" she says, grinning, and then she kisses me until her hands are warmer than mine.

Eventually, we end up back at my house, and when I let Dexter run free, he immediately scampers up the front steps.

"I should probably get home." Francine taps the red-brick border of the driveway with her shoe.

"I can walk you."

She shakes her head. "It's okay, it's not that far."

"All right," I reply. But neither of us budges, and then we both kind of laugh.

Francine glances at our front door. "I almost forgot—will

you thank your dad for me?"

"What?" Dexter's leash goes still in my hand.

"Your dad called yesterday," says Francine, looking surprised. "He said he was sorry he couldn't make it to see my a gūng and offered to pay all of his medical bills."

"My dad called?" I'm still stuck on the first part.

"Yeah, my mom was really shocked. They haven't talked in years, probably." Francine peers into my face. "I was sure you'd told him to."

"No—no, I hadn't."

"Of course, we couldn't accept."

"You should've."

She gives me a wry grin. "I have to go. For real." Then she kisses me again, quick and light this time, the breeziness itself exhilarating because it's a sign, suddenly, of feeling like we've got all the time in the world.

After she's gone, I head inside the house. Mom is awake, wearing a Cal sweatshirt that Isaac had bought for Dad. I've never noticed before how thin it makes her look.

"I feel like I haven't seen you in a while, Ollie," she says, tousling my hair. "Do you want coffee?"

"I'll get you some," I tell her.

As I walk by Dad's office, I pause at the open door. There's a lot I want to ask him, but for now, all I can see behind his desk—impenetrable glass on a steel frame, with everything down to the tray of paper clips left in meticulous order—is his empty chair.

26

Francine

"OPEN IT," SAYS OLLIE.

We're sitting on the couch in his family room, waiting for Jiya and Rollo to arrive, when he gives me a flat, narrow box.

"Another present?" I say, taking it with both hands.

"Just a small one," he says.

I undo the ribbon carefully and lift the lid. Inside, on silky black velvet, lays a gold bracelet. I'm too surprised to speak.

"What—"

"I know it's not the same," says Ollie. "But I thought you might like it, since you lost yours."

For a while, every time I remembered the bracelet was gone, despair would rise into a cold lump in the middle of my chest. I dreaded telling A Pòh what happened—especially because I couldn't even say *when* it had—and when I finally mustered up the nerve, I almost broke down in tears again. But A Gūng, overhearing me, shuffled over to pat my shoulder. "You don't need to cry over this, Fōng," he said. "Sometimes, it's just how things are meant to be."

"That's right," A Pòh agreed. "In Vietnamese, we have this saying: *của đi thay người*. Trade your valuables for your life. What else are they for?"

Of course, it wasn't lost on me that no amount of valuables would buy A Gūng any more time—or for that matter, A Pòh either—and after I nodded at them to show that I understood, I walked calmly to Ollie's house and cried for an hour in his kitchen.

Now, though, he's giving me this bracelet—a valuable to replace the valuable. As I lift it out of the box, I can see that it's delicate, like my old one, but with a more substantial chain. Here, multiple threads of gold have been braided into a rope and interspersed with shiny pearls all the way around.

"It's beautiful," I say, overcome by its loveliness.

"My mom is actually the one who wanted you to have it." A familiar flush appears on Ollie's cheeks. "When I told her what happened, she gave me this for you. She said it was a gift from Dad a few years ago."

"I can't take your mom's bracelet," I protest, setting it back on its little velvet bed. "What would your dad say?"

Ollie stops me before I can snap the case shut. "I think it would mean a lot to him if you had it." He takes the bracelet out again and lays it across his palm. "It would mean a lot to me, too."

After a moment of hesitation, I hold out my wrist and let him drape the bracelet around it. When I raise my arm, the sunset from the window makes the pearls sparkle.

"Thank you, Ollie," I say, smiling, just as the doorbell rings.

Dexter, who had been napping at our feet, jumps up and runs in a joyful circle.

"Hey, France." Rollo comes into the room and flops himself into an armchair. When he sees Ollie sitting back down next to me, he grins at us both. "You know, I'm really glad this worked out. I've been shipping you two since the beginning."

Ollie chucks a pillow at Rollo, but he's laughing. "Whatever, man."

"I'm serious! Who set up your first lunch date?"

"That wasn't a lunch date. And you didn't set it up."

"Wasn't it?" Rollo raises an eyebrow. "Didn't I?"

As with all things Rollo related, it's impossible to know.

A few minutes later, Jiya arrives carrying a stack of pizza boxes. "Rollo," she says, setting them down on the coffee table. "Why did you order so many?"

"There was a two-for-one deal," Rollo explains, grabbing himself a slice.

"So you ordered . . . four?" I say.

"It was a good deal!"

Jiya kneels on the floor and peeks into each box until she finds the veggie pizza. "Rolls, you know that just because something is a good deal doesn't necessarily mean it saves you money, right?"

Just then, the doorbell rings again, and everyone but Rollo looks surprised. "Who says it's always about the money?" he huffs. "Maybe I just want to make sure no one goes hungry on my watch."

Ollie squints one suspicious eye at Rollo, then leaps to his feet in a flash of understanding. Rollo races after him, but Ollie gets to the door first, flinging it open to reveal a delivery guy with his hands full.

"I've got two dozen doughnuts for . . ." The guy looks at his phone. "Rollo Chen?"

"Thanks, dude." Rollo elbows past Ollie to accept the delivery, then parades the boxes over to us. "Enjoy!"

I have no idea how the four of us are going to eat this many doughnuts on *top* of all those pizzas, but Jiya is delighted. "I'll never turn down sugar," she says, grinning.

But before she can even lift the lid to the top box, the doorbell rings again. This time, it's someone with several pints of artisanal ice cream. "There's lavender honey, salted caramel, birthday cake, and brambleberry crisp," she announces.

"Amazing," says Rollo. "Always good to see you, Stella."

Ollie stands back to let Rollo get by, but it's clear he has some questions. "What is—"

Once again, however, the doorbell rings, and Ollie has no choice but to open it. Standing on the front steps is a mustachioed man next to an old-school popcorn machine, fully outfitted with shiny trim and thin-spoked wheels.

"Where would you like it set up?" he asks.

Ollie spins around and points at the popcorn machine. "This is a little much, Rollo!"

"Really?" Rollo pops his head over Ollie's shoulder. "I got the smallest size, though."

Jiya watches as the man sets up the popcorn machine in the living room, then sweeps her eyes from the doughnut and pizza boxes to the ice cream in Rollo's arms. "Let me guess," she says, smirking. "It was *all* a good deal?"

"Like I said, Jee, don't worry about that—it's all on me," replies Rollo, puffing out his chest. "When it comes to movie night with my besties, I spare no expense."

Jiya only arches a brow, and Rollo responds by attempting a nonchalant toss of the salted caramel ice cream. He misses the catch, though, and it rolls across the marble floor, much to Dexter's delight. "And okay . . ." he admits, "maybe I got a little carried away on Groupon."

"Well, I think we should just enjoy ourselves." I pick up the carton of ice cream by my foot and open it, breathing in the sweetness. "Might as well, right?"

Ollie, who had disappeared into the kitchen, presses a spoon into my hand. "Good idea," he says, and smiles.

"Fine by me." Jiya hops onto the couch and turns on the TV, a slice of pizza in one hand and the remote in the other. "What should we watch?" She scrolls through options as we join her around the coffee table. "Something sad? Funny?"

"Let's do funny," I say, reaching over to scratch Dexter's ears. "Ollie doesn't like sad movies."

"Not true," Ollie objects. "I can appreciate the full spectrum of human experience."

"Ollie *is* good at wallowing in his emotions," Rollo agrees.

"I'm just *saying*." Ollie's glance travels over to me, his dimple appearing. "We should watch whatever Francine wants."

Jiya laughs and nods. "You got it."

Then I curl up against Ollie, whose arm is warm around my shoulders, and as we all settle into the night that's only just begun, I feel so happy I could cry.

Acknowledgments

This book was written during a very challenging time in my life, during a very challenging time for the world. As a result, much gratitude is in order:

Thank you to my agent Jenny Bent, who continues to be my favorite person of all time and a balm for my author soul. Thanks also to Gemma Cooper for her infinite loveliness, as well as the rest of the Bent Agency team, especially Victoria Cappello.

Thank you to my editors, Mabel Hsu and Stephanie King, for their excellent instincts, endless kindness, and unfailing patience as I wrangled, and then re-wrangled, this story. Many thanks to Fevik for the cover illustration and to the Harper team: Katherine Tegen, Molly Fehr, Amy Ryan, Sara Schonfeld, Julia Johnson, Rye White, Gretchen Stelter, Gwen Morton, Sonja West, Kristen Eckhardt, James Neel, Sabrina Abballe, and Katie Boni. Same goes to Kevin Wada for the UK cover illustration, and to the Usborne team, who are fabulous as well: Rebecca Hill, Alice Moloney, Kath Millichope, Sarah Cronin, Beth Gooding, and Jess Feichtlbauer.

Thank you to the wonderful family, friends, and colleagues who supported me throughout this journey and not once complained about the kind of person I became when on deadline. Special thanks to Mariko Turk for offering ever-ready wisdom and empathy, and for making writing and motherhood feel less lonely. Thanks also to Ayushee Aithal, for being a limitless well of emotional, intellectual, and spiritual support, and for appreciating the book even when I didn't want to let anyone read it.

Thank you to the caregivers who made it possible for me to work while also being a mother, especially Zach, and also my mom and dad.

And as usual, thank you to C., for the inspiration. You are so handsome, so wise, so brave. Thank you, bǎo bǎo, for existing. And thank you, J., for everything else.